G000143593

TORMENT

JOHN DEAKIN

authorHOUSE®

AuthorHouse™ UK
1663 Liberty Drive
Bloomington, IN 47403 USA
www.authorhouse.co.uk
Phone: 0800.197.4150

Published by AuthorHouse 03/09/2017

ISBN: 978-1-5246-7861-6 (sc)
ISBN: 978-1-5246-7858-6 (e)

Print information available on the last page.

Contents

Chapter 1

"Don't worry you won't be in there for long and there's plenty of room where you're going." Those words had haunted Tom since the fateful day in 1940 that had changed his life forever. He woke up abruptly on 28th May 2014, still haunted by memories of horrific events exactly seventy-four years earlier. Those happenings had blighted the long life which he had loved, the only positive anticipated from his inevitable death, which he had always dreaded, was that all memories would be erased. But he was not ready to give up on life yet.

He sat in the lounge at the Care Home where he had lived for the past eight of his one hundred years, feeling as comfortable as he could at his age. The small group around him, included his daughter and two sons and their own partners, all of whom were themselves in their sixties or seventies. They were accompanied by his six grandchildren, most of whom looked as though they didn't want to be there, but given the occasion had felt obligated to make the effort. At least it was a change from his normal daily routine which involved sitting for hours in this very same chair, taking little interest in the television in the corner of the lounge which was clad in depressing brown floral patterned wallpaper, making it dull in natural light.

It did make a change to have a coherent conversation which was not normally possible as most his companions, almost all women and were in various stages of dementia. One lady called Irene was in the habit of carrying her own wedding photograph around, showing it to anyone who had the time and patience. Tom had lost count of the number of times she had sat beside him and pointed out the main guests of an event that must have taken place at least 60 years before. Irene had a wonderful long term memory, pointing out her Mother, Father and two sisters, both of whom were obviously bridesmaids. It was only when she got to the bridegroom, that she dismissively exclaimed, "I don't know who he is".

Looking at the beautiful bride in the black and white photograph, Tom wondered why on earth is life so cruel that the years play havoc with minds and bodies, leaving such a lovely woman finding it difficult to walk and not knowing who she was most days.

He knew all about that having lived so long himself and seeing all his friends go, adding to the loneliness of old age. Tom wondered how he had lasted this long, he had not been much of a teetotaler and smoked cigarettes from his early teens, until he had finally given up for health reasons when he was 80. It had obviously worked as he had received a message from the Queen that morning, confirming that he had reached his century. He also had received a few cards from his not very large family, but none from friends because he no longer had any. The staff in the Home were kind, but somewhat patronizing and he found it difficult to understand why some of them talked to him as though he was four years old. Tom could remember adults' addressing him like that when it first became aware of what was going on in the new world around him. It seemed fine then but not now. He was also resentful that he had to be taken to the toilet, although he reluctantly accepted it was necessary, but at least he could keep himself clean.

He had been woken that morning by one of the more mature staff members, a somewhat large but happy soul called Anne, who was just about his favorite. The mornings had always been the best part of his day and he recalled with both pleasure and sadness waking up next to his wife who was usually still sleeping, but nearly always woke with a smile on her beautiful face. When she had died, he had been distraught and there had not been a waking moment since, when he hadn't missed her.

Anne, who was her usual breezy self that morning, drew back his curtains flooding the room with bright spring sunlight, reminding him:

"It's a big day today Tom"

"Why's that then?"

"You're a grumpy old bugger, It's your 100th birthday"

He laughed, "Oh I forgot, you know what my memories like"

"No you hadn't, you're just winding me up as usual, anyway Happy Birthday, what an achievement".

"Not from where I'm sitting, it would have been a lot easier and I'd been a lot less trouble if I'd have gone 20 years ago."

"You're no trouble and you know it. Come on let's get you up and you can make yourself presentable for your visitors"

"If I must, but I'd rather stay in bed"

Always having loved banter with women, who he got on better with than men, finding them far more interesting in more ways than one.

Anne helped him out of bed and after making sure he'd got everything he needed left him to his own devices. He was happy that he was still able to wash and dress himself, thinking it wouldn't be worth going on if couldn't. It took him a little time to, as Anne had said, "make him self presentable", after which he grabbed his walking stick, slowly making his way to the Lounge and taking his place in his usual armchair. Considering it to be his own, anyone else who sat in it did so at their peril. Breakfast was soon ready, served on tables at the other end of the large room. Not needing an invitation to move to the table, he had always considered it the most important and enjoyable meal of the day. It was somewhat less appetizing these days as many of his companions had to be fed by the patient staff, finding it difficult to locate their own mouths. He felt so sorry for them and gave silent thanks to whoever or whatever had protected him from many of the ravages that accompany old age. Finding it difficult to believe in God, concluding that any supreme being would not condone the profound evil that he had witnessed in his lifetime, although he had joked in the past that he should start going to church, "just in case".

After breakfast, Tom slowly made his way back to the chair, where he spent almost all his waking hours. He found this to be totally frustrating, having always been active and loving country walks. At the age of 60 he had taken up running, everyone considering and even saying that he was mad and would kill himself. A long gone neighbor, having had a Heart By-pass, had been standing at his garden gate puffing a cigarette, as he set off for a five miler one day, advising him that "jogging can kill you, you know", which he had found amusing.

These days the only exercise he got was a walk around the garden, where he was also able to sit in the summer. It was not particularly large and was enclosed by a six-foot-high wall, but there was grass and well tended flowerbeds, with enough furniture to accommodate all who wished to venture from the security of the building. There was no escape from the garden as the only exit was by the way of a security protected gate. One thing that did make him happy was the birdsong, particularly Blackbirds in the spring serenading prospective partners with whom they would soon produce new life.

A real treat was when Anne took him to a nearby shop, where he could buy a newspaper. They were generally only out for about 10 minutes, but nevertheless it was uplifting for him to see people go about their normal daily business. When he did go out he bought the Daily Mail which was as intellectually demanding as he could cope with, although on Sunday's he missed the News of the World, which hadn't contained any news to speak of, but much of the content had made him laugh.

The day of his centenary was wet, so even in May; he was unable to escape from the shackles of his armchair. One of the staff was kind enough to bring him in a "Mail", so at least he had something new to read and as always started at the back and worked his way in. He always found the sports news was less depressing than what was going on in the crazy World, even for a West Bromwich Albion supporter.

The Staff made a real fuss all wishing him "Many Happy Returns", they were a lot more optimistic than he was. He got so many kisses on the cheek that he was getting worried about bruising, although he enjoyed the attention. There was a party arranged for him after lunch and he was happy to see his family members turn up.

The eldest of his children was his step daughter Petra, who reminded Tom so much of her mother. Jack his eldest son was 67 and had spent all his working life in the Air Force, having been warned by Tom not to go anywhere near the coal pit where he had worked. Tom thought that Jack's main problem was that everyone said that he looked like him and he wouldn't wish that on anyone. George was two years younger than his brother and did well academically, getting a Master's Degree and had worked in High Tech in recent years, the mysteries of which Tom had never been interested to come to terms with.

"Hello Dad", they all said almost simultaneously, with Petra kissing his cheek.

Hello" replied Tom, "There was no need to bring a deputation"

Jack enquired," Are you having a good day?'

"I've had better, I was pissed off when I was your age, so you can imagine how I feel now"

"Come on Dad, cheer up it could be a lot worse", interjected George.

"Not much, the Vicar was in this morning to wish me happy birthday and tell me there's a space booked for me in the church yard"

"Always the optimist Dad", Petra laughed, "Come on, we're all here now, so let's have a good time"

And they did seem to have a fine time fussing over him to the point of being annoying. There were presents, which were all clothes, mainly designed to keep him warm in the winter, which was still several months away. Why was it that everyone seemed more confident of his continued survival than him? Then there was the cake, which was quite large, with "Happy 100th Birthday Tom" embossed on the iced top. There was also a single candle as they don't seem to make cakes big enough for 100. Invited to blow it out, he was happy enough to comply if only to keep the peace. This was followed by a rendition of Happy Birthday, after which his family seemed to be in a hurry to get out. Tom couldn't blame them as it was hardly a great atmosphere being surrounded by people, who no longer had any great interest in life, another negative being the constant background smell.

Petra was the last to leave, sitting with him, holding his hand. Even though she was over seventy, she was still his little girl, reminding Tom of her mother, although having had much fairer hair, which was now white.

Tom had got used to being alone, but this was somewhat alleviated by the presence of Anne, with whom he had a great relationship. He got depressed on her days off or when she went on holiday, counting the days until she was due back.

Not long after tea each day, the staff started to put the inmates to bed. As Tom was considered one of the less difficult, he was always one of the last to leave the lounge, but still thought 7.30 was early, particularly as he didn't sleep that well. By the time, it was his turn, Anne had long left for the day and he had to put up with one of her colleagues.

It was a bit of a lottery, but the Care Assistant that approached him was one of the newer additions. Tom had hardly spoken to Raj, who was

Asian, but had a strong Black Country accent, seeming to be outgoing and friendly. When they got to his room, Raj said that he would help Tom undress and get into bed, which irritated him.

"There's no need, I might be old but I'm not helpless"

"Sorry about that, but the most of them in here can't do anything for themselves".

"Well, I'm not most of them, so bugger off"

OK, if that's what you want, but I thought 100 years of experience would have taught you to be polite"

At that Raj left room with a brusque, "Good Night Tom"

Tom didn't reply, but afterwards was annoyed at his lack of courtesy and understanding of Raj, who had only tried to help. He vowed that he would apologize the next day. The main reason he was tetchy was the prospect of spending the next twelve hours alone with his thoughts in his small room, that was sparsely furnished with his single bed, an armchair, wardrobe and small bedside locker, which proved adequate for his meager possessions. There was a television in the corner that picked up the free view channels, but not much sport which was the only thing that interested him.

He knew that the only way he would permanently escape from his captivity was in a box. Getting into bed alone with his thoughts, when the inevitable did happen, he wanted to be remembered as a good man, but his hatred of the perpetrators of those events in France so long ago was undiminished. He had spoken as little as possible about his lucky escape from the massacre and the eighty of his comrades that did not were constantly in his thoughts. As was Paul Schiller, who had been executed because of Tom's testimony.

CHAPTER 2

Tom's first memories were of a semi-detached house, with the two properties divided by a dark entry, leading to a vegetable garden with a Pig Sty at the back. He remembered being fascinated by the two strange animals, with long snuffling noses peering over the gate of the pen, devouring with relish everything that was poured into their trough. No sooner finished, they were back at the gate seeking further sustenance. As they grew they became less easy for his strong father to manage and it was with some relief that he told his Mother,

"We're taking them to Hodgett's Butchers today".

"Whose helping you get them down there?" his Mother asked.

"Oh, three of me mates from the pit, I'll give them a bob apiece".

"You might need more than three; they're a big pair of buggers".

"No, we'll be alright; Charlie Hodgetts will be waiting with his knife when we get there".

So began an alarming ritual that Tom never felt comfortable watching. Men went to the Sty, where his Dad put a rope around the first animal's neck. This was followed by a struggle to get the condemned beast through the garden and along the narrow entry onto the road leading to their executioner's yard, which was mercifully only a short distance away. The pig seemed to know exactly what was going to happen at the end and struggled and screeched throughout, the noise stopping abruptly almost as soon as they got to the Butchers, which had a much wider entry at the side, leading to the enclosed yard. Fortunately, Tom was mercifully spared the final act of the process. No sooner had the first animal been dispatched than the by then heavily perspiring executioner's assistants, returned for his or her companion and the whole thing was repeated.

A few days later, Tom found two recently weaned piglets had replaced the Sty's previous occupants, who began emptying the trough with similar enthusiasm, fortunately not knowing what awaited them at the end of their short lives. In the meantime, large sides of bacon from those recently dispatched, could be seen hanging in the larder ready to provide the family with countless breakfasts. Tom wasn't keen on seeing the pigs to whom he had become attached go to what his Dad called the slaughter house, but the smell and taste of fried bacon tempered his discomfort.

Another significant event that awakened his senses was when he heard the bells in the church tower ring for the first time. A lot of the early conversations between his parents had been about something called "the war". He didn't know what that was, but on the day the bells rang he was taken by his mother in to the street where a lot of the people were cheering and jumping up and down, because apparently the "war" was over. Whatever that meant, it was obvious to Tom that everyone was happy about it, because the next thing was flags appearing from nowhere, being hung out of windows and anywhere else there was a space for them. People waved and hugged each other, which he had not seen happen before. He had never seen his normally reserved Mother look so happy and when Dad came back from the pit in the afternoon, his clothes filthy and face black as usual, she ran to meet him and kissed him on the lips in the street in front of all and sundry. They came down the entry to the back door which they and callers always used, his Mother's normally immaculately clean blouse and skirt stained with the black coal dust that had been transferred from his Dad's pit clothes.

"Well, it's over then me duck and about bloody time"

"Yes", his Mother replied, "the lads will be coming home now"

"A lot of the poor buggers won't, there's over twenty village lads laying dead somewhere"

"Yes, but at least there'll be no more and their wives and mother's can stop worrying about them."

"I wish I'd have gone myself, Clara, said Dad, "rather than stay in the pit."

"Well, I'm glad you didn't, what would me and young Tom have done if anything had have happened to you. You risk your life every day going down that black hole and they said they needed the coal anyway."

With that she lifted the metal bath from its hook in the kitchen, put it in front of the fire and filled it with water that had been heated on the black range adjacent to the open grate. She left her husband to rid himself of the grime as best as he could, telling him to call her when he wanted his back washed.

A few weeks later, it was something called "Christmas" and Tom was told that if he was a good lad, Santa Clause would fill his stocking with presents. He was somewhat confused by this, but the thought of presents certainly kept his mind on staying out of trouble. Christmas came and he did indeed get presents, the best of which was a wooden sword and shield, being complemented by an apple and some nuts. He also noticed that the main meal on the day was much more substantial than their normal meager fare, his Dad having procured a chicken from a local farm. When Dad arrived with the bird, he dumped it on the kitchen table, complete with head and feathers saying to his Mother,

"There you are me duck, do you want to pluck it, or will I?"

"Don't worry about it Henry, I'll have it ready for the oven in no time" was his Mothers reply as she set about the lifeless bird, first removing all the feathers, then cutting its head off and finally pulling the entrails out, saying that she would make gravy with giblets, whatever they were. Tom was fascinated by the whole process, being not sure that he liked what he witnessed, but thought it was well worth it when he tasted chicken meat for the first time in his life.

As time passed, he became aware of the seasons of the year and not long after Christmas experienced snow for the first time, being encouraged to go out into the street to play, but was not totally enthralled by the group of older boys who were making the snow into hard balls, considering Tom an easy target. After dodging most of the projectiles that came his way, he suddenly felt a thump on the back of the neck, leaving it uncomfortable with water dripping down the inside of his shirt. Turning around to find the identity of his assailant, he was surprised to see his Dad standing a short distance away laughing for all he was worth. But Dad was not finished and said,

"I saw what those young buggers were up to, let's give them what for."

And that's exactly what he did, throwing snow balls at his son's tormentors, who tried to retaliate but found they were up against an expert and soon made an expedient retreat.

Dad grabbed his hand and as they walked down the entry towards the warmth of the house saying, "There's the lesson for you my lad, never pick on anybody smaller than you, because retribution could be just around the corner"

Not to long afterwards, all the talk was of Tom starting school in the summer, where he was told he would have to go until he was 14. He certainly hoped that he would like what he found when he got there as 10 years seemed to be a long time. In the ensuing months, he looked forward to the summer, which seemed an awful long time coming.

In the meantime, he had experienced another awakening when one sunny day he walked through the nearby woods with his Mother to the next village, being dazzled by the sea of blue that carpeted the wood either side of the narrow pathway. Getting closer he saw that the ground was a mass of flowers and asked his Mother what they were.

"Bluebells" she said, "Do you like them?"

He didn't answer, but just stared in fascination at the beautiful display. Never forgetting that day, the wood became his play ground for all his formative years, his favorite time always being late spring, when the Bluebells appeared for what was an all too short few weeks.

Tom enjoyed the summer because he could spend many his waking hours' outdoors only going in when he was hungry, which in truth was quite often. He played all sorts of games with his friends, but his happiest times were spent on the top of the railway embankment which was quite close to home. The line was in constant use with express passenger and goods trains passing at regular intervals. There were also the less frequent local trains that he observed when they were either slowing or speeding up before or after stopping at the village station. Fascinated by the diversity of engines which were mostly bright red in color, expelling copious amounts of smoke from their chimneys.

During those long and warm days, the thought of school was uppermost in his mind, looking forward to the day when he could join the stream of boys and girls that he watched trudge past the house in the morning to the village school that was only a short distance away. He often waited for them on their return journey in the late afternoon and one thing that bothered him was that they mostly seemed to be much happier than they had in the morning.

The big day eventually arrived, his mother getting him up earlier than usual, taking him to the kitchen where she pumped some water into a bowl and washed his hands and face. The water was cold despite the time of year, making him flinch as it touched his skin, but he was certainly wide awake afterwards. His Mother dressed him in a new grey shirt and trousers which were just long enough to cover his knees, feeling somewhat rough on the areas of his body which were not protected by under clothing. Quickly eating his breakfast of bread and jam, he was soon ready for his new adventure and when his Mother put on his jacket and cap and tied his new boots, he was ready to go.

"Right Tom, I'll take you today seeing it's your first, but after that you can walk along with the other kids"

So off they went into the busy street where they found numerous groups of children making their way towards the school, chatting to one another about anything other than school. There were a small number of other Mothers who were accompanying new starters, the boys looking less comfortable than the girls having their hand held by a parent.

Arriving at the school gate, they were greeted by an older boy with a Monitors badge attached to his lapel, who told them to go through the entrance to Class Room Number Four, where a teacher would meet them. They were greeted by a severe looking woman who looked old to Tom, with short grey hair that just covered her ears. Her face was thin with deep lines, which were accentuated when she smiled as they walked into the room.

"Hello Mrs. Walton this must be Tom. Welcome to school young man."

"Yes, Miss Davis, this is Tom, it doesn't seem two minutes since you were teaching me."

"Well it must be fifteen years, is Tom your only one?

"He is now, but I'm expecting another early next year."

This was a bit of a shock for Tom, who had no idea that his Mother was going to have a baby, immediately wondering how it would affect him. He had to think quickly, when Miss Davis asked him.

"What do you think of that Tom? Do you want a brother or a sister?"

"A brother I think." was his immediate reply.

"Well that's something to look forward to, in the meantime, this will be your class room and your teacher will be Miss Kirkham, who is new like you and you will be meeting her presently. So, Mrs. Walton, you can leave now and we'll look after Tom. I hope everything goes well with the new baby."

With that his Mother quickly left saying, "Thank you Miss Davis, I'll see you when you come home, Tom, you be a good lad now."

Tom observed his new environment and was immediately struck by the bare walls. There were three rows of desks for about eight pupils with bench seats attached. There were two children already sat at their places, one girl and a boy.

Miss Davis told him that the two children were new like him and didn't want to go into the playground, but that he could go out if he wanted to and come back when the bell rang.

Not needing a second invitation, he was in the playground in the blink of an eye. A tirade of noise greeted him, with the boys mostly involved in games of tag, with others running around with little purpose. The girls were generally stood around in small and larger groups and seemed to be making less contribution to the noise level. Tom was attracted to a group of older lads in the corner of the playground who were kicking a ball about. Attempting to join in only to be told to "Bugger off" Tom slunk away and stood on his own until the bell rang signaling the start of his education.

CHAPTER 3

It soon became apparent that he was no scholar, particularly when it came to numbers. Finding it difficult to add and subtract and even more so when it came to multiplication, much to the frustration of Miss Kirkham, who seemed to like him despite his inadequacies. In turn, Tom thought that she was wonderful and always tried to be as helpful as possible, volunteering at every opportunity. His first teacher, was not particularly tall and quite round, with a kind face topped with short curly hair and didn't seem to be much older than some of the girls in the nearby senior school. She encouraged him a lot and was pleased that he had the ability to write and express himself well. He was also the first in his class, that was made up of seven other boys and eight girls, to be able to tell the time, this having been taught him by his patient Mother, who always seemed to have plenty of time for him.

This changed abruptly when his sister arrived not long after Christmas, being quickly christened Maud. It was quite a shock seeing his beloved Mother with another baby, the time she spent with Tom being significantly diminished. The main thing that he missed was being read a bedtime story, but fortunately he was also proving to be a good reader.

Despite this, he somewhat resented Maud, who seemed to be the centre of attention of both of his parents, Tom feeling that his life had changed forever. Whenever he accompanied his parents out for a Sunday walk with the pram, all everyone they met wanted to talk about was the baby, with his Father beaming with pride. He felt grateful when the odd person took notice of him with a "Hello Tom".

This established a pattern for the next few years, the frustrations at home being complemented by those at school, where anything other than reading and writing was a struggle. When he told his Father about this, he was brusquely informed not to worry too much about it because,

"You don't need to do sums down the pit".

At which his mother interjected, He's not going down the pit".

Dad grinned, "We'll see, if it was good enough for me and my Dad it'll be good enough for him"

And that was the family tradition; his Father had joined his Grandfather in the local pit when he was 13 years old, which he considered to be his only option, as did almost all the other village boys. It was hard work, but he enjoyed what he did and at least it had kept him out of the war. Some of his mates had joined up, although they didn't have to and most of them didn't come back. He had been married to Clara for only two years when the conflict began and had been happy enough to take his chances in the pit every day, rather than get shot at by Germans. When he had spoken to his wife about it, she agreed wholeheartedly, not wanting to be a young widow with a baby, Tom being then only three months old. Henry adored his wife, although he would have been the first to admit that he found it hard to show any obvious signs of affection. She had been in service for a Bank Manager in a nearby town when he met her and was immediately attracted to the smart well dressed young woman who was only 18 years old. Not thinking, he would have any chance it was a pleasant surprise when she had accepted his invitation to go out one Sunday and even more so when she agreed to marry him just six months later. It was a considerable relief that he didn't have to ask anyone for her hand as both of her parents were dead and he knew her elder brother well, who didn't seem to care one way or the other.

Tom learnt more about the war as he got older and when he was ten went to Village Square for the dedication of the Memorial to those who had been killed. It was a tall stone cross, with a wide rectangular base, on which were more names than he could count, noticing that there were three with the same surname as his. He had heard his parents talk about Jack and at the end of the ceremony, Dad pointed out the name of John Thomas Walton with pride,

"That's your Uncle Jack, he was only 18 when he was killed on the Somme, you should be proud of him"

"Where's the Somme Dad?"

"It's in France, where all the fighting was"

Tom knew where France was because he had seen maps at school, but realized that you had to go over some sea to get to it. He thought about his Uncle having been only 18, which worried him, thinking that it hadn't been a long time to live.

"Will I ever have to go to a war Dad?"

The reply was emphatic, "There's no need for you to worry about wars son, there won't be any more."

That was good enough for Tom and he went home in a much happier frame of mind.

Grateful that he lived in a happy home, with his own bedroom, the only thing that Tom didn't like was trips to the lavatory which was at the bottom of the garden near the Pig Sty, finding it an ordeal on a cold winter day. There was always plenty of food on the table and he tended to eat too much of it. This resulted in him getting heavier and his clothes tighter, which worried his Mother, but Dad wasn't at all concerned saying,

"Don't worry about it Clara, the weight soon comes off lads when they go to the pit."

"I keep telling you Henry, he's not going, I want better for him."

"Don't start that again me duck, there's nothing else for him to do around here."

"He can perhaps get a job in a shop, when he's 14. I'll start asking around."

Dad obviously didn't want to argue with his stubborn wife and went out of the back door saying "We'll see".

What angered Tom was that nobody asked him what he wanted to do. The one thing he did know was that he didn't want to go to the pit. He knew that his Dad worked long hours and was always moaning about the working day being increased and the pay being cut. This caused a family crisis when he was 12, when his Dad came home with a worried look on his face and said,

"There's going to be a strike."

Tom wasn't sure what this would mean, but knew from the look on his Mother's face that it wasn't good news. There was an uncharacteristically subdued atmosphere that evening and his parents sat at the table having tea in almost complete silence. This was eventually broken when his Mother said,

"What's gone on then?"

His Dad sighed, "They want to cut our pay by up to a quarter and put an extra hour on the day, but the Federation won't have it and there's talk of a lock out."

"What do you think about it Henry?"

"I'd rather work than go on strike, but if there's a lock out, there's nothing I can do about it."

"Maybe the owners are bluffing", said his mother.

"I don't think so; this has been brewing up for a long time."

And that's how the conversation ended and it was confirmed the next day, when his Dad returned from the pit with a clean face saying, "They wouldn't let us go down, but there's talk of a General Strike to support the miners. The railway men and other transport workers are going to come out, so the government could make the owners back down."

That was the start of an uncomfortable period with his Dad hanging around the house for weeks on end. The optimism brought on by the General Strike was short lived, the whole thing collapsing after just nine days. That didn't help his Dad at all as the miners were determined to stick it out, only to drift back to work a few months later the owner's terms, which were a 20% pay cut for an hour a day's extra work.

It left his Dad bitter, but despite this he was still determined that Tom would work at the pit, while his Mother was just as stubborn and adamant that he wouldn't. Things came to a head when he left school just two months after his fourteenth birthday, with his mother proudly announcing, "I've got Tom a job at Randall's".

CHAPTER 4

Tom was delighted that he wouldn't be going down the pit, which had never appealed to him. He was, however, somewhat alarmed when he was told that he had to go to Randall's for a writing and arithmetic test the following Monday morning. Never having been much good a school, his efforts being summed up in a brief leaving report.

"Tom is a helpful and polite boy and is good at writing and drawing. Apart from that, he has shown little academic ability throughout his time here."

Undaunted, off he went to Randell's, which was by far the largest shop in the village and must have supplied at least three quarters its inhabitants' food needs, from its well stocked shelves. Bread was also made on the premises, with a large Bake House situated in the yard behind the shop. Aromas of the baking dough drifted out onto the road, which Tom loved to inhale deeply passing on his way to school getting immense pleasure from what had become his favorite smell. The prospect of working so close to the Bake house excited him, being constantly on his mind that given time he might be able to graduate from being the shop boy to train as a Baker.

To achieve this dream, he would have to pass the dreaded test and it was with more than a little trepidation that he approached the shop on that Monday morning, where he was met by Mr. Randall, a short rotund individual with a florid complexion, which suggested a liking for whisky. He had a bald head, but had profuse amounts of hair growing from his nostrils and ears. It intrigued Tom that older men seemed to be able to grow hair everywhere except where it was supposed to be. A jovial man, he was popular with his customers and greeted his prospective employee with a broad smile making him feel just a bit more comfortable prior to his imminent ordeal.

Tom was ushered into a small back room where he was told to sit at a table and given a pencil and paper.

"Right me lad, I'll give you four or five sums to do with adding up, taking away and a bit of simple multiplication, after that I'll read out a few words that I want you to spell and write down. Are you ready?"

A petrified Tom replied nervously, "Yes Sir."

"Right here we go, I want you to add 6 pence, one and four pence, nine pence and a shilling, and you can write the answer down on the paper."

That set the pattern for another four similar problems, after which Randall said, "Right, now I'll read out ten words and you can write them down on your paper."

Growing in confidence, he knew was good at spelling and without hesitation wrote the answers to the first nine words, but the last one flummoxed him and he pondered, is margarine spelt with a "j" or a "g". After a few moments, he wrote down "marjarine", ending his aspirations of shop work.

Randall perused his answers and confirmed Tom's fears, dismissing him with, "I'm sorry young Walton your no good to me, you got two of the sums wrong and can't spell either."

Tom almost ran out of the shop with tears in his eyes, wondering how he was going to tell his mother of his humiliation. Instead of going home, he walked up the slight hill to a bridge over the canal and began walking along the towpath. So, embarrassed by his failure to fulfill his Mothers wishes for him, he seemed in a daze as he trudged aimlessly along the canal side. Approaching a bend in the path looking at the ground, he failed to see a giant horse towing a canal boat coming towards him and was almost knocked into the water, just managing to jump out of the way in time.

"Watch where you're going, silly young bugger" shouted the bargee, "you've frightened me orse."

The horse didn't look very frightened to Tom, continuing on its way seemingly completely unconcerned.

"Sorry Mister", said Tom, thinking that it might have been better if he had been nudged into the muddy water and drowned, at least he wouldn't have had to face his mother.

After wandering for the remainder of the morning it was pangs of hunger that influenced his decision to go home and face the music. He walked steadily down the dark entry and crept inside the back door, trying to delay the inevitable if possible. But there she was in the kitchen, peeling potatoes, greeting him with her usual smile.

"Well, how did you get along on your first morning as a working man?"

"I'm sorry mother, I haven't got a job, Mr. Randall says I'm no good for shop work because I can't add up and I'm not that good at spelling."

His Mothers smile disappeared, but her face remained sympathetic, "Never mind, it's not the end of the world, we'll wait for your Dad to come home and then we can talk about it."

Tom pottered around until late in the afternoon when his Dad returned from the Day Shift, covered in coal dust as usual, having left for work at six o'clock that morning. He knew straight away that something was wrong, "What's up then?"

His Mother came straight out with it "They're not going to take Tom on Randall's. Randall says he's not clever enough for shop work."

"Not clever enough be buggered, any bugger is clever enough to work in a shop. Any road, I can get him fixed up at the pit and he'll have a job for life."

"I don't want him down the pit, Henry."

"What else is there round here; all his mates are going anyway so it's settled?"

Giving a sigh of resignation, even though Tom's opinion hadn't been asked he knew that his destiny was decided.

Chapter 5

Three months after his fourteenth birthday, Tom walked along the Pit Lane with his Father to the Colliery where he expected to work until he retired, which if he was lucky was fifty long years in the future. It was five thirty. Dawn breaking, he thought that when the sun comes up he wouldn't be seeing much of it as it would be late in the afternoon when he emerged from the black hole, by which time he would be baptized with his first coat of coal dust. Loving the open air, he had spent as much time as possible in the fields and woods that surrounded the village. He had always been surprised that the countryside close to the pit, with its smoke and dust from the slag heap, was so unspoiled, with the hedgerows either side of the lane ripe with blackberries, providing refuge for diverse types of birds. This made his approach to the pit even more depressing and he grew angry with a God, if one existed, that had not made him, what his teachers had called, "clever".

Dad had told him a few days before, that he had got him a job and would be starting the following Monday, handing him a metal box, saying, "You'll be needing this for your snap."

His Dad continued, "You'll not be working on the face just yet, I've got you a job with the Osler."

"What's an Osler?"

"He looks after the horses, there are a fair few of them in the pit, they pull the coal tubs along the rails from the face to the pit bottom and back again"

"Do they stay down the pit all the time?"

"Nearly all the time, they get a week or twos break once a year, poor buggers."

That was to be his lot for the next four years and what surprised him was that he enjoyed it. Jack Harper, the Osler was easy to get on with from the start and after he laid the law down on the first day, Tom knowing exactly where he stood. Having not met Jack before as he was from another village, he was surprised that after looking him up and down he shook his hand saying, "Right me lad, I'm Mr. Harper and its my job as well as yours to keep these horses as well as is possible down here. We can't keep them clean, but we muck out the stalls and put clean bedding down so they're as comfortable when they're not working, because when they do they work bloody hard and the better they're looked after the more we get out of them. You will also have to take them to and from the face and don't worry about getting lost because the horses know their way around"

"What if we get a new one?"

"Good question lad, then we have to take special care of them until they get used to the dark, but they soon settle down."

Becoming increasingly attached to his charges, apart from being underground the work was not too arduous and there was a pay packet at the end of each week. Taking it home unopened to his mother, he never knew how much was in it but was grateful to be handed back a few shillings' pocket money. This was the pattern of his early working life, he developed an affection the placid animals, who like him he felt were not made for pit work and should be outdoors in the fields. It was therefore with relish that he could take pairs of them to the pit top each year, guiding them to a nearby field, where they would spend their all too brief summer holiday. A wonderful sight was to watch them gallop around the small enclosure with the freedom that they were usually denied. Fed by a local farmer, Tom would visit them every day making sure all was well and was distraught when he collected them to resume their bleak existence underground.

It all changed when be was eighteen his Father telling him, "Your days as a horse trainer are over lad, it's about time you did proper pit work on the face, it'll make a man of you."

Tom wasn't particularly pleased as he was perfectly happy with his lot, knowing that face work as well as being physically demanding could be dangerous, but knew that argument would be futile. Although his mother did speak up for him, saying that Tom was obviously content with working with the horses and shouldn't be forced to change.

His Dad had none of it ending the conversation with, "He's eighteen now and will get a lot more money on the face. Before we know it, he'll be leaving home and getting married, he'll need as much as he can earn then, so that's the end of it. Mind you, he won't be going onto the face straight away because he has to do his training"

Chapter 6

Realizing that his time with the horses, while enjoyable had in effect delayed his introduction to what his Dad referred to as real pit work. Finding himself in a group that were all younger than him, having to learn all aspects of life underground before being allocated to what was considered best suited to his talents. By the time his training period finished, having shed all the excess weight that had marred his teenage years, he was as strong as most face workers, so was an ideal candidate for "stripping". Each man was allocated a stint that had to be completed in the eight hours spent underground, which included twenty minutes "snap time", during which he consumed the sandwiches that his mother prepared for him. These were filled with cheese or occasionally beef dripping and washed down with water.

Looking in the mirror after ridding himself of the filth that was a bi-product of the job, he was content with the reflection, that showed his black neatly trimmed hair and almost olive skin, which he nurtured by spending all his time away from the pit in the open air. He tanned so easily that people often commented that he must have had Latin ancestors in the dim distant past. Another feature was the dark shadow on the lower half of his thin face, stubbornly refusing to disappear no matter how closely or often he used his razor. Wondering why he had so little success with girls, the fact was that while he was sure of his self in every other aspect of life, his confidence disappeared whenever he approached a young woman, even those that his mates referred to as being "rough".

On his twenty first birthday, his situation at home changed, his Mother telling him that from now on he wasn't required to bring his pay packet home unopened, but would pay his "board" and keep the rest. Set at thirty shillings, Tom was impressed that this would leave over two pounds for him to do with as he pleased. On the actual day, he returned from the pit with his Dad, who was on the same shift, being greeted by a special tea, which comprised of ham and beef sandwiches and an iced fruit cake that his mother had made, with "Happy 21st Birthday Tom" embellished in red icing on the top, with a single candle in the middle. His Mother and Maud, who was now sixteen and had proved "clever" enough to get a job at Randall's, stood proudly behind the table smiling broadly and together with his Father spontaneously serenaded him with "Happy Birthday to You."

After tea, his Dad said, "Right Me Lad, you're a man now so you can take me down to the "Oak" and buy me a pint and then I'll buy you one back and see where we go from there."

Tom had never been in a pub before, so he felt somewhat out of place amongst his Fathers mates, most of whom he knew. Duly buying his Dad's pint of mild and having the same himself, after taking the first mouthful he pondered, why do people pay for this stuff? He had nowhere near finished his drink when his Dad put another glass in front of him, which was followed by numerous others as the "Oak" regulars were intent on joining in the celebrations. Soon beginning to feel lightheaded, when "time gentlemen please" was called he was seeing double. Staggering home supported by his Father, who seemed totally unaffected by the celebrations, Tom was unable to walk up the steep staircase and thought it better to crawl. When he first got into bed, he was alarmed that the room was spinning, but this soon passed as he drifted into a comatose sleep.

Regaining consciousness with a start, his Dad came into the bedroom and shook him saying, "Come on lad, its gone five o'clock, and time to go to work."

Feeling as though his head was about to explode, his mouth tasted foul, concluding it impossible to get out of bed let alone do a stint on the coal face. Realizing he had little option, he dragged himself up into a sitting position, only to realize that except for his jacket and boots he was still fully dressed. Standing up, his head felt even worse and immediately vowed that he would never drink again. When he got down stairs his father was waiting for him seemingly having little sympathy, telling him you always had to pay for a good night's drinking and they'd be leaving in five minutes. At that, Tom went through into the kitchen and put his head under the pump that brought soft water from an underground well, keeping it there until it was time to leave, the last few seconds being taken up by drinking as much water that he could get down him.

It was a painful walk to the pit and confronted by the day's work arriving on the face, he thought this is bloody ridiculous; I can hardly hold my head up let alone a pick and shovel. Despite his discomfort, he set about the coal seam, but after only about fifteen minutes felt light headed and began to retch, depositing the earlier consumed liquid onto the ground. Afterwards he began to feel better, but wasn't working as fast as normal, he managed almost half of his allotted stint by Snap Time, when he was surprised that he was able to eat his cheese sandwiches.

Coming of Age didn't change Tom's life much, although he appreciated having the extra money. His first love was football and he was a regular in the pit team, which played in the local league, embracing other pit and village teams in the vicinity. He and his mates made a lot of the journeys to the various locations by bike, but for longer trips the club hired a charabanc. Although baths had been installed on the pit top, meaning that he and his father could clean themselves up after work, football was another thing, there being no showers at any of the grounds. If it was muddy, that's how he arrived home, relying on the trusted tin bath. At least for home games the changing rooms were located next to the pitch, but many of the village teams used huts or rooms above a local pub, players having to walk up to half a mile to games. Whether a weekend was enjoyable or not very much depended on results, but fortunately the pit team won more than they lost. Summer weekends were taken up by cricket, with most of Tom's group playing both sports, although the summer game saw some of the older miners involved.

There were trips to the Picture House and the local dances, held in various Parish Halls giving Tom the opportunity to meet girls. Failing to understand why he was totally ill at ease in female company, he lacked the confidence to approach any girls of his own age and watched almost every dance. Another problem was that he was renowned for having "two left feet".

Despite this he did have the occasional date, usually ending up in the Picture House, given his lack of aplomb on the dance floor. They never came to much and he concluded, it might be easier to give up on girls and remain a bachelor.

CHAPTER 7

Barbara Garrett came along when he was twenty-two. A friend of Maud's and the same age as his sister, she was five years Tom's junior. Barbara had been visiting their house for years and while Tom always thought that she was a nice little girl, he had always looked upon her as a child. Noticing that she was a lot more grown up these days, developing into an extremely attractive young woman, with quite short dark hair, a round attractive face and only slightly shorter than Tom's five foot ten. Another thing that was brought to his notice by one of his more observant mates was, "she's got a bit of meat on her, mostly in the right places and all."

Feeding the pigs, which was still one of his regular jobs, Maud looked over the Sty wall and dropped what to Tom was a bombshell.

"Barbara has asked me if you'll take her to the pictures on Saturday Night."

Somewhat taken aback, he replied, "She's only seventeen and I work with her Dad at the pit, he'll have my guts for garters."

"No, he won't, daft sod, you're not exactly an old man you know."

"I'm going to ask him first and if he says it's alright I'll take her."

Maud went back up the path shaking her head, "You're a funny lad Tom."

Tom was worried at the prospect of approaching Jack Garrett, even though they got on quite well. Jack was very much like Tom's Dad, being well built, but spreading at the waist as he moved into middle age. He had a swarthy dark complexion with what appeared to be specs of coal dust under his skin, apparently, the result of being involved in a minor explosion in the pit when he was in his teens.

Knocking on the door of the terraced miner's cottage about ten minutes' walk away, it was answered by Barbara's mother who looked surprised to see him.

"Hello Tom, she said, what can we do for you?"

"I'd like to speak to Mr. Garrett please if he's in." said Tom, hoping that he wasn't.

"Tom Walton's here to see you Jack."

"Tell him to come in, Edna."

Mrs. Garrett showed Tom into one of the only two downstairs rooms of the small cottage, the other being the kitchen. Jack was sat in an armchair with his pipe, clouds of smoke drifting up to the ceiling of the small room where the family lived and ate. Wearing a shirt without a collar, an open waistcoat and trousers held up with braces. Like most of the older miners, he also had a thick leather belt around his waist, the threat of the "strap" being regularly used to deter children from misbehaving.

"How do Tom? Sit your sen down."

Sitting in the other armchair, facing the large coal fire in the black range that was the centre piece of the room he overcame his trepidation, "Mr. Garrett, I've come to ask if I can take your Barbara to the pictures on Saturday."

"How old are you Tom?"

"Twenty-two."

"Well she's only seventeen, so don't you think she's a bit young for you?"

At that moment, the front door opened and in walked Barbara, who took one look at Tom and quickly ran up the creaky stairs to the refuge of the bedroom that she shared with her younger sister.

Jack was grinning, "What do you reckon, Tom?"

Not sure whether to persevere or just go, he plucked up courage, "You're right Mr. Garrett, but I like her and I think that she likes me and she's been friends with Maud since they started school."

"Right lad, you can take her if she wants to go, but let me tell you this, I hear a lot at the pit from young lads boasting about what they've done with girls and I wouldn't like to think anybody would treat either of mine like that. So, if you do take her, you can call for her here and bring her straight back after the Big Picture finishes."

"Most of the talk at the pit is wishful thing Mr. Garrett and you won't here anything like that from me. If she says she'll come, I'll call for her at half past five on Saturday and promise that I'll look after her."

Feeling pleased with himself he told Maud about his successful mission, asking her to tell Barbara that he would call for her at half past five on Saturday.

The three days until then seemed endless, but when Saturday came he dressed in the only suit he owned, made sure that his shirt collar wasn't frayed and fixed his tie as neatly as possible, given lack of practice as he seldom wore one. Leaving early and hanging around at the end of Barbara's road for a few minutes, he tried to avoid appearing too eager. At half past five exactly, he knocked on the door and was greeted by Barbara herself who smiled and came straight out. Tom thought that she looked wonderful in her floral summer dress that covered her shoulders and knees, with her almost black hair shining in the fading sunlight, but Tom had to hurry to keep up as she breezed enthusiastically along the street. Looking around she said,

"Come on Tom, we don't want to be late, there might be a big queue because it's Fred Astaire and Ginger Rodgers."

Walking briskly along Barbara said, "When you came to our house the other day and I saw you sat there, I didn't know where to put myself, because I twigged what was going on. Why did you ask my Dad if you could take ME out?"

"Because I thought it was the right thing to do, I work on the same district as your Dad and wouldn't want to fall out with him, after all I am five years older than you."

"Well there was no need, I'm the apple of his eye and I'm sure he would think I'd be safe with an old bloke like you" she said laughing.

As expected. there was quite a queue when they arrived at "The Palace", which was a somewhat pretentious title for a converted warehouse. Joining on the end, they were soon at the kiosk where Tom paid a shilling each for seats in the Balcony, mainly because his mates usually sat down stairs and the last thing that he wanted them to know was that he had taken his sisters seventeen-year-old friend out.

Pathe News was already on, which Tom wouldn't normally give a second glance, but it was interesting for a change, with pictures of the

Olympic Games that had recently been held in Berlin. Germany was seldom out of the news and even with his passive interest in what was going on in the World he was usually aware of the latest antics of Adolf Hitler. There was a glimpse of him in the report, which was predominantly about the black American runner Jesse Owens, who had won five Gold Medals. Tom whispered, "I wouldn't mind being a black man if I could run like that."

Barbara whispered a reply, "Well Mister, there's no way that my Dad would let me go out with a black man." Which made him laugh.

It was well into the program that they finally got to see the Big Picture, which was "Top Hat", that had been released the previous year, it always taking a long time for pictures to get to The Palace. Tom was enthralled by Fred and Ginger's dancing but would never admit it. When it started, he felt for Barbara's hand and she seemed happy enough to let him hold on to it, but he didn't feel confident enough to put his arm around her shoulders. At the end of the film, the lights came up and he suddenly realized how visible they were to all and sundry. With that in mind, he walked out in front of her and only turned to wait when they were some way up the street.

"Are we in a race or what?" She said breathlessly

"Sorry, I didn't want any of my mates seeing us."

"Why not?"

"It's just that they'd be on about it at the pit and I don't like the way they talk about girls."

"Well, you don't have to join in."

"You're right, but I did promise your Dad that I'd get you straight home."

Taking about ten minutes to get back to her house, nothing was said all the way until they got to the front door where she turned and smiled, "Thank you for taking me, I thought the picture was wonderful. Did you like it?"

Not wanting to expose his soft side, he replied, "It was OK, but I'm glad you enjoyed it."

At that she turned, brushed his cheek with her lips and was gone.

Chapter 8

Walking home quickly, he was soon in bed, realizing that he liked Barbara and couldn't wait to ask her out again. When he got up in the morning after his usual Sunday lay in, Maud was helping her Mother prepare Sunday Dinner, the only time in the week that roast meat found its way to their table. Maud was quick to ask, "How did you get on with Barbara then?"

"Not bad, she was OK but didn't say a lot."

"What about you, did you say a lot?"

"I suppose not."

"Well then, what do you expect?"

At that, he was out of the back door to feed the pigs, going out after lunch with his Dad and their black and white mongrel Mick to try and snare a rabbit.

Later that evening, Maud asked if he was going to ask Barbara out again.

"I don't know if she'd want to, I think she was a bit miffed that I walked out of the Palace in front of her and she had to catch me up, you ask her for me."

"Ask her your self" was the abrupt reply.

Taking him a couple of days to pluck up the courage, he was on day shift so got home in the middle of the afternoon. Knowing that she finished work at around five, he waited at the end of Church Road where she lived at about the time he thought she would be passing. Standing at the end of the road was not ideal, attracting glances from passers by, most of whom he knew. It was a relief when after about twenty minutes she appeared around the corner. The problem was that she was with her friend

Doreen, who took one look at him and giggled. That would normally have put Tom right off, but he wanted to go out with Barbara so much that he stood in their path.

"Hello Barbara, have you got a minute?"

They stopped and he was relieved when she said, "I'll see you in the morning Doreen."

He smiled saying, "Can we go out again this weekend?"

"It depends, are you sure you want to be seen with me in public?"

"Bloody Hell Barbara, I told you why I did that and it won't happen again."

"No need to swear me lad and your right it won't because if it does that will be that. Anyway, I'm going out with Doreen on Saturday night, but if it's fine we can go for a walk on Sunday afternoon. I'll meet you here at two if it's not raining."

Sunday's weather was uppermost in his mind for the rest of the week and it was with alarm that he woke up on Saturday morning to the sound of rain driven by strong wind against the window pane. Fortunately, it didn't last and playing football in the afternoon, while it was still breezy the rain had stopped. There was further improvement the following morning, with continuous warm sunshine only being interrupted occasionally by wispy white clouds. As was the case on the previous Saturday, Tom dressed in his best suit, collar and tie, with brightly polished boots, positioning himself at the end of Church Road by the appointed time. He had no way of telling the time but had left home allowing himself ten minutes to walk to the meeting place, which was twice that required, but his eagerness to get there early contributed to his alarm when Barbara failed to appear. He was on the point of giving up when she hurried along the street waving, looking flustered and breathlessly saying, "Sorry I'm late, dinner was later than usual and I had to help with the washing up."

"That's alright; it was really nice standing here in the sunshine and you're here now."

Walking out of the village along a lane leading to a pathway that took them into the woods Tom loved. It was on the cusp of early autumn but the leaves on the trees were still almost wholly intact, restricting the sunlight, but allowing bright beams to penetrate the canopy, giving them the benefit of warmth on an ideal late summer afternoon. As they had entered the wood, with its shelter and seclusion, Tom felt confident enough to put his arm around her shoulder. The exhilaration he felt when Barbara placed her arm around his waist, made it one of the happiest moments that he had ever experienced. Animated by her company, he chatted about his ambitions of getting work away from the pit one day and how he would never let his own children near the place. Trying to impart his love of nature, he pointed out wildlife, particularly birds that were so abundant, in what was their own private world. Time passed quickly and after what he thought was about an hour they began to walk back towards the village and as they were almost out of the cover provided by the trees he stopped, pulled her towards him and kissed her. There was no resistance when Barbara responded to his embrace more willingly than he had expected, gazing into his eyes saying, "Well, where do we go from here?"

"I don't know."

"Do you want to go out with me regular?

"If that's what you want and you like me enough."

"I wouldn't have let you kiss me if I didn't like you enough, daft beggar."

So, that's where they went, seeing each other every weekend and occasionally on weekdays, it soon being accepted in the village that they were a couple, who would probably get married one day. Tom knew that was unlikely to happen until Barbara was twenty-one, having been told by her strict parents that she would do as they told her until then. Happy enough to have time to save up enough money to ensure they had what his mother called, "a good start in life.", Tom became a regular visitor to the Post Office, depositing every penny he could afford.

That's how it was for the next two years, a contented Tom was proud of Barbara, being astonished that a girl who could have her pick of the village lads had chosen him. As was their want, workmates pulled his leg, enquiring if he was getting "it'. Not responding to their lewdness, he certainly wasn't and hadn't even tried, particularly as Barbara had made it clear that "it" was only for married people and of the possible consequences for them both if she "got into trouble". She had allowed him to touch her breasts on the outside of her blouse, but any attempt to go inside, was swiftly rebuffed.

Despite being happy with his lot, the possibility of escape from the pit was never far from his thoughts and he saw his chance. Taking more than a passing interest in the latest news, particularly from Germany, whose Chancellor Adolf Hitler was constantly making demands to expand his influence well beyond the frontiers of his nation. This came to a head for Tom in September 1938, watching the Newsreel at the Palace with Barbara at his side. Seeing Mr. Chamberlain come down the aero plane steps waving his piece of paper, saying that there would be "peace in our time", having capitulated to Hitler's demands regarding the Sudetenland.

"Barbara whispered, "What a wonderful man, nobody wants a war"

Tom's response was unequivocal, "Wonderful man be buggered, he's a coward and only delaying the inevitable"

After that Barbara hardly said a word until they arrived back at her front door, where she kissed him briefly and went straight inside.

Tom thought no more about that, but was angry at what he had seen on the Newsreel and during the week that followed decided to do something about it. Sometimes cycling the four miles to the nearby town, usually when he needed something, as he was on afternoon shift and it was a particularly nice morning, this time he did it on impulse. Wheeling his bike around the streets, outside the large Post Office, he was confronted by a poster. It was colorful and the centre piece was a young man in football kit, with a soldier's peak cap and unbuttoned tunic, standing in front of the globe. He had a broad smile on his face, a football under one arm and a cigarette in the other hand. Large red letters at the top heralded, THE FINEST JOB IN THE WORLD, surrounding the globe it invited the reader to, "Work and Play All-Over the Globe". While the largest black capitals at the bottom confirmed that to have the chance to avail yourself of these opportunities, all you had to do was JOIN THE ARMY and that's just what he did.

Thinking that if there was going to be a war, he was going to be ready for it and not stuck down the pit while others were defending his country, with the prospect of fresh air seven days a week being exhilarating. He didn't expect for one minute that he might be dodging bullets. It was a simple enough process, a trip to the nearest recruiting office, which was fifteen miles away, causing him to miss a day's work. The Recruiting Sergeant was a friendly middle aged chap with a row of medal ribbons on his chest, making it obvious that he had served in the war. He told Tom that he had spent four years in India and that the Army was a wonderful opportunity for any young man. Not needing to be convinced, he had already made up his mind prior to walking through the Office door. The Sergeant took his details and discussed what skills that he had. Tom outlined his career in the pit also mentioning his work with horses. The conclusion was that the best option for him would be the Infantry and that they would do their best to allocate him to his local County Regiment. At the end of the process, the Sergeant shook his hand saying that he would be contacted and told when to report for a medical, if it was satisfactory he would be in.

Going home to wait for the letter, he told no one of his plans. After a couple of weeks, it duly arrived, the brown envelope embellished with "On His Majesties Service", and fortunately he got his hands on it before anyone else saw it. He was to report back to the Office the following week, having to make yet another excuse to be off work. As expected, he sailed through the Medical Examination and was told to go home and await further instructions. Three weeks passed and he got back into his normal routine. Barbara had seemed to get over their disagreement about Mr. Chamberlain, being her usual ebullient self. Then one afternoon when he came in from the Day Shift, there on the kitchen table was a large brown envelope waiting for him. His Mother looking somewhat concerned asked, "What's that then, are you in some kind of trouble?"

"No I don't think so; I know what it is."

Opening the envelope in front of his mother, by which time his Dad had also come into the room. They both looked at him anxiously and he knew that now was the time to tell them.

"I've joined the Army and will be going in a fortnight's time."

His Mother was silent but looked downcast but his Father reaction shocked him,

"You're a daft young bugger, what did you do a silly thing like that for. Everybody knows that there's going to be a war, you'd be a lot safer in the pit."

"You know I've never liked it down the pit and war or no war this will give me a chance to see the world."

"If you don't end up with a German bullet in you."

"That's a risk I'll have to take, but I want the chance of a life away from this village."

His Mother interjected, "Have you told Barbara?"

"No", he replied, I haven't told anybody, I'll go around and tell her tonight", not relishing the thought one little bit.

After a not very enjoyable tea, he made the short walk to Church Road and knocked on the door. Barbara answered herself, looking surprised,

"Hello, I wasn't expecting to see you tonight."

"I need to tell you something, can I come in?"

"Of course, you can, Mum and Dad are in."

All three of them looked at him expectantly and deciding that there was no easy way of announcing his news said, "I've joined the Army and go in two weeks' time."

Barbara and her Mother looked astonished, but her Dad grinned, shook his hand and said, "Good lad, I don't blame you, I'd do the same if I was your age."

Barbara was not so understanding saying, "Well I think it's terrible, you could at least have talked to me before you did it", and ran up the stairs to her bed room.

"She'll come around Tom, it's just been a bit of a shock" said her Dad trying to reassure him. Tom wasn't convinced and even less so after she failed to reappear before he left twenty minutes later.

Chapter 9

The next two weeks passed quickly, giving notice at the pit, he would have a few days off prior to reporting to the Regimental Depot, only twenty miles away. Reaction around the village was generally positive, with more than one of his mates intimating that they were thinking of following him into the services. Several older men told him that they "would go tomorrow if they were young enough" and that the Army would "make a man of him." Gradually getting over her initial shock, his mother said that she would miss him, but if that's what he wanted to do, he would go with her blessing. Conversely, his Father was still far from enthusiastic, telling him that there was going to be war and it would be "bloody dangerous."

Barbara's reaction was the worst, initially sending a message through Maud that she wouldn't be going out Saturday night. It was obvious that she was upset with him, so he went around to her house on a peace-making mission after lunch on the following Sunday, only to find that she was out. Her Mother seemed a bit unsettled and not as friendly towards him as usual. It got worse when Maud told him that she had been told that Barbara had been seen out with Roger Holland on Saturday, who was the same age as she was. Feeling betrayed, Tom was livid but thought it better to calm himself down before confronting her. Knowing the time that she got home from work, he waited for her on the next Thursday afternoon. Looking sheepish at seeing him, she stopped in her tracks saying,

"What do you want?'

Shocked by the abrupt greeting, but trying suppress his anger, he asked, "Don't you think that you owe me an explanation?"

"What for?"

"Well for one thing saying you couldn't come out on Saturday and then going out with somebody else"

"You don't own me Tom and I'll go out with anyone I like."

"So, the last two years don't mean anything then?"

"Of course, they do, but you joined the Army without a word to me and that was cruel. I always thought that you put me first and that we would get married, but you've spoilt it"

"Look, soldiers can get married, I'll be able to come home on leave and I don't want to work in the pit all my life."

"And what do you expect me to do all the time you're not here, sit at home and nit?"

"No, but you don't need to go out with other blokes"

"Well I like going out and I like Roger, so you've made your choice and I've made mine."

Losing his cool, he shouted, "Well good luck to you, you spoilt little bitch. You're the only girl I've ever looked at, but Holland's welcome to you."

Bursting into tears, Barbara ran up the street seeking the sanctuary of her house, while Tom, immediately regretting his outburst turned on his heel, went straight to the pub, thoroughly miserable.

The following day at the pit Jack Garrett approached him outside of the canteen and put a conciliatory hand on his shoulder saying, "Our Barbara was upset when she came in last night, have you had a fight?"

Relating the events of the past few days, which provoked Jack's sympathy, "She's being unreasonable, but it's a common trait in women that we all have to get used to. I've never been able to weigh them up, but don't worry this Holland thing is probably a flash in the pan, she'll come round."

"Well, I'm off in a week's time come what may, but thanks for being so understanding Jack, you're a good mate."

The next week passed quickly enough and he didn't see Barbara again, not that he looked for her. After the disappointment of her attitude and subsequent actions, he tried to convince himself that he was better off without her and concentrate on his new life. On the day that he was to leave, he was awake early, dressed in his best and only suit and after eating his usual bowl of porridge was ready for his adventure. Grabbing his small bag, he had hoped to get out of the door without too much fuss, but his mother, who seemed close to tears, hugged him and told him to come back soon. Dad was on the afternoon shift and much to Tom's surprise, decided to walk with him to the small village station, where eight trains stopped each day, little being said during the fifteen minutes it took them to get there. Not long after arriving, a plume of smoke appeared about half a mile away. Shortly afterwards a grimy tank engine pulling two red carriages clanked into the station, when his Dad shook his hand and said, "Well this is it me lad, I still don't agree with what you're doing but if it's what you want, so be it. Make sure you look after yourself"

Finding an unoccupied compartment, Tom was quickly inside pulling on the window strap to bring it wide open. Hoping to have enough time to thank his Father for the unexpected good wishes, he was already walking along the platform towards the exit and didn't look back.

Tom's destination was a much larger station just three stops up the line, where he arrived half an hour later. Walking towards the exit, he saw a group of chaps standing around a small stocky man in khaki, wearing a peaked cap and holding a clip board. Approaching the man, who had two stripes on his arm and looked him up and down before almost shouting," Are you for the Warwick's son?"

"Yes sir."

"I'm not a sir lad; I work for a bloody living. It's only Officers you call sir. I'm a Corporal and that's what you call me. What's your name?"

"Tom Walton, Corporal"

"Right Walton, get on the back of that lorry, we're going for a ride."

Climbing onto the back of the lorry, just as it began to rain, he was relieved there was an iron frame covered by tarpaulin to provide shelter. Sharing the transport with ten others, just about allowing enough space for them to occupy the wooden bench seats either side of the tailgate. They were all around his age or younger and very much occupied by their own thoughts of what awaited them. Their far from luxurious conveyance set off on what the Corporal told them was the short journey to the depot. After around ten minutes they came to a stop, hearing someone say, "More lambs to the slaughter, bring them in." Setting off again, it finally came to a halt on a large tarmac square, where the tailgate was opened by two soldiers, one of whom said, "City Centre lads, off you get."

After jumping down, they were confronted by the smartest man Tom had ever encountered. Standing rigidly to attention, with highly polished boots, an immaculate khaki uniform with pressed creases on the trousers and sleeves of his tunic that looked as though could cause a nasty wound to anyone that was unfortunate enough to come into contact with them. No hair whatsoever was visible beneath his splendid peaked cap. Along his chest, this fearsome looking individual sported a row of medal ribbons and a broad red sash, while under his arm he carried what appeared to be a gold tipped cane.

As soon as they all had their feet on the ground the statuesque soldier shouted, "Right, line up in single file and keep quiet"

The recruits shuffled into line, placing their bags on the ground beside them, waiting in anticipation for this fearsome being to address them.

"Right gentlemen, let me introduce myself, my name is Sgt. Major Broadhurst and you will stand to attention in my presence and address me as Sgt. Major. I will be looking after you with the help of Corporal Winterbottom who met you at the station. He will be your Drill Instructor for the next three months, by the end of which you will be sick of the sight of both of us and the ground that you are standing on, which is a Parade Square and designed for marching up and down until you look something like soldiers. The first thing that the Corporal will be doing is to take you to your barracks, where you'll be given a bed and two lockers, one large and one small, to store your kit in. Then you will go to the Bedding Store, which is where you get blankets and sheets to keep you warm at night, we'll make sure that you're warm enough in the day. That will do for today, you can have the evening free and go to the NAFFI if you want, but make sure that your back in your barracks and in bed by lights out at 22.00 hours. For those of you that can't count to 24, that's 10 o'clock. Do you all understand?"

There were some mumbles of assent, which seemed to irritate the Sgt Major, who shouted, "If you understand me the way to show it is to shout." Yes, Sgt. Major. Do you understand?"

The line of recruits responded in unison.

That was the start of an intense period, during which Tom pondered whether he had made the right decision. For one thing, he was earning less than half of what he made at the pit, not that there was much to spend it on within the confines of the Regimental Depot. On the plus side, he enjoyed being outdoors for most of the time and was soon feeling much better physically because of the daily PT sessions. One thing that he found depressing was the amount of so called "Bull" that was expected, not that he minded keeping his uniform pressed and his boots shining. Polishing floors and cleaning toilets was another thing altogether and while accepting that everywhere should be clean, having to keep everything pristine for daily inspections seemed illogical.

They didn't see the Sgt. Major every day, but he could certainly be heard some distance away as he had a perpetual habit of shouting at everybody and everything. Their tormentor in chief, Cpl. Winterbottom, quickly became known as "Cold Arse" in their twenty-four-man barrack room. It was of wooden construction, with twelve beds either side of the highly-polished linoleum covered floor. Although somewhat Spartan it was comfortable enough, with a coal stove in the middle, providing barely adequate heating in the winter months. Just about managing to eke out the coal ration, the exhausted recruits gathered around the stove each evening to keep warm.

The reveille bugle sounded at 6.30 each morning, the Corporal appearing almost instantaneously to make sure that his charges were out of bed, always shouting the same greeting, "Hands off your cocks on with your socks." That summed Winterbottom up, fancying himself as a bit of comedian, but not getting too many laughs. They had an hour to wash and dress, tidy the barrack room and have breakfast, before having to be on parade for inspection at 7.30. Then it was a mixture of drill, P.T., weapons training and firing on the rifle range. That was an aspect of soldiering that didn't appeal to Tom at all. Not liking the incessant noise created by numerous rifles being fired simultaneously, he concluded that he would never be a marksman as his target invariably remained unscathed. This caused Cpl. Winterbottom some consternation, informing Tom that he'd never be a soldier as long as he had "an ole in his arse." According to the Cpl, the same conclusion applied to the majority of the Company and despite these shortcomings they all finished their basic training, passing out as fully fledged Privates and were rewarded with a forty-eight-hour pass.

Making the short journey back to his village, Tom was treated like a hero in the "Oak", with many of the older drinkers wanting to buy him to a pint. It was nice to see his Mum, Dad and Maud, who seemed proud of her big brother, wanting to know every detail of the three months since she had last seen him. He also enjoyed some home cooking, which was a pleasant change from what he had become used to in barracks. Maud also told him that Barbara had been asking after him, but was still going out with young Holland. Tom's only response was, "The best of luck to her, she can go out with every young chap in the village for all I care."

Returning to the Depot, Tom was informed that he had been allocated to the 2nd Battalion of the Royal Warwickshire Regiment, currently serving in India. Excited by this, India was somewhere that you only read about in books or got a glimpse of on Movietone News, he looked forward to receiving the details of his passage. Following a week of anticipation, he was called to the Admin Office expecting to receive his orders, but was deflated to be told that the Battalion was being brought back from India and he would join them in Yorkshire after their arrival, where they would be part of an Infantry Brigade based near York.

Having never travelled so far away from home before, despite his disappointment he looked forward to joining the Battalion at their new base. Strenshall Barracks was only eight miles outside of the City, which suited Tom, whose inquisitive mind found York fascinating, with its ancient Minster and City Wall, finding ample time to explore when he was granted a pass. Many of his colleagues spent their time off seeking comfort from the female population, but that didn't appeal to him, his split with Barbara having convinced him that he would be better off keeping away from women. Not that he had much time for that sort of thing anyway, given the intensity of the training that the Battalion was subjected to, and it becoming clear from the attitude of his Officers and NCOs' that they expected to be fighting Germans before the year was out. Returning home for short periods of leave, it was on one these visits that news came through that Germany had invaded Poland and that the Government had delivered an ultimatum in Berlin that they must withdraw.

Since he had left home his Mother and Father had acquired a Radio that was powered by a large portable battery. It had been in the newspapers that the Prime Minister would make a radio broadcast at 11.15 am on 3rd September. Gathering around with his family, they listened in eerie silence, Mr. Chamberlain giving details of the ultimatum to the German government, which had been ignored and consequently the war that Tom had anticipated had started. Soon after the broadcast the air raid siren that had been installed in the village sounded, not that it made much difference because they had no shelters to go to. His father's reaction summing it up,

"What a bloody waste of time", "there's bugger all to bomb here."

Tom was under instructions to return to his unit immediately in these circumstances and left for the journey back that afternoon, not knowing when he would see his parents and Maud again. Maud and his Mother seeming aware of the dangers that Tom was likely to encounter, making his departure even more emotional, with both in tears. His Dad was more pragmatic, again accompanying him as far as the station, his parting shot being," keep your head down lad"

Chapter 10

Arriving back at the Depot, he learned that the Battalion would be leaving for France in days rather than weeks and soon found himself on a packed troop train heading south, taking several hours to reach the coast and the ship that would take him away from England for the first time. Following a choppy crossing, Tom was happy to climb on to the back of a lorry, taking him to his destination on the Franco- Belgian border where the hierarchy expected the Germans to attack.

That heralded a period of intense boredom, with very little happening. They were unable to relax, being told that the Germans could attack any time and they had to be ready, but apart from a few skirmishes which they heard about along the long defensive line, the enemy was only conspicuous by its absence. Continuing throughout the cold winter spent in tents, spring brought reports of a few naval actions, Tom feeling that the war was passing him by.

It came as a shock when in May they heard that the Germans were attacking, making significant gains through the Netherlands and Belgium, being expected to arrive at the Warwick's position within days. It never happened and a retreat was ordered towards the Channel, having a significant negative effect on morale. Marching towards the coast across flat terrain, it was apparent that the retreat was not orderly, given the amount of equipment that had been abandoned on the roadside, but spirits lifted when they were told to dig in approaching a village called St. Jean du Becq, which they were told was only twelve miles from the coast. Troops from other Regiments were in the vicinity, including the Cheshire's, Royal Artillery as well as some French soldiers. Ordered to defend the position at all costs, it being vital that the German advance was delayed to allow as much time for as many members of the B.E.F as possible to reach the channel and hopefully cross it.

Not having long to wait, immediately the Germans engaged them it became clear they facing far superior firepower and numbers. Pinned down by incessant mortar and machine gun fire, despite sustaining casualties they did succeed for some hours in frustrating their determined adversaries. The next problem was insurmountable, their ammunition supplies being almost exhausted, with the enemy infantry close. Word passed along the line that their only option was to surrender and white flags were raised. The only Officer present, a Captain, who Tom didn't know, said that they would be taken prisoner and likely spend the rest of the war in a POW camp in Germany. Although the thought of captivity was depressing, Tom and his mates all thought it was better than being dead.

By the time the enemy appeared, Tom and the others had discarded weapons that were useless without bullets and raised their hands above their heads. The German soldiers had strange epaulets on each shoulder of their tunics and were very aggressive, causing considerable unease amongst the vanquished troops. One of the Warwick's NCO's saying that they were from the SS who had reputation for brutality, adding to the anxiety of the captives which numbered around a hundred.

Corralled into a group, a German Officer addressed them in excellent English, telling them that they would be taken to a place to be be sheltered until arrangements could be made to transport them all to POW camps in what he called, "The Fatherland" and warning anyone attempting to escape would be shot.

After a short time, they were told they were to be marched to a barn, where they would be held until transport could be arranged. It suddenly occurred to Tom that it was his twenty-sixth birthday and certainly the first one that he had spent in a barn. Telling his friend Al, a long serving professional soldier who had returned with the Battalion from India, since when he had "adopted" Tom treating him almost like a son. He responded with a grin saying, "Happy Birthday, perhaps the Krauts will bake you a cake when we get to the Hotel."

Laughing Tom replied, "Well, I hope it's a big one, because there are a lot of us and I suppose some of them will want a piece."

Having sustained wounds in the fighting, several of the captives were having difficulty standing, let alone walking. The unsympathetic Germans, lifted them up and almost threw them towards their comrades, who did their best to support them. The Captain approached the German Officer, asking how far these men were expected to march, but was brusquely told to return to his place. Ushered on their way, their captors continued to be aggressive shouting insults and prodding them with rifle butts, it becoming clear that the two most badly wounded were unable to walk even with the assistance of colleagues. When the first of them fell to the ground, a German soldier pushed the two men who had been supporting him out of the way, before firing three bullets into his chest. After the initial shock, the whole group became agitated with a Corporal shouting towards the Germans.

"You vicious murdering bastards haven't you heard of the Geneva Convention."

The Captain looking equally distraught, shouted to the men to calm down. By this time the German Officer had left the main party and as it appeared that he was the only one that spoke English, communication was impossible. They reluctantly resumed their painful march, leaving their dead comrade on the side of the road.

Several minutes later, a second soldier fell and despite frantic efforts of to pick him up an identical situation unfolded, this time a different German did the shooting. Tom, like the others felt helpless and wondered who would be next. Trying desperately to calm the situation, the Captain shouted, "Steady lads, when their Officer gets back, I'll make an official protest and those two pigs will be arrested and hopefully shot."

Continuing towards their unknown destination for what must have been around half an hour, they were continually abused and harassed. Their discomfort was exacerbated by the oppressive heat from the strong sunlight, unusual so early in the summer. It was some relief when the bedraggled party, all of whom had not washed for days, were guided into a large field bordered on three sides by tall trees. At the far end, there was a small barn, obviously recently occupied by cattle if the pungent smell emanating from the open doors was anything to go by. On the verge of exhaustion after battling against overwhelming odds for the past two days, Tom despaired when it became clear that this was to be their temporary prison. It was obvious that the barn was far from adequate to accommodate almost a hundred men, but they were forced to enter it and were standing almost shoulder to shoulder when the doors were closed behind them.

After they had been incarcerated for over five hours, it began to get dark and the men started to complain that if they were to be kept their overnight there was no room to sleep.

The Captain again protested, demanding to see an Officer and shouting,

"For God's sake open the doors there's not enough room in here. This is contrary to the Geneva Convention"

The immediate reply in perfect English was, "Don't worry you won't be in there for long and there's plenty of room where you're going."

Somewhat relieved Tom said to Al, "That's the Officer who was in charge this morning, perhaps they will treat us better now that he's back." Al looked unconvinced.

Tom and Al who standing close to the back of the barn, decided to share their last remaining cigarette. Before they could finish, the doors were opened and there was panic among those closer to them, with the Captain shouting "get down".

This was difficult due to the restricted space, but Al pulled Tom down just prior to two deafening explosions. Totally disorientated, it was soon apparent to Tom that a significant number of his comrades were either dead or injured, there being a great deal of groaning and cries for help. Relieved that he was seemingly unscathed, he was petrified when Al, who was bleeding from his left arm, said, "The Krauts threw grenades in, they're trying to kill the lot of us, we've got to get out of here". The question was, how?

In a short while, several of their captors appeared at the door again and started taking small groups of the survivors outside, followed almost immediately by gun fire, making it clear what was happening. There was increasing panic among those who remained and once again the doors were thrown open, followed by indiscriminate rifle fire. Tom lay on the ground, to suggest that he was already dead, hoping to avoid the inevitable. When the firing stopped, Tom was again surprised that he was uninjured, thinking it could only be a matter of time before his luck ran out. Al, who had also survived the latest onslaught, noticed that the doors had not been properly closed, the Germans perhaps concluding that there were no survivors.

Tom was terrified, but not prepared to give up and whispered to Al, "Our only chance is to make a run for it."

"They've probably got the door covered, the bastards will shoot us down."

"We've nothing to lose, because that's exactly what they'll do if we stay in here."

"Your right lad, do or die ah."

Creeping towards the door with difficulty, both trying to avoid the bodies of the comrades, all of whom appeared to be dead. Tom peered through the narrow gap and was heartened to see that the nearest enemy soldiers visible, were some distance away.

"It's now or never mate", said Tom, carefully pushing the door open enough for them to pass through. Once outside, they crept to the back of the barn and ran towards the tree line. Tom, thinking if they could get to the trees undetected, they had a chance, but hopes were dashed when he heard shouting, followed by the zing of bullets, Hearing Al cry out, Tom didn't turn and soon reached the trees, giving him a little cover. Just beyond the tree line, he saw a small pond which he ran towards. As he got to the edge, he felt that his shoulder had been hit with a hammer, causing him to fall into the cold murky water. There being no sign of Al, Tom was resigned to his fate, hearing his pursuers approaching. The water was waist deep, but Tom stooped, thinking his best chance was to get as low in the water as possible. Only his head remained above the surface and astonishingly the German soldiers passed by the pond. Knowing that they would probably retrace their steps, Tom stayed put, but was alarmed when a solitary figure came to the edge of his refuge, stopped and lit a cigarette, Tom catching a fleeting glimpse of his face, before he turned and walked away.

After what seemed about an hour, he decided that he needed to get away while it was dark. Crawling out of the pond with difficulty before staggering in the direction which he thought would get him further away from the barn. Cold and wet, his shoulder seemed to be on fire, but he made progress through sheer will power. At least there was no sign of his tormentors who he hoped had given him up for dead, but he was getting weaker as the result of the loss of blood. In this condition, he concluded that getting it to the coast was not an option, so resolved to try and seek shelter. hoping that he might be found by retreating British troops.

Finding the dark night somewhat reassuring, the only sanctuary that he could find was a hedge and being almost in a state of collapse, slumped down beside it. Laying on his back looking at the stars in the cloudless night sky, he drifted into an uneasy sleep, dreaming of his life at home with his Mum, Dad and Maud. Then he saw Barbara and they were back walking in the woods, looking forward to their future together. Pain in his shoulder abruptly brought back the reality of his plight, realizing he was unlikely to ever see his family again and of all the things that he would like to say to them. It was Barbara that he longed for, the only person outside of his family that he had ever loved and tears came to his eyes, thinking what could have been and the life that she would have without him, wondering if after what had happened between them she cared if he lived or died.

Not having eaten or drank since the previous morning, his stomach griped with hunger, while his tongue seemed to be swollen in his dry mouth. Fatigue was overwhelming him and feeling that he couldn't last for too much longer unless he was found, he decided he needed to look for help. Getting up with difficulty, he felt unsteady on his feet but managed to find a narrow road and decided to walk in what he thought was the direction of the coast. It was not long before exhaustion overcame him, causing him to stagger to the edge of the road, where he tripped and fell and finally accepted that he was going to die.

Once again, he found himself far away from the battlefield, walking hand in hand with Barbara among the late spring bluebells, emerging from the shelter of the wood; elated to feel the warmth of the sun on his face, closing his eyes to take pleasure in the moment. Opening them, it was not Barbara that he saw, but the swarthy unshaven face of a man in a grey uniform, which had a white band with a red cross on the left arm. Taking him only a moment to realize that he had not been found by retreating colleagues as he had hoped, but was once again in the hands of Germans. Becoming fully conscious, he realized what a pitiful state he was in, unkempt, unwashed and hungry, with the pain in his shoulder almost unbearable. The only consolation was that now that the enemy had recaptured him, he was unlikely to be in pain for long. But this German seemed different, smiling and speaking in broken English, "My name is Klaus, I will look after you tommy. What is your name?

Despite his parched mouth, he whispered, "Tom"

Seemingly smiling sincerely, he said, "A tommy called Tom that is funny. Congratulations Tom, your war is finished."

CHAPTER 11

Barbara was ecstatic when in the autumn of 1940, she learned from Maud that her parents had received a letter from the War Office informing them that Tom had been taken prisoner. Nothing had been heard of him since May, it being presumed that he had been killed in France. Despite this, whenever Barbara had seen Maud, she had been inspired by his sisters' optimism that he would come back. Answering the door, she had found Maud with tears in her eyes, shrieking, "He's not dead, I told you that he'd come back one day."

Barbara hugged her asking, "Where is he?"

There was a pang of disappointment when Maud said; "He's in a prisoner of war camp in Germany. We'll have to wait until the wars over, but at least we'll see him again"

Thinking that it could be a long time, but didn't want to spoil Maud's happiness and asked, "How are your Mum and Dad?"

"Happy, I've never seen Dad cry before, but when he opened the letter, he blubbered like a baby and me and Mum thought it was bad news, but when he told us what was in the letter we all cried. It's bloody marvelous; we all thought that we'd lost him, Dad's looked like an old man over the last few months."

Regretting her treatment of Tom, Barbara had been unhappy when he was not among those that had escaped from Dunkirk. The relationship with Roger had petered out and while she had been on dates with a few boys, Tom that had always been in her thoughts and the fact that she had lost the opportunity to express her feelings haunted her.

She had worked in Randall's since she had left school, but a month earlier, on her twenty first birthday had told her parents that she intended to join the WAAF's. Her Mum's initial reaction had been less than supportive, saying she wouldn't let her go as she was needed at home, but her Dad was quick to chip in saying.

"Come on Beth, I'll miss her as well, but she's an adult now and we can't really stop her. We've always said she can go her own way when she's 21 and we should support her."

"Thanks Dad, I really want to do something positive to help the war effort. There is lot of RAF boys being killed and I feel guilty in a shop selling tinned vegetables. I also cannot get Tom out of my mind, he volunteered even before the war started and it looks like he won't be coming back. I let him down and will never be able to forgive myself. At least if he knew I was doing this he might be proud of me."

"So will your Mum and me girl, you're doing what I would do in your shoes", said her Dad reassuringly with Mum finally nodding in agreement.

Things were already under way when the news about Tom arrived. She had contacted the Recruiting Office in Birmingham, who arranged an interview. This was conducted by a male officer and included several questions that she guessed was to gauge her intelligence and IQ levels. Another aspect of the exchange was to play an important part in her destiny, as she mentioned that as well as working in the shop at Randall's, she helped with the accounts. It seemed over in less than thirty minutes, after which she had been told that she would be accepted subject to passing the medical examination and could be suitable for work in Accounts. She was quite pleased with this as she didn't fancy ending up as a driver or cook.

A few weeks later, she received a brown envelope with "On His Majesty's Service" on the front, which she excitedly opened in front of her parents.

Dad asked; "What does His Majesty have to say then."

Laughing Barbara replied, "I'm to report to the Office in Birmingham next Wednesday to be taken for a medical and if I pass will start my training straight afterwards, so I need to take clothes and washing stuff with me."

"What happens if you don't pass?" Mum asked.

"Then that's it, they just send you home."

"Well that's not going to happen is it", Dad confidently exclaimed, "So you'd best pack everything you need."

The next few days passed quickly, her Dad soon seeing her off on an early morning train for the short journey to Birmingham. Some of her friends had laughed when she told them what she was going to do and when she had given notice to Mr. Randall he had said that she should work a full week, but as she was going to work for the King he wouldn't insist on it.

Birmingham New Street Station was a hive of activity when she arrived at 8.30, with at least half of the passengers on the platforms wearing uniforms. A grimy dirty place, with palls of smoke emitting from the chimneys of the numerous steam engines trapped by the enormous canopy that covered the whole station. Barbara couldn't wait to get out into the fresh air to make the short walk to the Recruiting Office, where she arrived ten minutes later, finding several girls standing outside, all clutching small suitcases. The tallest of them who had a broad Black Country accent told her that she had to report to the Sergeant inside to get her name ticked off. After this, she returned to the group to wait for transport to a nearby hall, where the medicals were being conducted. Ten minutes later the WAAF Sgt. emerged with her hat on, shouting above the din of the traffic, "Sorry girls there's a problem with transport, so we're going to have to walk. It will be good practice for what most of you will be doing for the next few weeks."

"How long will it take?" asked the tall Black Country girl who was obviously not lacking in confidence.

The Sergeant, whose generous figure had not been adversely affected by wartime rationing, seemed less than impressed and snapped, "It depends on how fast you walk, so no more questions, just save your breath."

Proving to be a laborious process, the Medical Examination took over three hours, with the would-be recruits having to join numerous queues to confirm that various parts of their anatomy met service requirements. As not one of the male doctors showed any emotion whatsoever throughout, Barbara became increasingly pessimistic about the outcome and was more than relieved when to be told that she had passed.

In midafternoon, Barbara together with around twenty others were told that they would be transported back to the station for a train to their destination. On arrival, they were each presented with a railway warrant, which they were told to exchange for a ticket. After a short time, each of them was clutching a small rectangular green card, with Third Class Single, Birmingham New Street to Gloucester printed on the front. Prior to leaving them to their own devices, the Sergeant told them that their train was due in 20 minutes' time from Platform seven and that they would be met at Gloucester.

Duly arriving fifteen minutes later than scheduled, the group clambered aboard only to find the carriages already quite full with many passengers squatting in the corridors, but they all managed to squeeze in. Several them including Barbara were offered seats that were occupied by men, for which they were grateful. It was proving to be quite an adventure for Barbara, who had seldom ventured beyond her locality, apart from a couple of motor coach trips to Blackpool. The journey only lasted an hour and twenty minutes, with one short stop at Cheltenham Spa, but she enjoyed it, particularly the view of the Cotswold Hills on the left-hand side as they approached Cheltenham. As the train slowed down on the outskirts of Gloucester, Barbara's stomach was invaded by increasing numbers of "butterflies" as she contemplated her immediate future. Coming to an abrupt halt in the station, the doors soon opened and it seemed that a lot of passengers were getting off.

Barbara had sat close to the tall girl, who had upset the Sgt. Edna was from Wolverhampton, where she had been working as a Bus Conductress. Transpiring that she was Barbara's senior by five years and had joined up for some excitement and to meet some good-looking blokes, there being precious little of either in Wolverhampton. Chatting throughout the short journey, they had learned a fair bit about each other and together followed the exit signs towards the station forecourt. As promised there in a prominent position was a WAAF Corporal with a clipboard, standing next to a sign that read, "WAAF RECRUITS"

Ticking off their names, the Corporal told them to climb on to the back of one of two Lorries that were parked nearby. This was easier said than done for some of the less agile girls, but it was a process that they would all become familiar with. Managing it with without difficulty, Barbara and her fellow-recruits were soon on their way to the WAAF Training Camp that had recently opened at Innsworth. Following what had already been a long day, all of them were looking forward to a rest and hopefully a hot meal. Only to be disappointed when the Lorries stopped outside a row of long wooden huts, the Corporal taking them inside the closest one where they were told to find a bed, leave their cases beside it and "Form up in two ranks outside."

Having complied with the instruction, the Corporal stood in front of them shouting, "Right, I'm Corporal Bradley and I live in the bunk at the end of your billet. I'll be looking after you for the three weeks that you're here, by the end of which you should be fit to wear His Majesties uniform in public and not look like a load of shop girls like you do now".

At this Barbara smiled, which provoked a swift response from the Corporal.

"What have you got to smile about girl?"

"I worked in a shop, so it's not surprising that I look like a shop girl"

"Oh my goodness, a comedian, we just love comedians here." resulting in laughter. "You won't be laughing when I've finished with you." Confronting Barbara she asked, "What's the comedian's name?"

"Barbara Garrett"

"Barbara Garrett, Corporal if you don't mind funny girl. Whenever you address an NCO you call them by their rank. Whenever you address an Officer, its Sir or Ma'am."

"Yes Corporal, I'm sorry."

"And you should be, we've certainly got off on the wrong foot haven't we, I hope it's not a sign of things to come or it could be painful three weeks for all of us, particularly you Garrett."

Following the altercation, Corporal Bradley turned them to right to march to their next stop, the Clothing Store. On arrival, they were ushered to a long counter that was piled with various garments. The process started with the issue of a kitbag to each recruit after which they moved along the counter and were presented with their entitlement, which included trousers, a skirt a robust looking pair of black shoes and basic black thick knickers, causing some amusement then and afterwards. Finally, they were each given a knife, fork, spoon and mug, before having to lug their fully laden kitbags back to the billet, where much to their relief they were told that they were finally to be fed.

Arriving at the cookhouse, which smelt of stale cabbage, the fare on offer was far from appetizing, watery stew and powdered mashed potatoes. This was washed down with a brown liquid dispensed from a bucket into their newly acquired enamel mugs, provoking Edna's damning review. "What a load of shit."

With the by now exhausted group's hunger having being belatedly satisfied, after a fashion, it was past 10pm when they arrived back at their new home only to have to make up the basic steel beds, with the two sheets, three blankets and what proved to be a lumpy pillow provided.

Corporal Bradley then came to the end of the long billet and shouted, "Wright it's after lights out, so get into bed and I don't want to hear any noise until I come to wake you up from your slumber at six in the morning. Then the fun really starts." Turning on her heel, she switched off the lights leaving most of them to undress in the dark, which some of them were grateful for.

Clambering into their uncomfortable beds, for what for Barbara proved initially to be a fitful sleep and given the amount of tossing, turning and the occasional sob emitting from her companions, she thought that she was not the only one having a problem. Waking several times during what seemed to be an endless night, she wondered what she had got herself into, but Tom's plight was never far from her thoughts. Whatever she was going through, she thought it was nothing compared to being corralled behind a barbwire fence, hundreds of miles from home. What would he be thinking; would it be of her? She certainly had no expectations after what she had done, would he ever forgive her? Come what may, she pledged to try to make it up with him when he came home. When deep sleep finally came, she and Tom were back in the Palace entranced by the elegance of Fred and Ginger.

The dream was abruptly terminated by the shouts of their mentor, "Right Time to get up, let's see all of your feet on the floor. You've got twenty minutes to get dressed and then it will be "brekie" time."

That started an exhausting three weeks, during which they had no spare time, being kept on the go from six in the morning until ten at night, with three short breaks for what passed for food at Innsworth.

Barbara having at first found living in the same large room as nineteen other girls somewhat claustrophobic, soon got used to it and became good friends with most of them, particularly Edna Thrupp, who soon emerged as their leader. Being almost thirty, she had seen more life than most of them and had the group in stitches, when she recalled her experiences in the back of parked buses, with her favorite driver or drivers. She concluded her story by telling them, "A clippie's day involves a lot more than selling bus tickets."

Predominantly occupied by drill and physical training, despite being exhausted at the end of each day; Barbara certainly felt the benefit and could soon run a long way, without gasping for breath. Just a few days before they were due to leave Innsworth, they were lined up on the parade square and informed of the trades to which they had been allocated and where they would be going to train. Numerous groans emanated from girls, whose names were read out, followed by the word "Cook", with Barbara becoming increasingly nervous that she too would be consigned to the kitchen, but was relieved when Corporal Bradley shouted,

"Garrett, Pay Accounts"

Edna whispered, "You're a lucky bugger, there's no chance of me getting a cushy number like that"

Predicting her fate accurately, soon afterwards the Corporal pronounced, "Thrupp, Barrage Balloons."

"Bugger it; I've heard that that lot has to work bloody hard in all weathers. But it's better than being in the cookhouse. If I'd have got that, I'd probably end up getting hanged for poisoning."

Going their separate ways, vowing to keep in touch, Barbara travelled to an Accountancy School in South Wales, while Edna was sent to Cardington in Bedfordshire, where the giant Airship Hangers were now occupied by the Balloon Unit.

It was a relatively short journey from Gloucester to Cardiff and then on the local train for Penarth, where once again she was met by an NCO with a clipboard, being told that she would be accommodated in a hostel close to the seafront. Barbara was grateful to have been allocated a place in a hostel, with several other girls as she had come to enjoy the communal life. Some on her course were billeted in houses in the locality, with land ladies who did not treat them at all well, being denied access to their rooms after breakfast until 5pm each evening. The course was intense, but enjoyable and they were lucky enough to have a helpful male Corporal instructor, whose teaching skills ensured that most them passed. As at Innsworth, they were informed of their destinies on a parade that was held on the seafront and after hearing the word "pass" after her name had been called out, she was excited to learn that following a few days' leave, her posting was to the Bomber Command Station at Binbrook in Lincolnshire.

CHAPTER 12

Barbara was happy to be able to spend some time with her Mother and Father, but was impatient to get to work at her new station. Five days passed quite quickly, but she did make time to visit Randall's shop, where Maud still worked. Mr. Randall seemed pleased to see her, beaming as he pronounced, "They've made a fine-looking woman of you, Barbara."

Pleased with his reaction she replied, "Thank you, Mr. Randall, it's the best thing I've ever done"

Maud looking on with envy and said, "I wish I could do the same, but it would really upset Mum and Dad, with Tom being so far away"

"Have you heard from him?"

"Yes, we've had a couple of brief letters through the Red Cross, he seems alright"

"I don't suppose he asked about me"

"What do you think? "Maud said, turning on her heels and walking to the back of the shop, "it was good to see you."

Barbara was soon making the slow train journey in packed carriages across country to Lincolnshire, having to make a couple of changes along the way. It was quite late in the afternoon when she arrived and was again met by the statutory lorry, throwing her kit bag over the tailgate and climbing after it to find a place on wooden benches fixed on either side. Only four boarded the transport, which dropped them outside the Admin Offices in Station Headquarters, where she was told that she would be in the transit hut overnight before being allocated a permanent billet the following morning. Finding out immediately what a busy place Binbrook was, with constant noise of aircraft taking off and landing and the din from engines being run up and tested on the ground.

Allocated a place in a hut like that which she occupied at Innsworth, she was directed to the Pay Accounts Office, finding that she would be part of a team of five, with a male Sergeant, Paddy Lehane from Londonderry in Northern Ireland, a WAAF Corporal who introduced herself as Gail Bennett, who appeared to be in her mid thirties and wore a wedding ring. The staff was completed by a LAC and a LACW, John McNally and Margaret Wilson, both only having arrived in the last few weeks. As an ACW 1, Barbara was the "office junior" and although Sgt. Lehane was friendly and helpful during the arrival briefing, he did tell her that when there was tea to be made, she would be making it.

Binbrook had two operational squadrons, flying Vickers Wellington Bombers on nightly raids over Germany. Some of the aircrew came into the office from time to time, most of them looking close to exhaustion. Barbara knew the pitiful amount they were paid for putting their lives at risk every night. Despite this, she found them friendly, but kept her distance, not wanting to get close to anyone whose future was so uncertain. That changed about three months after her arrival, when a newly posted in Flight Sergeant Gunner came into to check on his pay increase, having been recently promoted. Dealing with his query, she looked across the desk at him and was struck by his fresh round face, blonde wavy hair and sparkling blue eyes. Unlike others flyers she had dealt with, he looked fresh, with no sign of dark circles under his eyes. She saw from his Pay book that his name was Peter Stanford and that he was born in August 1919, two months earlier than her own birth date. He had a broad smile on his face, not seeming to have a care in the world, Barbara wondered how long that would last, when he got into the nightly routine of bombing raids.

"What do you do if you get any time off around here?", he asked.

Barbara laughed, "We don't get much and Lincoln's twenty-five miles away, so it's the NAFFI or the pub"

"The Pub sounds good to me; perhaps I'll see you there sometime"

"Perhaps you will."

"I certainly hope so" he said with a glint in his eye.

Working together, Barbara and Margaret got on well and soon became best friends, spending much of their precious off duty time together. On odd occasions, they went to the nearby town of Market Rasen, but most of their off-base time was spent in the Lamb and Flag pub, which was the most popular haunt of many from Binbrook being only a mile away from the main gate. Margaret was a somewhat rotund girl from South East London with dark long hair, that took her a long time to pin up to ensure that most of it stayed under her hat. Speaking with what Barbara thought was a cockney accent and while she would never be deemed attractive to most observers, Margaret's outgoing personality more than made up for it. Soon after Barbara had arrived she had told her, "Don't go out with the first bloke you see. Look for a Pilot, preferably an Officer from a well to do family, who'll keep you in the lap of luxury after the war."

Barbara asked, "Have you found one yet"

"No", she replied laughing, "but it's not for want of trying"

The main advantage of going out with Margaret was that Barbara seldom stopped laughing, because there was hardly any situation, of which she couldn't see the funny side. Constantly flirting with the boys in the pub, but never latching on to anyone saying that she would know the right one when he came along. They went to the "Lamb" at least once a week, mainly on a Saturday when it was usually packed, getting to know a lot of the regulars, who were mainly, like them, off the camp.

Barbara had remembered her brief conversation with Peter Stanford and had kept an eye out for him, both on and off the camp, but to no avail. So, it was quite a surprise when she felt a tap on the shoulder, on a night out with Margaret two months later, turning around and there he was, beaming, "Remember me?"

"How could I forget", she replied, the first thing that striking her was much older he looked than on their previous encounter, having probably flown several operations, experiencing all the stress that entailed and consequently had developed dark circles under his bright blue eyes.

"I've only been in here a few times, because I'm on ops a lot, but I've looked for you every time", he continued.

"Why on earth did you do that?" She said smiling back at him.

"Because when I left your office, I had already decided that I was going to marry you one day."

Somewhat taken aback by his totally unexpected declaration, she laughed.

"Oh yes, after you've known me all of five minutes, you don't even know my name."

"Yes, I do, Barbara, I made it my business to find out"

"Well you don't lack confidence I'll give you that. Anyway, what makes you think I'd want to marry YOU?"

"Well, you haven't got a boyfriend; I made it my business to find that out as well, so you've obviously been waiting for me to come along."

She didn't quite know how to deal with the situation, being both flattered and annoyed at the same time, "I might have a boyfriend at home, Mr. Know-it-all."

"I hope not, don't break my heart on our first date" he said, trying to appear forlorn.

"Cheeky bugger, we're not on a date, I've just come out for a drink with my mate." looking around for moral support from Margaret, who to her dismay was in conversation with another group on the other side of the bar.

"Well we could make it one, lets have another drink and then I'll take you for a spin on my bike."

"What are you going to do, give me a ride on your cross bar?"

"Nothing so exciting" he replied with the almost constant broad smile on his face, "I'm afraid I've only got a motor cycle, so you'll have to make do with the pillion. We won't be able to go far because I haven't got much petrol, it's hard to come by."

"I should feel flattered then, if you're prepared to use your precious petrol on me. Never mind the drink, let's go."

And that's how it started; she had enjoyed the exhilaration of her brief pillion ride, with the wind in her hair and had consented to being kissed when he dropped her back outside her billet. Following that they spent as much time as they could together, time being restricted by Peter's flying commitments, which they didn't talk about much. She knew that the odds of him not being shot down were not good, being constantly worried about him and arranging to get a message from the squadron every time he touched down safely.

As they got to know each other, she found that he was an only child, his parents living in South East London, from where his father commuted each day to his job as a tailor in Saville Row. He had gone to a local private school as a day boy and had hoped to go to University, but instead, following the Munich Crisis, had joined the RAF Volunteer Reserve, intending to be a Pilot, but finding that he did not have the aptitude required. Despite the disappointment, he was desperate to fly so was happy to be placed on a Gunnery Course and while it had been quiet initially, he was now on his second operational tour. Despite the hazards, he was totally optimistic about surviving the war, and always scoffed at the danger that came with spending so much time in the front of a Wellington over Germany.

Still thinking of Tom stuck in a prison camp somewhere, while she would never forget him, she found herself falling totally in love with Peter and was soon convinced that she would indeed be his wife. When he could find some precious petrol, he would take her on longer excursions, even as far as Lincoln, which was dominated by its beautiful Cathedral on top of a steep hill. Walking hand in hand past some impressive half-timbered houses. Peter was like a small boy in his enthusiasm, saying "I love these old buildings, can you believe it's been here for over 800 years and is reputed to be the finest Cathedral in England." His interest was infectious as he pointed out the various styles of architecture in a building that had evolved over the centuries, Barbara finding it difficult to come to terms with how this cultured educated young man found her so special.

Chapter 13

After they had been going out together for three months, he told her that he had almost completed his tour of missions in Wellingtons and was due some leave, intending to spend it with his parents. Barbara was shocked when he asked her to try and get leave to go with him to meet his Mother and Father, also expressing a desire to go to meet hers as soon as possible saying, "I need to pop the question to your Dad."

"You haven't popped it to me yet me lad, what if I say no?"

"In that case, I'll have to kidnap you and lock you away somewhere until you change your mind, but you won't say no."

"No chance", she replied, "I can't wait to be Mrs. Stanford."

"That's settled then, unless your Dad says no and he probably can't wait to be rid of you", he said with a broad grin on his face.

"Cheeky Bugger", was her spontaneous reply, thinking she really would have to stop swearing, not wanting to slip up at the Stanford's.

When she initially approached Sgt. Lehane, he was not enthusiastic, explaining that they were far too busy to sanction people going on seven days' leave, but when she explained her reasons for asking, he relented, saying she could have four. Happy with that, even though Peter had got a week, they would at least be able to spend part of it together and have the time to visit his parents.

Looking forward to spending so much time in each other's company, Barbara was living on her nerves while Peter completed the final two trips of his tour. She was working the day after his final night flight over Cologne, so he could get plenty of sleep prior to their journey south the following day. Excited, having never been to London, despite her apprehension of her forthcoming meeting, with what Peter described as her future "in laws". Arriving at Kings Cross around lunchtime, they fought their way through the crowded terminus to the steps that led to the Underground Railway, where the platforms were just as busy as those above ground. They were soon at Charing Cross and on another train for the twenty-minute journey to the station closest to Peter's home. She did notice that there was a significant amount of bomb damage close to the railway, but it became increasingly less noticeable as their journey progressed. Peter saw the concern on her face and reassuringly said, "Don't worry about bombs, they seldom get this far out and they don't seem to come every night now."

It was a thirty-minute walk to their destination, initially along busy streets lined with shops, then passing through neat rows of houses, most of which had well tended gardens, predominantly growing vegetables. As the houses got larger, she began to wonder what Peter's parents would think of her, but felt more relaxed, when she saw a well-dressed lady who must have been around fifty waving to them from outside her garden gate.

"That's Mum", said Peter, "I told her that we would be about this time. She must have been looking out for us."

"Hello Bonny Boy", it's wonderful to have you back for a while." she said hugging him, "This must be Barbara, Welcome dear, we've heard so much about you."

Barbara was immediately taken by this still attractive woman, who was quite tall, slightly built, with remarkably unlined skin and fair hair, which was showing the first traces of grey. Holding out her hand, Mrs. Stanford took it and leaned forward to kiss her on the cheek.

"I'm really pleased to meet you Mrs. Stanford, thank you for inviting me to your home."

Peter's Mother took her arm saying, "You must call me Grace, Trevor is at business but will be back in a couple of hours. He's really looking forward to meeting you."

Enormous compared with her own parents modest terraced home, the house had large bay windows and stained glass in the front door. Inside there was a long hall leading to a large lounge, separate dining room and kitchen at the back, which was four times the size of that which she was used to. Grace took her upstairs, showing her what she described as the Guest Room that overlooked the long rear garden, which once again was three times the size of the one she shared at home with her sister. "I'm sorry this is the smallest bed room in the house, but I hope that it will suffice for three nights."

"It's a lovely room Grace, I'm used to sleeping in the same room as twenty other girls, this will be like heaven."

"I'm happy that you like it, just take your time and freshen up, while I go down a make us a cup of tea."

By the time she went downstairs, Peter's father was back and Barbara was immediately struck by how much like Peter he was. Wearing a smart pin striped suit, having thick wavy hair like his son, but his was almost white. As she went into the lounge, he was quickly out of his chair and with a broad smile said, "Hello Barbara, I'm Trevor, welcome to our home. Peter has been telling us how beautiful you are and he certainly wasn't exaggerating."

Feeling herself blush as she shook his hand saying, "Thank you Mr. Stanford, Peter is renowned for his exaggeration and certainly looks at me through rose tinted glasses."

Peter laughed, "I wasn't exaggerating, neither is Dad, he's always had an eye for lovely women, just look at Mum."

Sitting down and having tea together, Barbara felt very welcome at what she hoped was the beginning of three blissful days together. They in fact only had two clear days, with the first and last of Barbara's precious leave being taken up by travel. They spent the first of them close to home. It was a beautiful early summer day and Peter asked his Mother to make them up a picnic lunch, which he carried in a rucksack to a large park only ten minutes' walk away. There was a wide green space, surrounded by thick woods and after they had eaten their food, they lay on the grass together looking at the clear blue sky. Afterwards they strolled hand in hand in the woods, causing Barbara to fleetingly wonder what Tom was doing behind a wire fence somewhere in Germany.

At breakfast on the following day, she was excited when Peter suggested that they get the train up to Charing Cross so at least she would be able to see some of the sites of London. They had a hectic time looking at Westminster Abbey, Trafalgar Square and the widest river that she had ever seen, despite restrictions resulting from the considerable bomb damage. They even had time to squeeze in a free lunchtime concert at St. Martin's in the Fields, where almost all the audience were in uniform. Barbara couldn't wait to write and tell her Mum and Dad about a day that she would never forget. Throughout the journey back to the suburbs, they held hands, with Barbara becoming engrossed in her own thoughts, knowing that Peter would soon have to return to operations and the hazards that came with it. It was then she decided that they should be properly together and Peter seemed shocked when she suggested that he should come to her room that night, when his parents were asleep.

"Are you sure?"

"As sure as I've ever been about anything", she replied, "We're going to get married anyway, so why should we wait. I love you and I couldn't bear it if I lost you and we'd never done what married people do together."

"Let's hope there's not an Air Raid to spoil our conversation then", Peter said with a broad grin on his face.

Peter's parents went to bed quite early, Barbara soon followed and was quickly undressed and into bed, nervously waiting for Peter to join her. It seemed an age, but was probably only about half an hour until she heard him come into the room. Unable to see him because of the black out curtains, she felt his warm body move beside her, whispering. "I've never done anything like this before, so you'll have to help me."

"Neither have I, so it should be fun for both of us" she giggled.

Taking her in his arms and caressing her breasts, he lifted her nightdress, stroking her between her outstretched legs, "Will it hurt", she asked, becoming increasingly aroused, spreading her legs to allow him to explore further.

Breathing heavily, Peter was clearly excited, but trying to reassure her whispered, "I'll be careful, but tell me if I'm hurting you."

Climbing on top of her, he supported himself so that she hardly felt his weight, but it was a shock when he entered her. It felt painful, but the discomfort didn't last, soon beginning to feel sensations that were delightfully new, making her sure that what they were doing was right. Peter moved slowly at first, but this soon changed and it was over quickly, Barbara feeling the spasms of his body as he let out a subdued cry, after which he relaxed and hugged her tightly.

The first thing that Barbara thought was, well is that what all the fuss is about as the whole thing must have been over in less than five minutes, but clung to him asking, "Are you alright?"

"That was wonderful", he whispered, "I love you so much, we'll have to get married soon, did I hurt you?"

"Hardly at all", it will be even better next time."

Not having to wait long for the next time, within an hour they made love again and this time his slow but probing movements lasted so much longer, as she moved her own body to meet his she became increasingly excited, experiencing moments of ecstasy that she could not have imagined. Finally crying out, as once again feeling similar spasms from Peter as he made a final thrust deep inside her.

Afterwards he held her in his arms for a long time, but then went back to his own room, leaving Barbara to contemplate how her life had changed in the last couple of hours, praying silently that Peter would be kept safe, to ensure the happiness she had experienced would last a lifetime.

They were both up early the next morning, for Barbara's journey back to Lincolnshire, Peter feeling duty bound to spend the remainder of his leave with his parents. Barbara thought that she caught Grace giving her knowing look, causing her to wonder if she had heard anything in the night. Reassuringly, when it was time to leave, Peter's mother hugged her saying, "Trevor and I have really enjoyed having you and you'll always be welcome."

Peter took her to the station after which it was a lonely journey back to her mundane life at camp. Managing to get a seat on the crowded train from Kings Cross, as they parted, Peter said, "After last night, we really need to get married soon, shall we plan to get a special license on our next leave?"

Gazing into his eyes Barbara said, "Well you're the Flt. Sgt., so if you say so I'd better do as I'm told."

"Quite right too, it's important that you minions know your place."

Punching him playfully on the shoulder, she said, "Cheek, I'll have to write and tell my Mum and Dad that I've been ordered to get married."

As the train sped north, she gazed out of the window contemplating the events of the previous night. Despite her tenderness, she felt more fulfilled than she had ever done, thinking about their future together and the children they would raise. She was sure that her parents would love Peter and hoped that they would be able to meet as soon as possible, but probably not before they were married. Prior to meeting him, she had believed that she and Tom would be together one day, despite the acrimony between them and wondered what he would think when he heard she was someone else's wife.

CHAPTER 14

Returning to the village in the autumn of 1945, Tom looked back on his period of captivity with mixed emotions. Thinking of five wasted years, but still having a life to look forward to, unlike his comrades that were slaughtered in a French barn. He had found his years behind the Stalag wire frustrating, but also had felt reasonably safe, relishing the prospect of being reunited with his loved ones when the war was eventually over.

He had received infrequent letters from Maud, keeping him up date with events at home. While in return, Tom attempted to provide reassurance that he was as well as could be expected, given his situation. Maud told him that Barbara had joined the Air Force, but after that, there had been no mention of her, despite Tom having asked for news from time to time.

For much of his time as a POW, Tom and his comrades had been well treated and fed, their diet being supplemented by Red Cross parcels. In return, they had regularly been employed helping their enemy's war effort on nearby farms, keeping them reasonably fit and healthy. That had all changed in the final months of the war in Europe, when it became clear that things were going far from well for the Germans. Food had become scarce and the supply of Red Cross parcels gradually dried up, while the formally friendly guards became increasingly intolerant to the point of aggression. Tom thought that some would need little excuse to shoot them, also occurring to him that they might do just that as the Allied advance progressed, or at least relocate them.

As it was they had been lucky, waking one morning in the early summer of 1945 to find that their guards had disappeared, followed by the arrival of American soldiers three days later. Tom had never met a "yank" in his life, but he and his mates cheered them to a man, in return their liberators seemed to have unlimited supplies of chocolate, which they distributed freely.

Two days later, there had been no nostalgia when they clambered into the back of lorries for the first stage of their journey home. It took over a week for them to get back to England, where they were taken to an Army Camp in Wiltshire for processing and de-briefing prior to what was hoped would be impending discharge. When he was being medically examined, the M.O. had noticed the scar from his shoulder wound, his passive disinterest completely changing when Tom described the circumstances in which it was sustained. A few days later he was interviewed by young Major from the Intelligence Corps, who was adamant that if any of the perpetrators of the outrage could be identified they would probably be tried as war criminals and that Tom would be required to give evidence against them.

Having been back in England for three weeks, much to his relief, he was told that the five-year commitment, for which he had volunteered had been fulfilled. As he had been a POW for so long, he would be among the first to be discharged. Formalities didn't take long and after being issued with a set of civilian clothes, which comprised a grey pin stripe double breasted suit, shoes, shirt with two detachable collars and studs, a tie and a raincoat, he was presented with a railway warrant for the last leg of his journey back to the Midlands.

Getting off the train at the village station, he was somewhat emotional, there having been times during the past years when he had convinced himself that he would never see his family again. Although his Mum and Dad knew that he had been repatriated and was back in the country, he had not been able to tell them that he was on his way home. There were tears in his eyes as he walked down the entry to the back door and up the steps, which led straight into the kitchen. His Mother was at the sink peeling vegetables, but when he walked in she dropped the knife, screamed with delight and hugged him with her hands still wet. He had never seen his Mother cry before, but her body was convulsed with sobs as they embraced saying "I've waited for five years for this moment, Welcome home son."

She then shot out of the door and Tom heard her shout, "Henry, come up here and look who's come to see us."

Hearing the familiar sounds of his father's boots on the garden path, he stood behind the door so that he was not seen immediately it was opened, but when his parent walked into the kitchen said, "Fancy a pint tonight, Dad?"

His Father spun around with a broad smile on his face, grabbed Tom's hand shaking it vigorously almost shouting, "Course I bloody well do, you're a daft bugger. Why didn't you tell us you were coming, we could have put the flags out"?

"I didn't know myself until yesterday and I wouldn't want any fuss anyway."

"No fuss be buggered, after five years in a prisoner of war camp you deserve a bloody fuss."

In the meantime, his Mother had collected her thoughts and having had time to look at him properly said, "The first thing we need to do is feed him up, he's a bag of bones."

Tom had lost over three stones during his time in captivity, but had already started to put the weight back on, despite the far from appetizing fare that had been available since his repatriation and said to his Mum, "I can't wait, I think I could eat a horse."

She laughed, "Well we haven't got a horse, but we've got plenty in the larder", as she opened the door to revel the familiar sides of bacon hanging on hooks.

It was now quite late in the afternoon and Tom decided that he would like to surprise Maud. Walking the familiar path to Randall's in the Centre of the village, he waited across the road until she breezed out of the shop just after five o'clock. Turning sharply left on the footpath, having not seen him, he crossed the road, and grabbed her elbow saying, "Do you want to walk home with me?"

"Tom", she screamed, "are you home for good?"

"Well, I hope so, unless you've given my bed to a lodger."

Walking along arm in arm, chatting happily, Tom once again felt emotional, thinking how lucky he had been to survive the horrors that befell him in France, to spend a normal life with his family.

True to her word, his mother cooked bacon for tea and just the smell of it frying in the pan was enough to satisfy Tom, but when it arrived on his plate he demolished the generous portion in no time. The conversation got around to what had happened in the village for the past five years, the highlight being the single bomb that had been dropped; fortunately, landing on the Council Rubbish Tip. At the pit, there had been intense pressure to increase production throughout the war, which hadn't been easy with the workforce being supplemented by "Bevin Boys". His Dad had been generally impressed by the mainly reluctant conscripts, one of whom on his district underground had come straight from Oxford University. His Dad concluded, "I don't think he'll be staying after he's demobbed."

The conversation turned to the various village lads and girls that were or had been away in the forces, there had been eight who would not be returning, but his Dad seemed relieved when he said, "At least, it's not nearly as many as were lost in the last lot"

Tom looking at Maud said, "Have you seen anything of Barbara Garrett?"

Before she could answer his Dad quickly interjected, "You don't want to have anything to do with her lad, she's damaged goods. She's been out of the WAAF's for three years and brought a baby back with her. Her poor Mum and Dad were heartbroken."

Chapter 15

On her return to Binbrook, Barbara had settled down into a normal work routine and managed to spend time with Peter infrequently as he had resumed operational flying. The first time they did manage to see each other, he had enough petrol to get to Lincoln and back, so off they went, feeling the wind in their hair, speeding through country lanes. When they arrived, they took the familiar walk up the hill towards the Cathedral, finding a busy Tea Room close by. Holding hands and chatting about the future, Peter told her that as soon as he had completed his next ten missions, he would be entitled to another week's leave. This would be their opportunity, as he put it, "to tie the knot". There was another surprise for her, when he produced a small blue velvet box from his jacket pocket and handed it to her. Despite knowing exactly what it was, she couldn't suppress her delight when she opened it to reveal a gold ring, embellished with a single diamond.

"Try it on then", he said.

Slipping it onto the third finger of her left hand, it was a perfect fit.

"It's beautiful", she said, "How did you know what size to get?"

"I took a chance and had it made to fit my little finger."

Never having felt so happy, she suddenly thought that she hadn't mentioned Peter to her parents and here they were talking about marriage.

"You really need to meet my Mum and Dad, is there any chance that we can get a 48 hour pass together so we can go and see them?"

Peter frowned, "I'll try, but it's not easy when I'm constantly on call for ops."

"Well, if we're going to get married, they'll have to know. My Dad will probably want to give me away."

"That could be complicated; I was thinking of getting a special license and doing it here, what do you think?

"I don't mind, but they may be disappointed. What about your parents?"

"I spoke to Mum and Dad about it before I came back and they're OK with it given the circumstances. Both like you and would be really happy for us."

Barbara spent that evening writing a letter to her parents, telling them about Peter and her visit to his parents. She told them that she had accepted his marriage proposal and their intention to get a special license in Lincoln. When the reply came, she tore the envelope open desperate to know what their reaction would be, but was dismayed as she read.

> *Dear Barbara,*
>
> *Your Mother and I were shocked to receive your letter telling us that you are going to get married. We can't stop you because you're over 21, but it all seems so sudden. What do you know about this lad Peter? Have you just been dazzled by his wings?*
>
> *You say that you have been home with him to meet his parents. Don't you think it would have been a good idea to bring him here, so we could have had a look at him before you decided to get married?*
>
> *Another thing that is worrying your mother and me is that we always thought that you would marry Tom one day, despite the shameful way you treated him when he joined the Army. I know that he worships the ground you walk on and goodness knows what he will think if he hears about this when he's stuck in a prison camp.*
>
> *Barbara, you get married if you must, but don't expect my or your mother's blessing.*
>
> *Love,*
> *Dad.*

Sitting on her bed reading the letter, Margaret looked on from the other side of the billet and realized straight away that something was wrong and came across to sit beside her. Seeing tears in Barbara's eyes, the letter hanging limply in her hand, she put her arm around her friend's shoulder, asking, "What's wrong Babs?"

"It's from my Dad, look at it"

After reading it, Margaret said, "I take it he won't be giving you away then?"

"It's not funny Margaret, I thought that they'd be happy for me."

"Well, they're obviously not; I think that you need to take Peter to see them. He's such a gentleman that I'm sure they would change their attitude if they met him."

"I've already asked him to come home with me and he's trying to wangle a Forty-eight."

"OK then, write back and tell them that's what you're going to do. Mind you from the look of that letter Peter probably will be sleeping in the garden."

Barbara sighed, "Thanks for trying to make me laugh Mags, but I'm going to marry Peter whatever they say."

Replying straight away, she told them how unhappy she was with their attitude and how much she thought they would like Peter when they met him. As for being dazzled, she told them that there was nothing glamorous about being an Air Gunner in a Wellington Bomber and that he was putting his life in danger every time climbed into one.

Telling Peter about her parent's letter, he agreed that he needed to meet them and would come home with her as soon as he could get a pass. The wait was not long, Peter telling her that he could get a pass two weekends later. Barbara explained the circumstances to Sgt. Lehane and he immediately approved her own, enabling her to write and tell her Mum and Dad that they would be coming.

The next two weeks dragged, but they planned to leave after work on the Friday and come back on the Sunday morning. In the meantime, she received another letter from her Dad, saying that Peter would be welcome to stay, but would have to sleep in a chair. When she told Peter, he laughed out loud saying, "A chair will be luxury after a Wellington gun turret."

Chapter 16

Peter was apprehensive at the prospect of meeting Barbara's parents, but was looking forward to the weekend away, even if there was no bed involved. Having resumed operational flying, despite not wanting to admit it, he was tired.

As he and his five colleagues were driven out to their Wellington in the receding August light, he thought about the prospect of marriage to Barbara, who he had fell for on the day that he walked into the Admin Office when she had asked, "What can I do for you, Flight?" Immediately thinking of a lot of things, on that day he had to be satisfied with her sorting out his pay query.

Walking into the crowded smoke filled pub a few weeks later, he saw her close to the bar with another girl he recognized. Making straight for her, he had been surprised that after only a brief conversation she agreed to let him take her for a spin on his beloved two stroke motor cycle, that he had saved for before the war. His mind was made up that she was unlike any girl that he'd met before, not that he had much experience. Their relationship flourished, spending as much time together as possible and he was happy when she agreed to go home with him to meet his parents. Obvious that they were taken with her as much as he had been, he was happy when she declared, "They're really lovely aren't they." On the night she asked him to go to her room, as well as being excited, he hoped that his parents would not be disturbed. Wondering if Barbara had been with other men, the talk around the Sergeants Mess was that most WAAF's at Bimbrook had, he hoped she wouldn't be disappointed with his lack of experience.

Laying together that night it had been obvious that what they shared was new to them. It was also a relief, because it had often been on his mind that he might get killed without ever having been with a woman. Afterwards, Peter thought that the best thing was to get married as soon as possible and was elated when she agreed to his proposal. He was looking forward to meeting her parents, even after she had told him of her father's misgivings.

Still, that was tomorrow's problem. In the meantime, there was a job to do over Cologne. He was the second youngest of a youthful crew, all of whom got on well together. The Pilot was Flight Lieutenant Jock McLaren, who at 22, was just a year older than Peter, while at the other end of the plane in the Rear Gunners turret, was Peter's 19-year-old roommate Sergeant "Doc" Halliday.

As usual, little had been said on their way out to the Wellington and as they climbed in, assuming familiar positions, Peter tried to put the forthcoming weekend out of his mind, needing to concentrate on the job in hand. Even after so many missions, he did not feel comfortable in the cramped Front Gunner's turret and looked forward to the next four hours with little enthusiasm.

About five minutes later after the preflight checks were completed the heavily laden Wellington taxied out onto the grass runway and Peter noted that they were airborne at 9.35.

Crossing the North Sea towards their target was uneventful, but after the Dutch coast they encountered intermittent light flak. Peter was unconcerned, but as they approached Cologne, as always, he could see that the sky was flooded with search lights and the anti-aircraft fire was intense. They were over the City for less than two minutes before the bombs were released and Mac's voice came over the intercom, "Right, let's get out of here." But within seconds, the Wellington shuddered violently, the pilot exclaiming, "Bugger it, we're hit."

Almost immediately, Peter heard one of the engines splutter and Mac reported, "It's the starboard engine chaps, but hopefully we can get back on one." Setting off on the one good engine, all seemed to be going well, but just after Peter saw the Norfolk coast ahead, the plane began to lose height, with the port engine beginning to sound as though it too was failing. Mac sounding reassuringly calm said, "We're almost out of fuel chaps, I don't think we've much chance of reaching base, but, I'll try and find an alternative." By this time, Peter could see the search lights over Norwich, but the aircraft was by now dangerously low. Having always felt safe with Mac at the controls, he thought that if anybody can get us out of this mess it's him. But it was obviously a losing battle, with the beleaguered bomber crashing through power lines. Peter thought, this is it, but his heart leapt when Mac shouted, "I can see the lights of an airfield, stand by for a crash landing." Peering out of the front of the beleaguered aircraft, Peter looked for a runway, but all he could see was a railway line. Thinking about Barbara and his weekend with her parents, he suddenly saw a bridge right in front of him.

Chapter 17

Having arranged to leave as soon as she could get away on the Friday afternoon, it meant that Peter would be able to get some sleep after flying the previous night. Barbara heard the Wellingtons take off on the Thursday evening, before drifting into a fitful sleep. She was up early, packing a small weekend bag, which she took to work to help with a speedy getaway. About thirty minutes after arriving in the office, Sgt Lehane, looking perplexed went over to Margaret's desk, who put her hand to her mouth in shock and Barbara wondered what could have happened, when they both crossed to her desk she knew.

"My god no."

"There's nothing certain yet, come into my office and I'll tell you what I know."

The three of them went into the Sgt's. cramped office and unusually Barbara was invited to sit down, "Look Barbara, I've had a call from 12 Squadron Admin and Peter's aircraft came down on the way back from Cologne about twelve miles away from base. Three of the six are in hospital, but at this stage they don't know who."

"What about the other three?"

"Apparently the other three bought it."

Feeling sick, it was all she could do to avoid throwing up over the desk. Regaining some sort of composure, she willed that Peter would be one of the survivors, despite knowing that all the others would have loved ones waiting for news.

Lehane said, "Look your no use to me here, go back to the billet and wait for news, you go with her Margaret."

"Thanks Sarge, but I'd rather stay here, at least I'll have something to do, rather than stare at four walls."

She didn't have to wait long to be called back in and knew the worst before he opened his mouth to say, "I'm sorry Barbara, Peter was one of the unlucky ones."

Margaret hugged her, but she felt strangely composed, thinking more about how Peter's parents would cope with losing their only child. The next few days were a blur, until she was told that Peter's body had been recovered intact and that his funeral would be at a Military Ceremony in Surrey, one of the Pilots from the Squadron would represent the Station. The senior WAAF at Binbrook, Squadron Officer Passmore, who must have been approaching forty, interviewed Barbara and asked her if she would like to accompany him. Previously, Barbara had considered her to be a distant unemotional figure, but found her kind in these circumstances. Not knowing if she would be able to cope with the funeral, she initially declined. Passmore was, however, adamant that she owed it to Peter and his parents to be there and if she failed to make the effort would regret it in the future.

She and the pilot, Flt Lt. Ashworth, who had a DFC ribbon above his breast pocket travelled to Brookwood together. It was the largest cemetery that she had ever seen, with an abundant variety of trees surrounding the various areas, which included a significant military section. The lovely late summer day made the occasion even more difficult for Barbara, as did the number of new plots that had been added to the neat rows of crosses. There were very few people there to commemorate her lover's short life and she was shocked to see Peter's father, who looked to have aged ten years. He was distraught, sobbing throughout, making her feel guilty that her own tears did not come, having shed so many in recent days. Speaking to her afterwards, he apologized that Grace had been unable to face the trauma of her only child's burial, but he said that she had told him to tell her that she would always be welcome in their home.

Barbara had to face the long journey back to Lincolnshire alone, as Flt. Lt Ashworth was travelling on to Portsmouth for the funeral of the Co-Pilot from Peter's aircraft, which was to be held the following day. Alone with her thoughts, believing that her whole future had been destroyed and wondering how she would be able to carry on. When she arrived back,

Margaret, who like all the other girls in the billet, had been supportive, hugged her and said, "We're all here for you Babs, we'll get through this together."

It was only at that moment, that it struck Barbara that her period was two weeks overdue.

CHAPTER 18

Tom's Mother was true to her word about feeding him up and his weight increased quickly; this was supplemented by regular trips to the "Oak" with his Dad, whose regular parting shot to his wife was, "We're just off out for two pints", which on most occasions was a somewhat conservative estimate.

On one of these visits, when he had been home for around three weeks his Dad asked, "Have you thought what you're going to do now then?"

"Well, I suppose I'll have to get a job, because if I don't I'll soon be as fat as a pig with the amount of "snap" Mothers putting on my plate."

"Are you coming back to the pit?"

Tom grinned, "No I don't think so, I can spell margarine now, and so I'll go and ask old Randall for a shop job."

"Daft bugger, there's no money in shop work."

"I'm joking Dad, of course I'm coming back to the pit, it's the only thing I know about, apart from firing a gun and I didn't get much practice at that."

So, the following Monday he was back on the Pit Top for the first time in seven years, applying for a job underground.

The Colliery Manager, Mr. Beasley took him into his Office shook his hand saying, "Welcome home Tom, it's been a long time. I'll be glad to have you back, but do you think that you'll be strong enough for face work straight away after five years in a POW camp. It might be better if you stay on the "bank" for a few months."

"I'll be OK Mr. Beasley, it's a couple of months since I got out and I feel a lot stronger than I did."

"OK, if that's what you want. What shift is your Dad on next week?"

"He's nights this week, so he'll be on days."

"Right then, you can start on days on Monday morning, after that you can go on a three-shift pattern, Days, Afternoons and Nights, stripping on the Top Bench Seam."

Feeling a lump in his throat as he walking along the pit lane with his Dad on Monday morning, knowing that there had been times over the past years when he had convinced himself that he would never do so again. Jumping into the Cage enthusiastically, he enjoyed the colliers banter while they were being lowered for eight long hours' underground. He tackled his "stint" with vigor, but soon realized that it was not going to be as easy as he thought and was relieved to hear the shout of "Snap time" from along the Face. Sitting next to his Dad, with their backs to a Coal Tub he said, "Bloody Hell; I'd forgotten how hard this is."

"You'll soon get back into it lad; by this time next week you'll feel that you've never been away."

At the end of the shift, Tom felt exhausted and went to bed very early, knowing that he would have to be up at five in the morning to do it all over again. When he did wake up, every sinew of his body ached and even getting out of bed was an effort. This was the pattern for several days, but his Dad had been right, because after the first week his aches and pains subsided and while he found face work demanding, his body soon adjusted to it.

During the second week, he was sat in the Canteen having a cup of tea prior to the Afternoon Shift, when he felt a hand on his shoulder. He turned to see Jack Garrett who grasped his hand saying, "Welcome back Tom, me and the Mrs. thought about you a lot while you were away. How are you lad?"

"I feel good, thanks Jack. I struggled a bit on my first week back at work, but I'm getting used to it. How are you and Mrs. Garrett?"

"We're fine Tom, getting a bit older but apart from that we can't complain."

Chatting for a while, as the conversation was coming to an end Tom nervously asked, "How are Barbara and Jean?"

"They're both fine Tom, but what happened to Barbara in the war was a bit of a shock to us and she doesn't go out much these days. I tell you what, if you want to see her come around for your tea on Sunday. I won't tell her that you're coming, it will be a surprise."

"Or a shock", joked Tom.

"Don't be so bloody daft, come around at about five."

On Sunday afternoon, Tom didn't tell his parents where he was going, but dressed in his demob suit and made the familiar walk to Church Road. He knocked on the door and when Mrs. Garrett answered was surprised that she held both of his arms and kissed his cheek," Come in, Tom it's lovely to see you looking so well."

Jack was sat smoking his pipe, by the immaculate open black range, where a small fire burned. He didn't get up, but said, "Come in Tom and make yourself at home, Barbara and Jean are out with the baby but will be back in a minute. Do you fancy a Woodbine?"

Accepting the cigarette, before there was time to finish it, he heard front door open and the sound of Barbara and her sisters' laughter. When they walked into the room, the laughter stopped abruptly when they saw their visitor.

Looking perplexed Barbara said, "Tom, I wasn't expecting to see you."

"Why not, I've been back a while now and I thought it about time that I came around to see your Mum and Dad. Who's this young lady?" he said looking it the beautiful blonde little girl that Jean was holding, who had the deepest blue eyes that Tom had ever seen.

Barbara took the child from Jean, leading her by the hand over to Tom and said, "This is Petra."

Stooping down in front of the surprisingly confident little girl he smiled, "Hello Petra, I'm Tom, I'm a friend of Mummies."

Putting a thumb in her mouth, she looked at him before taking it out and smiling, "Hello Tom", before turning to seek the security of her mother's skirt.

"Tom's staying to tea", said Jack, "so get yourselves sorted out and we can all sit down together."

Settling down to Meat and Fish paste sandwiches, these were followed by small rock cakes that had apparently been made by Barbara. The only conversation involved Jack and Tom and was mainly about what was going on at the pit and the prospects for West Bromwich Albion in the FA Cup that was being resurrected in the autumn, prior to the Football League restarting in 1946. Tom and Barbara said little to each other, but there was the occasional smile. As he was about to leave he was surprised when she said, "I'll see Tom out Dad", following him into the small hallway. Opening the door himself, as he was going out she touched his arm and said, "If it's nice next Sunday afternoon, perhaps you'd like to go for a walk with Petra and me?"

Thinking only briefly about the reaction of his parents, he realized that the invitation had made him as happy as he had been since he had arrived home, replying, "I'd like that, what time?"

"Come around at three, providing it's not raining."

Tom was on nights that week, so spent most of the daytime sleeping and the rest of it looking forward to seeing Barbara on Sunday. Praying that it would be dry, he was rewarded with a warm autumn afternoon, once again putting on his grey pin stripe suit and a collar and tie, causing his Mum to ask, "Have you got a lady friend, then?"

"No, I'm just going around to a mate's house"

"Wearing your best suit?"

"Well it is Sunday", he said making a hasty exit.

Barbara was ready when he arrived, wearing a plain blue summer dress, with a white cardigan to protect her from the autumn chill. She looked older than her 26 years, with fine lines having appeared at the sides of her dark eyes the slightest hint of grey in her jet-black hair. Petra was already in her push chair, seemingly quite determined to get out, but Barbara stooped over speaking quietly to her daughter, before saying to Tom, "Don't worry, she'll go off to sleep as soon as we start walking."

Walking towards the edge of the village and into lanes, bordered by hedgerows, which had lost some of their summer foliage, they passed several other couples, enjoying ritual Sunday afternoon walks. Most of the men, greeting them with, "How do, Tom", but he noticed that many the women either ignored Barbara or gave her a cursory nod. Surprisingly Barbara didn't seem phased by their attitude and said, "I'm used to the way a lot of people treat me, they think I'm what my mother calls a "loose woman". If you want, I'll tell you what happened to me."

She was surprised when Tom said, "I prefer not to know really, a lot of things happened to people in the war, including me, and I want to look forward not back. In all those years in the camp the only thing that kept me going was the thought that I would see you again and that I'd be able to put right what happened before the war."

"There's nothing to put right Tom, what happened then was due to my selfishness, but whatever you think, things have changed. What about Petra?"

Tom smiled at her, "I think Petra is lovely, almost as lovely as her mother."

Tears welled in her eyes, "Oh Tom, I don't deserve you, you could do so much better than me"

"The last time I saw you before I went in the Army; I said that you were the only girl that I'd ever looked at. Well that's still the case and whatever happened to you while I was away, I still want to marry you."

"Despite me having had a baby?"

"Look Barbara, I'd feel the same if you had ten babies and I don't give a bugger what people think of you or me for that matter. I'll care for Petra as if she was my own, which believe me won't be difficult."

They said little else on their way back to Church Road, but as he was about to leave her he said, "Look if your happy with it, I'll talk to your Dad as soon as I can get him on his own and providing he's got no objection, we can get engaged."

"If you're sure you know what you're taking on Tom."

"I've never been as sure of anything in my life."

Chapter 19

When Barbara got home, she was no sooner through the door when her mother asked, "How did you get on with Tom then?"

"It was really nice", she replied, "it was lovely in the lanes and we had a really good chat."

Surprised how well that they had got on, considering everything that had happened, she was sure that he would be a kind and loving husband. He obviously loved her, but she knew that she would never be able to care for him as much as she had for Peter. She was also relieved that Tom didn't want to hear about what happened to her in war, which she still found heartbreaking.

When she had found that she was pregnant, she had mixed emotions, but predominantly joy that Peter would live on through the unborn child, which outweighed the stigma that unmarried motherhood would bring.

After missing her second period, she reported sick for the first time since she had joined the WAAF's and was confronted by a middle aged bespectacled Medical Officer, who abruptly asked,

"What can I do for you, Garrett, you look pretty healthy to me?"

"I've missed two periods, Sir"

"I see, have you been sexually active?"

"Yes sir, but my fiancé was killed a month ago,."

"I'm sorry for you and him; let's have a look at you."

Following a brief examination, the M.O. sat back in his chair, wrote a Memo, which he put into a brown envelope, handed it to her saying, "Take this to the General Office, they'll arrange for you to be discharged from the service straight away."

Not surprised by the outcome of her visit to the Medical Centre, on reporting to the General Office she was informed that she would be discharged within forty-eight hours. In the short time that she could think about her situation, her main worry had been her parent's reaction, deciding that rather than turn up on the doorstop unannounced she would send a telegram telling them what had happened. There was an abrupt reply the following day, which read. "We are ashamed of you, please don't come back here."

Despite expecting their anger, the telegram had been a shock and she didn't know what to do or where to go. Margaret suggested that she might seek help from Peter's parents, but Barbara was not sure that this was the solution to her plight. In desperation, she thought that she had little to lose, so the following day left Binbrook for the final time travelling apprehensively to London. Having had time to think about it, she decided that it would be better to contact Peter's father, rather than turning up at their home, so after arriving at Kings Cross she made her way to Saville Row. Feeling very conspicuous entering the large oak paneled tailors shop, she was immediately approached by slim immaculately dressed middle aged man who said, "Good afternoon Miss, can I help you?"

"Good afternoon, I wonder if Mr. Stanford is available?"

"I'll check; may I ask your name please?"

"Barbara Garrett, He knows me."

Disappearing through the back of the shop he quickly returned followed by Trevor, who had a broad smile on his face and a tape measure hanging around his neck.

"Hello Barbara, what a wonderful surprise, you should have told us that you were coming."

Finding it difficult to control her emotions and embarrassment, she had tears in her eyes, making Trevor quickly aware of her distress. Holding her arm he led her to an office, that had his name on the door.

"What's the matter my dear?"

"I'm sorry to turn up unannounced, but I've nowhere else to go and I'm at my wits end. I'm going to have Peter's baby and have been discharged by the Air Force."

Looking shocked, he calmly asked, "What about your own parents?"

Barbara burst into tears and handed him the telegram that she had received the previous day.

"I see; don't worry we'll sort this out. You can wait here for an hour until I finish work and then you must come home with me. I'll get you a cup of tea."

Leaving promptly at five o'clock, Trevor hailed a taxi, which took them to Charing Cross and within an hour they were walking up the short garden path to the suburban semi-detached house which had been Peter's home throughout his short life. Trevor opened the front door with his key and shouted, "Grace, we have a visitor."

Grace came into the hall, looking delighted to see her and said, "Oh Barbara, how good of you to come and see us. How long can you stay?"

Barbara looked at Trevor who said, "It's not quite like that, dear."

Grace was sympathetic and hugged Barbara, "Don't you worry, my dear, they'll always be place for you here. I know how much Peter loved you and I'm pleased that we are going to be grandparents."

Trevor, as he said, would "sleep on it" before deciding how to handle the situation. The following evening, they sat together in the lounge explaining that he and Grace had a small weekend cottage in the village of Westcott near Dorking. They had decided that Barbara would be much safer there than in London and that they would spend as many weekends there with her as possible. As she got closer to her confinement, Grace would stay with her the whole time and any neighbors they knew would be told that Barbara was their son's widow. He also told her that he would contact her parents at the appropriate time, probably after the baby was born, to hopefully influence them to change their attitude.

Overwhelmed by their kindness, Barbara found Westcott to be a delightful old world village, bordered by the North Downs. There was a pub on the village green and woods nearby, where she could walk. The only problem was loneliness, as she had no friends, the only contact being with people she saw in the village shops. It was better at the weekends, when Trevor and Grace came and were always kind and considerate. There were photographs of Peter at various stages of his life throughout the cottage, finding the one by her bed side to be of comfort through the long lonely nights.

Throughout the winter, Barbara adapted to her situation, but longed for the weekends when she enjoyed Trevor and Grace's company. She had registered with a local Doctor, who arranged for the baby to be delivered in a hospital in Dorking, less than two miles away. Six weeks before the due date, Grace moved in permanently and was on hand, when Barbara went into labor three days early. Eighteen hours later, totally exhausted, she gave birth to a 7lb 4oz baby girl. Initially disappointed, she had longed for a boy, as much for Trevor and Grace's sake as hers. Then she saw the baby's wonderful blue eyes, which were so much like Peter's, thinking how proud he would have been. If his parents were disappointed that it wasn't a boy, they didn't show it and when Trevor held her that weekend, he was in tears as he said, "I'm sorry Grace, but you're out of the picture from now on."

Barbara had intended to name the new arrival, Peter, had she been a boy, but settled on Petra Grace, which seemed to delight the new grandparents. One thing she did insist on was that Peter's name was on the birth certificate and that his daughter would have his surname.

Everyone decided that it would be better for everyone if Barbara, Grace and Petra stayed in the cottage away from the bombing for the immediate future, with Trevor visiting at weekends. This arrangement seemed to be working well, until after around three months, sitting together one Saturday evening, Trevor surprised Barbara by saying, "Grace and I have been talking and I would like to contact your Mother and Father. We really like looking after you, but we're not comfortable with the estrangement from your parents and feel that if they are agreeable you should go back and live with them."

"Well, after what my Dad put in that telegram, I don't think they will be very pleased if I turn up with a baby and I'm really happy here."

"We know you are, but that's how we feel, but I won't contact them unless you are agreeable."

"What will you do, write to them?"

"Yes, but I will show you the letter before it's sent."

"Alright, but I don't expect for one minute that they'll want me back."

The next day Trevor asked Barbara to read the letter.

Dear Mr. and Mrs. Garrett,

First, let me introduce myself. My name is Trevor Stanford and my son Peter was engaged to your daughter Barbara, prior to losing his life when his aircraft crash landed last August. Peter had brought Barbara home to see us only a month before he was killed and my wife Grace and I, were immediately taken with her and think that she would have made our son a wonderful wife.

Alas, that was not to be, but as you know, at the time of Peter's death, Barbara was expecting his child and she gave birth to a daughter, Petra on the 16th May. When you told Barbara that she would not be welcome in your home, in desperation she came to us, having nowhere else to go. Grace and I were happy to help her, having previously told her that she would always be welcome in our home. As you can see from our address, we live in the London suburbs, but fortunately have a weekend cottage just outside Dorking in Surrey, where Barbara has been living, as we thought it safer to be away from the bombing in London.

We are happy to be Petra's grandparents and hope that you are too. She is a beautiful baby and while I know the circumstances are not ideal, I am sure that you will be delighted when you see her for the first time, which I hope will be very soon.

While Grace and I are happy to take care of Barbara and Petra indefinitely, we do feel that it would be better for them to come and live with you. Barbara was very unhappy with your rejection of her, I know that she misses you both and hope that you will reconsider your position and agree to take them back into your home. We would miss them terribly, but feel it would be best for all concerned

We look forward to hearing from you soon.

Yours Sincerely,
Trevor Stanford

Happy with the content of the letter, they agreed that Trevor would post it on Monday in the hope of getting a reply by the following weekend.

It was a nervous wait until the following Friday evening, but Barbara was disappointed when Trevor arrived to tell her that there had been no reply. Knowing how stubborn her Dad could be, she wondered if he would respond, but her fears were allayed on the following weekend, Trevor arriving and immediately presenting her with a neatly opened white envelope.

Nervously removing the enclosed letter, Barbara was conscious of both Grace and Trevor watching as she read.

> *Dear Mr. Stanford,*
>
> *Thank you for your letter, which was a real surprise for us. We had wondered what had become of our daughter, having not heard from her for a year. It was a great shock to me and her mother when she told us that she was expecting a baby, but now we are more aware of the circumstances it is easier to understand. The thing is unmarried mothers are not viewed very kindly in our small mining community and that was why I reacted so abruptly to her telegram. Me and her mother have talked about it a lot since and realize that we did act hastily, being unfair to Barbara.*
>
> *We only have a very small house, with a living room and kitchen downstairs, two bedrooms upstairs, with a lavatory in the yard. It is not ideal for a new baby, but we are willing to take her back. If you could let me know when they will be coming, I will meet them at the station.*
>
> *Me and my wife, Beth would like to thank you both for what you have done for Barbara and we would be happy if in the future, you wanted to visit your granddaughter although it's a long way here from London.*
>
> *Yours Sincerely,*
> *Jack Garrett*

Not knowing quite how she felt, she was relieved that her parent's attitude towards her had changed and knew that she would have to go back to them, despite being content with her life in Surrey. She hugged Trevor saying, "I'll miss you both so much, you have been a mother and father to me for the past year and I love both of you. I'll never be able to repay you for what you've done for me and Petra."

It was Grace who replied, "Oh Barbara, we feel the same, we've come to love you like the daughter we never had, you gave us Petra and Peter will live on through her and her children. You must bring Petra to see us after the war"

"When will I have to go?"

Trevor said, "Look you're not going all that way on your own, I'll come on the train with you. We'll write to your Mum and Dad and tell them when we'll be travelling."

Barbara knew that she would miss the comfort and security of the cottage and was apprehensive how people would react to her in her home village, but looked forward to seeing her parents and sister. It was just over a week until she, Petra and Trevor travelled to Waterloo and across London to Euston to catch the north bound express to Nuneaton, where they had to change for the stopping train that would take Barbara and her daughter home.

When the small tank engine edged its two-coach load into the village station, as promised her Dad was waiting for them. Barbara was relieved when he shook Trevor's hand, kissed her cheek and took Petra in his arms clearly intent on carrying her.

Trevor carried both cases as the small party made the fifteen-minute walk to Church Road, attracting the gaze of curious villagers. When they arrived, Barbara was surprised when her Mum hugged her tightly saying, "We've missed you here Barbara and we'll do everything we can to make you and this lovely baby happy."

Putting down the cases in the tiny hallway, Trevor, hugged Barbara and shook her father's hand saying, "Well, it's been nice to meet you, and I hope that Petra makes you as happy as we have been with her. Now I must be off Barbara, because I need to get back to "town" tonight."

"You're not going before you have a cup of tea and a sandwich", said Beth, we're really grateful for what you've done for our family."

"Thank you, it's been a pleasure for us, but I really must go if I'm going to get back to London tonight."

Reluctant to part Barbara hugged Trevor again, saying their emotional farewells; both pledging to keep in touch, Barbara promising to make sure that they could see as much of their granddaughter as distance allowed and then he was gone.

The remainder of the war passed Barbara by, with the village being far removed from the action and she could concentrate on Petra, who brought back constant memories of Peter. Life with her parents, was as she expected, nowhere near as comfortable as that she had become used to since leaving the Air Force. Appreciating their renewed support, she especially enjoyed the company of her sister, who was always eager to help with the baby, the three of them sharing the small bedroom. The times that she ventured from the house was with Petra, she found attitudes towards her, while not being hostile were far from friendly, particularly among women of her age with babies. On the few occasions, she saw Tom' parents they ignored her, but at least Maud still acknowledged her albeit somewhat distantly.

There were muted celebrations in the village on VE Day with several houses displaying flags, but no dancing in the street. It was almost three months later when she heard her Dad say to her Mum. "I saw Tom Walton at the pit today, my word he looks older and has lost a lot of weight, although his Dad told me that he's not as skinny now as he was when he first got back"

Barbara had often thought about Tom during the war and wondered what he would be like when he came back, never even giving it a thought that he might not. Hearing that he had returned to the village, she was sure that given what had happened, the last thing that he would contemplate would be to spend the rest of his life with her, making her totally unprepared for what happened on those two autumn Sundays.

CHAPTER 20

Reflecting on his five years of captivity, Tom was relieved that his misery had not been compounded by the knowledge that the only girl he had ever loved, was back in the village with a baby. It had been a shock when his father had told him, but it became clear that whoever the child's father was, Barbara was no longer with him. When Jack invited him to tea, he had looked forward to it but with apprehension, unaware what her attitude towards him would be. Soon finding that his concern was misplaced, he was pleased when she asked him to go walking. Knowing that most people in the village would not understand him wanting to marry Barbara after what had happened, he didn't care, being sure she would make him happy.

Neither did he care, what his parents thought, but decided to put off telling them until he had spoken to Jack. A few days passed before they bumped into each other in the pit canteen and Tom took the opportunity to ask him to have a drink in the "Oak" the following evening. Both were on "Days", so they met quite early, while the pub was quiet. Sitting down with their pints, Tom offered him a Woodbine, which Jack declined preferring to stick to his pipe. Giving him time to fill and light it, as the plumes of smoke drifted towards the stained ceiling, he came out with it, "Jack, I hope you and Mrs. Garrett, don't mind but I'd like to marry your Barbara"

"Bloody Hell lad, I wasn't expecting that. It's a bit sudden, isn't it?"

"Sudden be buggered, look Jack, I've been waiting since 1940 to ask her to marry me"

"But what about the baby, don't you think things have changed?"

"What happened while I was away is nothing to do with me. We had our fall out before the war, which was my fault, I feel lucky to be given a second chance and I promise I'll take care of Petra as if she were my own."

"You're a good bloke Tom and Barbara's bloody lucky, her mother will be as pleased as punch. What about your Mum and Dad?"

"They'll be alright." He said unconvinced.

After two pints, they each went their separate ways, Jack knowing his wife would be delighted with his news, but Tom thinking that his parents would be anything but.

Not wanting to delay what he knew would be a difficult conversation, he got back from work the following day to find his parents sat drinking tea in front of the roaring fire, he said, "I've got some news for you and I don't want you flying off the handle Dad"

"It can't be that bad, lad. Come on, out with it."

"I've seen Barbara a couple of times since I came home and I asked her to marry me when we were out walking last weekend."

"Well it could be worse, but not much, you must be mad wanting to take on some fly boy's bastard."

For the first time his mother intervened almost shouting, "That's enough of that language, Henry. You can't blame the baby for what her mother's done, but I agree with your Dad, Tom. I don't think you should be marrying her."

"Look Mother, I'm thirty-one and time's passing me by. Barbara is the only girl I've ever wanted to marry and I feel lucky that she said yes. I spoke to Jack last night and he's really happy about it."

At that his father unrestrained exclaimed, "I bloody well bet he is. He's got a chance to get damaged goods off his hands, but if that's what you want, so be it, but don't expect to see me and your mother at any wedding."

"Well you speak for yourself, Henry. I'm not particularly happy about it, but there's no way on earth that I'm going to miss my only son's wedding."

That ended the conversation, with his Dad going out of the back door saying, "I'm going to feed the pigs."

Tom followed him, but turned left up the entry, thinking he needed to walk. He decided that he would meet Maud out of work, to tell her what had happened before she got home.

Maud was almost as tall as Tom, with dark hair and brown eyes. He considered her round face attractive, but a generous figure suggested that she had a liking for Randall's cakes. She had been engaged for two years to Les Draper, who worked in the bake house at Randall's and had told Tom that they were saving up to get married, but wouldn't do so until they had enough money for a deposit on a small house. Leaving the shop, she seemed surprised to see him, but crossed the road to where he stood.

"Hello Tom, this is a surprise."

"I need to tell you something before you get home."

"Is it anything to do with you being seen out with Barbara Garrett last Sunday?"

"How do you know about that?"

"You get to know everything what's going on in this village working in that shop."

"Well it is, I've asked her to marry me and told Mum and Dad this afternoon and he wasn't impressed. He said he won't come to the wedding."

"I'm not surprised, he is a bit old fashioned and I know he doesn't think much of Barbara."

"He's not marrying her."

"Perhaps given time he'll change his attitude Tom, but from my point of view I'm pleased for you both. I always thought that you were made for each other, but that you might have been upset by what happened to her, but she's not the first and won't be the last."

Following Tom's news his Dad carried on as if nothing had happened, never asking Tom about his social life or mentioning Barbara. He had always got on well with his father and was determined that the rift would not spoil the atmosphere in the home or his relationship with Barbara.

The first thing was to take Barbara to Birmingham to choose an engagement ring, which she displayed proudly to Jean and her parents. Becoming a regular visitor to the house in Church Road, Jack and Beth treated him like a son. Tom decided that they would get married as soon as they found somewhere to live, which Barbara thought would mean paying rent, but was delighted when he said that he had five hundred pounds in the bank and they could afford a deposit on a house. Jack told them about a three-bedroom semi in the Station Road, that as he put it "needed a lick of paint", but was on the market for 400 pounds and within a week they had arranged to buy it.

Jack and Tom worked hard to make it habitable, so the wedding could be arranged. He and Barbara had decided to go to the Register Office in the nearby town, but Jack would have none of it, saying, "They'll be no Register Office jobs here, if you're getting married you can do it properly in church."

Determined to avoid any conflict, they happily agreed and Barbara walked to St. Paul's Church which was just fifty yards away from the family home, wearing a Powder Blue suit and matching hat. Tom was waiting for her with his best man, Maud's fiancée, Les Draper. Jack gave her away, with the tiny congregation being completed, by Barbara's mother and sister, who held Petra, while on Tom's side of the aisle stood Maud and his mother. Afterwards the small party walked back to the house in Church Road, where Beth had prepared sandwiches and sausage rolls, while Les had made them a small iced wedding cake, which was all washed down with tea. There was to be no honeymoon, so in the afternoon the newlyweds walked to their new home in Station Road to begin their life together.

Tom had been nervous about the wedding night, being totally inexperienced and even wondering how Barbara would compare him with Petra's father. Needing not to have worried, because after some initial fumbling he found the experience well worth waiting for, with Barbara seeming happy and eager when on the following morning, they consummated their union for a third time. As they settled in to their new home, Tom found Barbara to be house-proud, the place shining like a "new pin." Beth and Jean where almost daily visitors, while Maud came around at least twice every week, sometimes with Les.

Chapter 21

Almost every minute of every day Tom counted his blessings, thinking how lucky he was to have a wife who seemed totally contented with their married life, and a ready-made daughter who he adored, the fact that he was not her real father never crossing his mind. Thinking that nothing could upset their happiness, he was brought back to reality when they had been married for six months. Arriving home from his day shift, he immediately sensed that Barbara was tense and asked what the problem was.

"I know that you don't want to know what happened to me why I was in the WAAF's Tom, but I do need to tell you something."

Apprehensive, Tom said, "Tell, me as much as you have to."

"Look, when I got pregnant, My Mum and Dad didn't want to know me, so in desperation I went to Petra's father's parents, who were really kind to me and looked after me for over a year. They haven't seen their granddaughter for nearly four years."

"Where was her father?"

"He had been killed."

"I see, but why do I need to know now?"

"Because they've written and say they want to come and see her."

"That's fine, but do they know about me"

"Yes, I wrote and told them when we were getting married and they seemed happy, you'll like them and I'm sure that they will like you."

"Where do they live?'

"South East London, but they've got a car so want to drive up for a couple of days and stay in a hotel."

"O K, just let me know when they're coming."

"You don't mind then?"

"If I did I'd say so. It's only right that they should want to see their granddaughter."

Tom did mind really, having completely shut all thoughts of Barbara's experiences in the war out of his mind. Knowing that she must have loved Petra's father, his parents visit would be likely to rekindle the memories of her time with him. Contrary to that, he was sure that if he had a grandchild in the future, he would want to be involved in its life and to deny them that would be unkind.

Just over a week later, Barbara announced that they were coming the following weekend, asking Tom if he would mind if they came to tea on the Saturday. Of course, I bloody well mind he thought, but said, "Yes, I'll look forward to meeting them."

At just after three o'clock on the Saturday a black pre-war Austin Seven drew up outside the house. Barbara had been looking out of the front window constantly for the past hour and excitedly announced, "They're here, come to the front door with me and meet them", which didn't improve Tom's uneasiness. But he picked up Petra and they went outside to greet their visitors.

A tall distinguished looking man, who was slim with grey hair, dressed in an immaculate dark three-piece suit got out of the right-hand side and walked around to the opposite door, opening it, from which an elegant woman emerged, who herself was dressed in a tailored suit and brimmed hat that covered most of her own graying hair.

Walking quickly down the garden path to meet their visitors, Barbara hugged Trevor and then turned to Grace. Standing behind to allow his wife to greet their visitors, he put Petra down, who showed no hesitation before toddling towards her grandparents, Trevor picking her up and saying "My word, you are a big girl, we've brought you a little present which you can open when we get inside."

Still standing behind Barbara, not wanting to impinge on the reunion, Tom felt it had nothing to do with him, but Trevor strode up to him offering his hand, while saying, "Hello, you must be Tom, Grace and I have been really looking forward to meeting you."

"I'm pleased to meet you Mr. Stanford, you and your wife are very welcome in our home"

"Thank you, Tom, but please call me Trevor and this is Grace"

"It's nice to meet you Tom", said Grace, who like her husband shook his hand.

"We've been looking forward to seeing Barbara and Petra after such a long time and we were really pleased when Barbara wrote to tell us how happy she is", said Trevor, "you certainly seem to have found a nice home here.

As soon as they were through the door, Petra tore at the paper covering a rectangular box, which she opened to reveal a doll with blonde curly hair and a pink dress, causing her to shriek with delight and run towards Tom to show him.

Pleased that the visitors had made his step daughter happy, Tom felt a lot more at ease with the situation, suggesting to Barbara that she show Grace around the house and inviting Trevor to sit with him in front of the fire. He offered him a cigarette, which he declined, saying that he had never smoked. Tom found this strange to say the least because he could not think of any other man that he knew that didn't.

Trevor said, "I understand you were a prisoner of war."

"Yes, for almost five years. It wasn't easy, but a lot better than getting shot at. At least, I've got my life to look forward to, while a lot of the blokes I went to France with in 1939 haven't. I consider myself really lucky, but also a bit guilty."

"Well, you shouldn't, I understand that you volunteered, just as our son did. We were very proud of him and I'm sure that your parents felt the same."

"They weren't best pleased at the time, but with what was going on in Europe it seemed the right thing to do and I wanted to get away from the pit anyway."

"And now your back, so how do you feel about it?"

"Not great, but it's all I know and it gives me the security to give Barbara and Petra the good home that they deserve"

"Good for you Tom how did you and Barbara meet?"

"We went out together before the war, but she was madder than my Mum and Dad when I joined up, so we had a bust up and I thought that was that. She's the only girl that I've really been interested in and when I came back from Germany her parents asked me round to tea and it went on from there."

"Well, we're happy for you both and really grateful that you invited us to come and see our granddaughter. Our son, Peter was an only child and we were absolutely devastated when he was killed, but it is some consolation that he lives on through Petra. Do you and Barbara intend to have more children?"

"I really hope so, but its early days. We really think it would be good for Petra to have a brother or sister or even both."

"Quite right too, I really wish that we'd have had more than one."

Surprised at how much he liked Trevor, Tom had relaxed by the time Barbara and Grace completed their tour and the five of them sat around the table for a tea comprising of sandwiches and Barbara's homemade sponge cake. Happy to be the center of attention, afterwards Petra went into the back garden with her grandparents, leaving Tom and Barbara to clear the table and wash up, Barbara asking nervously, "What do you think of them?"

Tom smiled, "They're really nice, and I've been worrying all week, but I got on really well with Trevor, while you were upstairs. I'm glad that they came, not just for them but for you and Petra as well."

Suggesting that they come back the following day, when, providing the weather was agreeable, they could take Petra for a walk to get to know her a little better. They seemed delighted and even more so when the following day was warm and sunny. After being with them for just over an hour, Petra seemed to have enjoyed her time with her grandparents, insisting that they take her for a ride in their car before setting off on their journey south.

Prior to leaving, Trevor asked Barbara if she had a tape measure. She seemed somewhat surprised but duly produced one. Trevor surprising Tom by saying, "Right Tom, let me take your measurements and I'll make you a suit."

"There's no need for that, although it's a real kind offer, what with the clothing ration."

"Look Tom, it's no problem to me, we often have remnants of cloth and I might as well put them to good use. It will take me a few weeks and I'll post it to you."

"Well, I never thought I'd ever own a suit made in Saville Row, it will make a change from the one I was given when I was demobbed."

Taking their leave, they said that they should all come to London, for a holiday the following summer.

Chapter 22

Following the visit, Tom and Barbara barely had time to settle into their normal routine, before being abruptly interrupted by a letter from the War Office, asking Tom if he was prepared to assist the War Crimes Investigation Unit who were considering an incident in 1940, which would involve him travelling to France in the next few weeks. Tom's only concern was making Barbara and Petra happy, dimming memories of that terrible time having not occupied his mind as predominantly as had previously been the case. Knowing that the contents of the letter were upsetting, she asked her husband, "What's that about then, love?"

"It's something that happened to me in France in 1940, which I've never told you about"

"Well, if it's worrying you, it's about time that you did."

"Look Barbara, I've never spoken to anyone about it since I came home and you would find it hard to believe what the Germans did to us."

"Tom what you have done for me and Petra is wonderful, I'm so happy and I know that I've never said it before, but I love you and I can't stand seeing you upset, so please tell me."

The declaration of love lifted Tom's spirits and he recounted what had happened, by the end of which Barbara was in tears, having had no idea that he had experienced anything as horrendous. To have witnessed his comrades treated so brutally, together with his own guilt about surviving, had caused him nightmares, telling her that the last thing that had ever crossed his mind was going back. Despite this, he felt obligated to see those responsible held to account.

"Then you must go, nobody should be allowed to get away with murder."

Replying the following day, Tom informed the War Office he was prepared to help in any way he could. Another letter soon arrived with a travel warrant to Euston enclosed, being told that he would be met at the station. Asking for leave of absence from the pit, it was granted without pay. Catching the train to London a few days later, he was taken to a Hotel, given a room for the night and told to report to the War Office the following morning at 9.00 a.m., to ask for Major Thornton.

He was immediately put at ease by the Major, who shook his hand firmly saying, "Thank you so much for your help in this matter Mr. Walton, I'm sure that you are not looking forward to going back to France, but we'll try and make it as painless as possible."

Thornton briefed Tom on the objectives of the investigation, which in effect was to identify those who had been responsible for the deaths of over eighty British soldiers on 28th May 1940 and subsequently bring them before a War Crimes Tribunal. They would be leaving for France later that morning, taking the Boat Train from Victoria to Dover for the short crossing to Calais, where they would stay that night, travelling by road to St.Jean du Becq the following morning.

Somewhat apprehensive about the boat journey, Tom was sure that it would rekindle memories of the crossing that he had made with his comrades in 1939, many of whom must have been killed in the retreat to the coast or at St.Jean du Becq. Considering himself fortunate to have survived, he was determined to assist as much as he could, so that those responsible could be held to account.

The short crossing was pleasant on a calm sea and as he looked back at the white cliffs, he was reassured by the fact that he would be making the return journey in two days' time, while in 1939 he had wondered if he would ever set foot on English soil again, despite the optimism of most of his colleagues, many of whom had thought themselves indestructible. The Hotel Pacific was small but comfortable, with Tom having his own room with a pleasant view of a large church.

Joined in Calais by two other Officers, a young Captain and a much older man who was introduced as Lieutenant Colonel Blackman and was obviously in charge. They were picked up in two jeeps in the morning, to travel the twelve miles to their destination. On arrival, Tom was immediately familiar with the site where the barn that had been rebuilt after the war was situated, with the pond that had been his salivation only 100 yds. away. The weather was so different than had been the case in 1940, Tom recalling the stifling heat on the march and in the barn compared with the strong autumnal wind and showery rain which welcomed them. Blackman asked Tom to recount his experiences as they toured the site, which he found very difficult bringing back fear and terror that he had tried to forget.

Major Thornton told him that they had been trying to identify soldiers from the SS unit who had survived the war. Of those that had been questioned, all except one Corporal had denied all knowledge of being present at the incident. The Corporal had been eager to identify the SS Officer in command on that day, who was living with his family in Hamburg. Tom was shown several photographs, one of which sent a chill down his spine, as it was undoubtedly the SS Officer who spoke such perfect English. He could well remember him shouting, "Where you are going there will be plenty of room", just prior to grenades being thrown into the barn.

After being at the site for almost three hours, Tom and the Officers travelled back to the hotel, where the Colonel shook his hand saying, "When we have reviewed the evidence it will be decided if any charges are to follow. If that is the case, you must go to Germany to testify. I don't suppose you will have a problem with that?"

"I'd be glad to. Sir. I'd do anything to get justice for my mates."

"Good man, it's been nice to meet you Walton, you've been a great help to us."

Following a restless night, Tom and Major Thornton were back on the boat in the morning, hoping to arrive in London in early afternoon. Getting on well with Thornton, he was interested to hear of his wartime experiences. Having seen service in North Africa, he was among the first to land in France on D Day, where he was wounded, his injuries having consigned him to desk since. Thornton bade him farewell at Victoria and while he was keen to get back to Barbara, on a whim he decided to take a taxi to Saville Row to see Trevor.

Arriving at Anderson and Shepherd's, he was struck by the racks that supported reams of material, although there didn't seem to be any customers. He was greeted by a smartly dressed young man, with sharp features, a pale face and dark hair slicked back with Brylcream. He had a tape measure around his neck and viewed Tom with disdain, obviously unimpressed by his Demob Suit. "What can I do for you, sir?"

"Is Mr. Stanford available, please, he's making me a suit."

Looking at him with incredulity, the young man asked, "Does sir have an appointment?"

"No, just tell him it's Tom Walton."

Turning towards the back of the shop he said, "Just wait sir, I'll see if he's available."

A beaming Trevor emerged from the back of the shop and grasped his hand, "Hello Tom, this is a pleasant surprise. What are you doing in town?"

Briefly relating the reasons for his journey, saying that it concerned his time in the army. Trevor didn't press him, being more interested in the welfare of Barbara and Petra. Tom could reassure him that they were both thriving and that he was looking forward to seeing them that evening, this being the first time they had been apart since their marriage.

Trevor said, "It's really fortuitous that you have come. I've finished your suit and you can try it on. If it fits you can take it with you."

For the first and only time in his life Tom tried on a suit made in Saville Row, which was an absolute perfect fit tempting him to discard his Demob Suit there and then, but thinking it smart enough for the pit. As it was, it was wrapped for him and after thanking Trevor profusely he set off for the last leg of his journey.

Although he had only been away for three nights, Tom couldn't wait to get home to Barbara. They made love almost every night and he wondered how he had remained celibate for so long.

Arriving in the middle of the evening he let himself in, Barbara ran towards him and was soon in his arms. He kissed her and asked, "Are we going to have an early night?"

"Not this early, me lad, I've made your dinner and you're going to eat that before any early night."

"I'm not hungry for food"

"Yes, you bloody well are, show a bit of self-control"

Laughing, he knew that the only way to get her up the stairs was to eat dinner, which they enjoyed together. He told her about his trip and the visit to Trevor and she insisted that he show her his new suit before bedtime. More bloody delays, he thought, didn't this woman know that he'd slept on his own for the last three nights. Mind you, so had she.

After they had made love, holding Barbara in his arms, she turned and kissed him whispering, "I've got a nice surprise for you."

"Oh yes, what's that?"

"Well, Petra is always saying that she wants a brother or sister and as you know she always gets what she wants."

Despite loving Petra as his own, the fact that Barbara was going to have a child which would be Tom's own flesh and blood made his happiness complete. He couldn't wait to tell his Mother and Maud the news and while they both seemed overjoyed, his Dad maintained his usual indifference. In contrast, both of Barbara's parents beamed with pleasure on being told the news, both prospective grandmothers occupying themselves by knitting baby clothes at every opportunity.

Following her marriage to Tom, Barbara found she had been treated a lot kindlier in the village, having made and cultivated friendships with several other young mothers.

After looking forward to the impending birth of their own second child the following spring, Jack duly arrived right on time just two days before Tom's own birthday. Tom went to tell his parents as soon as the midwife had left, Barbara's mother and sister being on hand to look after mother and baby. Walking into his boyhood home, his mother and father sat close to the fire, while Maud was at the table, and seeing it as an opportunity to make peace with his father said, "Congratulations, you've got a grandson."

Maud jumped up from her chair to embrace Tom saying, "That's brilliant, when can we come and see them."

"Tomorrow would probably best, because Barbara' a bit tired now, you as well Dad."

His mother said, "We'll be around tomorrow morning, before your Dad goes to the pit, he's afternoons."

"I won't be coming", said his father, "so no need to bother about me."

For the first time in his life Tom heard his mother shout in anger, "Yes you are, stubborn old beggar, it's time that you stopped this nonsense. You can see that Barbara has made Tom happy, and you are going to see your grandson."

Tom, having been a spectator to this altercation, was taken by surprise when his Dad said, "Alright Clara, have it your way, I don't suppose you can blame the child for the sins of the mother."

Tom was livid and before storming out pointed at his father shouting, "If that's what you think about my wife, don't bloody well bother, you won't be welcome in our house anyway. I'll see you and Maud tomorrow, Mother."

Walking home, he was determined not to let his father's bigotry spoil one of the happiest days of his life. When he got back, going straight upstairs to his wife who had the baby in her arms, with Petra sat on the bed looking at her brother with fascination. Tom thought that with his family now complete, he was the luckiest man alive. What could possibly go wrong?

CHAPTER 23

Early in 1948, with Petra almost six years old and Jack in his eighth month, Tom and Barbara had almost forgotten their wartime traumas and were blissfully happy, having the support of their extended families, except for Tom's father, with whom he did not communicate. Having done well since his return to the pit, Tom had started to go to Night School to gain the qualifications to enable him to become a Deputy. They even had a social life, being able to go to the pictures or Miners Welfare Club from time to time with Maud and Les, who were saving to get married themselves, usually happy to baby sit.

Then one day at the end of January, when Tom came home from the day shift Barbara, looking worried, handed him a brown envelope with the ominous "On His Majesties Service" embellished on the front.

Opening the envelope apprehensively, Tom suspected that the contents would not only upset him, but would also concern Barbara. The letter informed him that the man that he had identified had been arrested and charged with murder by the War Crimes Commission and that a trial would be held in Hamburg, commencing on 9th May. Tom was required to appear as a prosecution witness and to confirm that he would be in attendance, following which he would be sent further instructions. Having mixed emotions, while not wanting to be reminded of the massacre, he was keen not only look the perpetrator in the eye but to help get justice for his comrades.

Hugging Barbara to alleviate her concern he told her, "It's alright love, I've been half expecting this. They've caught the bastard responsible for the massacre and they want me to go to Germany in May to give evidence at his trial. I'm not looking forward to it, but I owe it to my mates."

"I agree me lad. I know you're still haunted by what happened and this might help to finally put it to bed. What will they do to him?"

"Hang the bastard I hope, I'm not normally in favor of hanging, but he deserves to die for what he did."

Having replied the following day, a couple of weeks later he received a railway warrant to London, being told to report to Major Thornton at the War Office by 9am on the 5th May and that a room had been booked for him in the Bedford Hotel in Southampton Row for the night of the 4th.

Not relishing the prospect of being apart from his family yet again, particularly as he was unsure for how long he would be away. The weeks passed quickly and the time for his departure soon came around. After he and Barbara had made love the night before she sobbed in his arms, saying that she didn't want him to go.

"You know that I have to" he said, "but I promise that this will be the last time. In future, the only times that you'll have to sleep on your own will be when I'm on nights."

Once again, Tom made the journey to Euston, taking the underground to Covent Garden, which left him with only a short walk to his destination. Following a restless night, he arrived at the War Office at fifteen minutes to nine to be warmly greeted by Major Thornton, who informed him that they would be picked up at 9.30 and driven to Northolt, for a flight to Hamburg. This added further to Tom's stress, flying having never appealed to him. Despite this apprehension, once the RAF Dakota took off he relaxed and could glance out of the small windows and on what was a clear day could see ground or water for most of the journey. On arrival, they were taken to a Barracks close to the City, but to reach their destination they drove through the Centre, Tom being shocked by the scale of the destruction. He had seen the bomb damage in London, but bad as that was it paled into insignificance with what he was witnessing. One thing that he found amazing was that the Cathedral remained almost intact, surrounded by piles of rubble. Perhaps there was a god after all.

Despite the damage, he was surprised by the volume of traffic on the streets and was fascinated by the crowded red and cream trams, with three cars running in tandem.

Surprised to find that he was to be accommodated in the Officers Mess along with Major Thornton, Tom didn't feel totally out of place in his Saville Row suit. Thornton informed him that they would be meeting the Prosecuting Officer the following morning to discuss Tom's witness statement that he had provided in advance and to prepare him for giving his evidence and the cross examination by the Defense Lawyer, who was German.

The defendant was Paul Schiller, who had been living and working as a teacher close to Hamburg since the war with his wife and three children, the youngest of whom was just one-year-old. Schiller had been a Hauptsturmfuhrer in the SS, serving in France in 1940 and had been named by an SS Corporal, who had admitted having been involved in the massacre at St.Jean du Becq, saying that Schiller had been his Commanding Officer. This together with Tom's positive identification was key to the case as Schiller, who, although admitting to being in the area at the time was adamant that he had not been involved and was indeed appalled when made aware that atrocities of this nature had been perpetrated by his SS comrades.

The Prosecution was led by Colonel Laurence Hastings from Army Legal Services, who was a Kings Council in civilian life, but had remained in the service after the war specifically to pursue the prosecution of German War Criminals, having participated in the major trials at Nuremburg. Making Tom totally at ease, Hastings took him through his evidence point by point, emphasizing that he should not be deflected or intimidated by the Defense Councils inevitable cross examination, when he would attempt to undermine the evidence, however compelling it was. In preparation, Tom was questioned by Colonel Hastings' Assistant, who played the role of Defense Council asking all of the questions that were likely to arise during the trial. At the end of the process, Hastings explained that the tribunal would comprise of three British Officers, two civilian lawyers and a Judge Advocate who would rule on points of law. The trial was expected to last three days and after giving his evidence Tom would be welcome to observe the remainder of the proceedings.

The court was to convene in the Centre of the City, the Berghof having been specially prepared for war crimes trials. Tom was instructed to wait in an anti-room until called to give evidence, which would not necessarily on the first day as it was expected that the defense would put forward a series of legal arguments challenging the charges. Having had warning, he had brought a book with him in the hope of making the wait bearable, but was unable to concentrate and spent the time with his own thoughts. It was a relief, when early in the afternoon his name was called. Entering the court, he looked at the defendant in the dock, who had put on some weight since he had last seen him. He was in no doubt that this was the man who had overseen the German soldiers that had taken him and his comrade's prisoner in 1940. Despite Tom looking at him, Schiller continued to stare straight ahead.

The members of the court and Judge Advocate sat behind a long desk on a slightly elevated platform, facing the accused, who was flanked by two Military Police NCO's, enclosed on three sides by waist high wood paneling. Tom was shown to the witness box, which was to the right of main platform and faced two tables on the opposite side of the courtroom which were occupied by the two Prosecuting Officers and the German Lawyers wearing long black robes, who represented Shiller. Court administrators sat behind, with seating on the opposite side of the court room being occupied by observers. There were earphones provided for all the participants, with two booths for translators at the rear of the court.

After taking the oath, Colonel Hastings asked him to confirm his name and occupation.

"Mr. Walton, you have confirmed that you currently work as a Coal Miner, could you tell the court exactly what your occupation was during the war?"

"Yes sir, I volunteered for the Royal Warwickshire Regiment early in 1939 and was sent to France with the British Expeditionary Force later that year. I was captured by the Germans on 28th May 1940 and spent the remainder of the conflict as a prisoner of war."

"Thank you for that Mr. Walton, I would now like you to tell the court of how you came to be captured and the events between then and your incarceration in the POW camp."

Initially nervous, Tom grew in confidence as he addressed the Judges, beginning with the surrender and the subsequent march to the barn, including the murder of the wounded prisoners.

Hastings interrupted him asking, "Was there are German Officer present in command of the unit to whom you and your colleagues surrendered?"

"Yes sir."

"Is that Officer present in court today?"

"Yes, he is, it was the defendant."

"Are you certain?"

"I've never been as certain of anything in my life."

"Was the defendant also present during the subsequent march, when several of your comrades were shot?"

"No sir, by that time he had left."

"Thank you, when did you see him again?"

"I didn't actually see him Sir, but I heard him reply to our Officer when he protested at the conditions inside the barn."

"How could you be certain that it was the accused if you didn't actually see him?"

"He had spoken to us early in the day and I was surprised how well he spoke English with the only the slightest accent. I would have recognized his voice at anytime and anywhere."

"Can you recall the exact words used?"

"Yes Sir, I'll never forget them, replied Tom glancing towards Schiller, who appeared to be taking notes, he said, "Don't worry you won't be in there for long and there's plenty of room where you're going."

"What happened then?"

Tom then described the subsequent terror that he and his colleagues had been subjected to and what he termed his lucky escape, being as far as he knew the only survivor. Relating the circumstances of his capture by the Ambulance Unit, which after his previous experience, he had been overwhelmed with relief and gratitude at the kindness that they had shown him. Despite being a prisoner for the remainder of the war, he had never again been subjected to cruelty, but as soon as he was released informed Army Intelligence of the circumstances of his capture in 1940.

Colonel Hastings finally asked Tom to describe events since the war and his visit to France with the war crimes investigators. After which the Court President decided that as it was 3.30 in the afternoon the court would be adjourned, resuming with the Defense Lawyers cross examination the following morning. While Tom was relieved to have completed giving evidence for the prosecution, he was frustrated that he would have to wait until the next day to face what would doubtless be the most traumatic part of his contribution, when Schiller's lawyers would do all that they could to undermine him. Driving back, he told Major Thornton that he would have been prepared to carry on and that he doubted that he would get much sleep.

"You did fine", said Thornton, "and leave it to me to sort the sleep thing out."

After dinner that night Thornton said, "Let's go to the bar for a pint Tom and you can wash these down with it", as he handed him two tablets.

Tom enjoyed his pint, swallowing the tablets as instructed. It was not too much later that he began to feel drowsy. Excusing himself, he was bed as soon as he got back to his room and the next thing he knew was when Thornton's batman woke him with a cup of tea at seven the next morning. Apart from what felt like a slight hangover, Tom felt fine and refreshed for his ordeal, walking confidently into the court room to take his place on the witness stand.

One of the German Lawyers was a tall man of around sixty with grey thinning hair. He was very slim, with hawk like features and had a slight stoop. Wearing half-moon spectacles, he looked over them, smiled at Tom saying, "Thank you for taking the time to come all the way to Germany, Mr. Walton, to hopefully clear this matter up so that my client can get back to his normal life as soon as possible."

Hasting didn't seem at all happy with these remarks and was on his feet almost shouting, "I must object to these remarks, can I suggest that the Defense gets on with the cross examination.

The Judge Advocate looking straight at the Defense Lawyers said, "I think that Colonel Hastings has a point and that it would be helpful to the court if you proceed with your cross-examination Herr Muller."

Ignoring the rebuke, he addressed Tom, "As you heard my name is Muller and on my left, is Herr Steiger and we represent the defendant. First, Mr. Walton I have no doubt whatsoever that you have given a true account of the incidents in question as you remember them, but as you said in your evidence, no German Officer was present on the march from where you and your comrades where captured to the barn close to St. Jean du Becq."

"Yes sir, I agree, that is correct.

"However, you have identified my client as the Officer who commanded the troops that captured you."

"Yes sir"

"How close where you to the Officer in question?"

"About ten yards, was the nearest he got."

"And you are absolutely sure it was Herr Schiller."

"Yes sir, absolutely."

"You have said that the Officer concerned was not present during the march to the barn. When did you next see him?"

"When I walked into the courtroom yesterday."

"So, you are unable to confirm that the Officer that was present when you were captured was also present at the barn."

"I can confirm that he was there because I heard his voice, when he replied to our Captain. He spoke almost perfect English."

"At that time, how many German people had you encountered who spoke English?"

"He was the first."

"And since?"

"Oh, any number from the time I was captured by the Ambulance Unit and in the Prison Camp"

"So, you accept that other German soldiers were able to speak English?"

"Yes sir."

"But you are convinced that the voice that you heard from outside of the barn was that of Herr Schiller?"

"Yes sir, I would recognize his voice anywhere."

Pausing to look at his notes and removing his spectacles, Muller pronounced, "I put it to you Mr. Walton that after eight years there is no way whatsoever that you can be sure that the voice that you heard shouting from outside of the barn was that of Herr Schiller."

Realizing that the Defense would do all that could be done to undermine his evidence, he was not phased and looked towards Schiller before replying "I heard his voice clearly earlier that day and was totally convinced that it was the same voice that I heard from outside of the barn."

Muller persisted, "I put it to you Mr. Walton, you were under unbelievable stress at the time and it therefore it could have affected your judgement at the time and since. I ask again how can you be sure it was my client's voice that you heard from the outside of an enclosed barn?"

"I admit that I was extremely frightened, but I am absolutely certain that it was the same voice that I had heard earlier that day."

"Thank you, Mr. Walton, I have no further questions."

The President said, "Colonel Hastings do you wish to re-examine the witness?"

"Yes sir", replied Hastings, "I have just one further question, Mr. Walton, you said that the first time that you saw the defendant after 28th May 1940 was in court yesterday. Could you confirm, however, that you did identify him from a series of photographs that you were shown by the War Crimes Investigation Unit?"

"Yes sir, that is correct."

"Thank you, I have no further questions for this witness."

The President smiling at Tom said," Thank you Mr. Walton you are discharged but are free to stay and watch the remainder of proceedings if you so wish."

Tom took his place in the seats designated for observers, which were almost full. The occupants were predominantly male, but he did notice one of the few women looked at him intensely as he took his seat and concluded that she must be Schiller's wife and the mother of his three children. Speculating that she was around forty years of age, with short fair permed hair, which was showing the first signs of greyness and wore a neat blue suit with a white blouse. The trial was obviously proving to be an ordeal for her, with Tom feeling more than a tad of sympathy, the likely outcome almost certain to result in her husband being sentenced to death.

The next witness called was Herr Wolfgang Kohl, who it transpired was the SS Corporal who had identified Schiller as the Officer in Charge of his Unit in France. Speaking in German, he told the court that prior to the capture of a large group of British soldiers on 28th May 1940 they had been involved in intense fighting and had sustained many casualties, which hardened attitudes towards enemy prisoners. When the white flags had been raised, he and his colleagues had advanced and collected the arms of around 100 enemy soldiers, who he automatically thought would be taken prisoner and spend the remainder of the war in Germany. Schiller had ordered them to march their prisoners to a barn around three miles away, where they would be confined prior to being transported out of the battle zone. After giving the order Schiller had left the unit to report to Field Headquarters.

At this point, Colonel Hastings asked, "Where you aware of any order given by Schiller regarding the treatment of those prisoners that were wounded?"

Kohl immediately replied, "Nein."

"Are you aware of who took the decision to shoot those wounded prisoners who were unable to keep up with the group?"

"I think it must have been Sergeant Major Dietrich, who was left in charge when the Officer left us."

Hastings again interjected, "I must advise the court that Sergeant Major Dietrich was killed on the Eastern Front in 1943."

Kohl then confirmed what had occurred during the march, with some stragglers being shot and left on the side of the road. When asked how he had felt about this at the time, he replied.

"I was appalled and still have nightmares about it."

Hastings continued, "What happened when you arrived at the barn?"

"Dietrich instructed us to force the prisoners inside, close and secure the door, with two sentries posted outside."

"What happened then?"

"After around an hour, when it was getting dark, I saw Hauptsturmfuhrer Schiller arrive in a jeep. In the meantime, I had heard shouting from inside the barn. I did not know what was being said because I do not understand English"

"Did the accused reply to the shouts from the prisoners?"

"Yes, he shouted back in English, but once again I did not understand what he said"

Asked to describe the subsequent events, Kohl confirmed that the doors were opened and several of his colleagues threw stick grenades inside, with Schiller looking on. The Sergeant Major then instructed that any left alive were to be brought out and shot. He had thought that all the prisoners must have been dead, but a short while later the alarm was raised that some had escaped. Schiller and several others had pursued them and returned saying that they had been killed.

"So, it was a surprise to you, when you heard that there had been a survivor?"

"Yes sir, a pleasant surprise, I wish that there had been more."

"What happened afterwards?"

Kohl then described, how the bodies had been dragged back into the barn, which was set alight.

Hastings concluded by asking, "In your opinion was it the accused that gave the order for the prisoners to be killed?"

"Yes sir, I never heard any such order given but, I thought it must have been him as it all happened soon after he arrived on the scene and that he must have been acting on orders that he had received during his absence."

Herr Muller stood up to begin his cross examination, pausing and looking intensely at Kohl before asking, "Herr Kohl, how long did you serve under Hauptsturmfuhrer Schiller?"

"For around a year, including throughout the campaign in France in the spring of 1940."

"Did you consider him to be a good Officer?"

"I really had no opinion, as far as I was concerned Officers are there to make decisions."

"Was the accused responsible for you being disciplined because of which you were demoted?"

"Yes sir, he wrongly accused me of insubordination and I did lose my stripes."

"You must have been very bitter.?"

"I was at the time, but I've never been one to hold a grudge"

"Herr Kohl are you telling the court that you do nor bear a grudge against an Officer who in your words wrongly accused you of insubordination because of which you lost pay as well as status?"

Kohl looking uncomfortable replied, "Yes sir, I am"

Herr Muller removed his spectacles and began cleaning the lenses with his handkerchief before continuing, "So Herr. Kohl, you are the only survivor of your unit who came forward to say that my client was present at the barn immediately before the prisoners were killed, I put it to you that you did not see Hauptsturmfuhrer Schiller on that day after he left to report back to Field Headquarters?"

Looking annoyed, he responded in a raised voice, "That is not the case, you don't know what you're talking about"

Remaining calm, the Lawyer quietly retorted, "Please confine yourself to answering the questions Herr Kohl and don't be impertinent"

Seeming to ignore the rebuke, Kohl continued to answer in a combative manner, being persistently harassed by his interrogator, who emphasized that the witness had cause to hold a grudge against Schiller. Attempting to press home his advantage, he concluded by suggesting that his client had not been present when the massacre took place. Kohl, however, was adamant that he had.

Following the cross examination, the prosecution rested its case and the court adjourned. On the journey, back to the Mess, Major Thornton told Tom that the Defense would probably only take one day and that the trial would likely conclude in two days' time, which cheered Tom up, feeling that he had been away from Barbara and the children for long enough.

Chapter 24

Arriving in court early the following morning, Tom was one of the first to take his seat. He was surprised when a couple of minutes later Frau Schiller arrived, smiled at him and in near perfect English said, "Good morning Mr. Walton." Replying with a curt "Good Morning", he did not return the smile.

Soon afterwards, the Prosecution, Defence and Members of the Tribunal took their places closely followed by Schiller, who as always was flanked by two Military Policeman.

Herr Muller stood, saying, "The Defence calls Paul Schiller"

Walking confidently to the witness box, Schiller took the oath in German. Kohl informed the court that his client intended to give his evidence in English to enable members to conclude how "perfect" his command of the language was.

It was established that he was a 40-year-old schoolmaster, living in a suburb of Hamburg. He had returned to the profession in 1946 after his war service which had concluded with a short period of captivity after he had been captured by the British early in 1945. A member of the Nazi Party since 1935, he had enlisted in the SS in 1937 and had progressed to Hauptsturmfuhrer by early 1940, joining the invasion force in France after service in Poland.

Muller guided him through his evidence, Schiller answering questions confidently and concisely. Admitting that he had been in the vicinity of St.Jean du Becq on 28th May 1940. Recalling the fierce resistance of the British troops, prior to their capture, he told the court that his Unit had sustained heavy casualties, which had hardened their attitude towards the enemy. He had ordered that they be marched to a collecting point on the instructions of his Field Headquarters. Afterwards he had returned to the Headquarters to receive further instructions at which time he was assigned to another unit who were pursuing members of the BEF towards Dunkirk. Having heard what happened to the British soldiers at St.Jean du Becq, he was appalled, believing that those responsible would be held to account. Serving in France for the remainder of the war prior to his capture, he had been re-employed in the school that he left in 1937 following his release by the British authorities.

Muller asked him if he had been surprised when he was arrested and charged with the murder of the British Soldiers. Schiller answered without hesitation, "I was not surprised, I was shocked, because I knew that I had done nothing wrong."

"There have only been two witnesses that gave evidence against you, can we deal with Cpl Kohl's testimony first. Can you remember him serving under you in France?"

"Yes sir, it's always easy to remember the "bad apples". Cpl Kohl had a long history of insubordination the result of which caused me to have him demoted. He was moody and resentful of authority and was lucky that he did not receive more severe punishment. When I heard that it was him that had denounced me, it was no surprise. I think he saw it as an opportunity to take his revenge."

"Thank you for that Herr Schiller, now could we deal with Mr. Walton's evidence. You have admitted that you were in command of the Unit that captured him and his colleagues. After they surrendered, were you present at the time of any of the deaths of those soldiers that were in captivity and therefore prisoners of war under the protection of the Geneva Convention."

"No sir, I was not. After the capture of such so many enemy soldiers, I went back to our Field Headquarters to ascertain how they should be dealt with, knowing that they should be removed from the battle zone as soon and as safely as possible. When I arrived at Field H.Q., I was told that the prisoners were being dealt with and that I had been reassigned to another forward Unit, all their officers having been killed. I left within an hour of arriving."

"So, you categorically deny re-joining your original unit at St. Jean du Becq?"

"Yes sir"

"Mr. Walton testified that he heard your voice from outside the barn, just prior to the massacre, having previously heard you speak at the time of his capture. What do you say to that?"

"All I can say is that he was mistaken, I have every sympathy for Mr. Walton, no human being should be treated like he and his comrades were even in wartime, but he must have been under considerable stress at the time."

At this Hastings was on his feet objecting that Schiller was in no position to Judge Tom's state of mind at the time and should stick to his evidence.

The Judge Advocate sustained the Objection and advised the accused accordingly. To which he replied, "My apologies."

At that Herr Muller said, "Thank you Herr Schiller, stay where you are please."

Hastings was on his feet in an instant and barked, "Herr Schiller you have admitted that you joined the Nazi Party voluntarily, did you also volunteer for the SS?"

"Yes sir", replied Schiller, "in 1937."

"Why particularly the SS?"

"Because they were elite troops and I wanted to be with the best."

"Do you admit that throughout the war, the SS had a ruthless reputation and were not inclined to take prisoners?"

"Some factions were, but I would not deem myself to be like that, I was responsible for capturing many enemy troops in the war and I treated them all correctly."

"Apart from Mr Walton and his comrades."

"I've already told the court what happened then. I heard afterwards what had happened to those prisoners and was appalled, but I was nowhere near that barn when the murders occurred."

"So, you are saying that Mr. Walton is lying?"

"No, that is not the case, I admit to being the Officer in Charge of the Unit that captured him and his colleagues and that he could identify me as such. However, he was mistaken when he testified that it was me that shouted in English from outside the barn prior to the massacre."

Appearing exasperated Hasting continued, "How many soldiers in your Unit spoke what Mr. Walton described as near perfect English?"

"Very few, but Sgt Major Dietrich was one of them. His English was just as good as mine."

"Very convenient for you that he's not here to defend himself. I put it to you that Mr. Walton was not mistaken and that you returned to your Unit and gave the order to kill the prisoners."

"That was not the case."

"If it wasn't you, then who was responsible?"

"I wish I knew, sir."

"So do I Herr Schiller, so do I, No further questions."

Believing that Schiller had stood up well to Hastings' cross examination, it occurred to Tom that he might get away with it and that opinion strengthened when the Principal of the school in which Schiller taught was called to give evidence. Herr Rongen stated that he had held Schiller in high regard both before and since the war. Respected by his colleagues and parents, he enjoyed good relations with pupils and was an outstanding teacher. He stated that his finest qualities were his quiet, gentle nature and his willingness to assist those with problems. Concluding, "That is it was both inconceivable and incomprehensible that he could have been involved in such an atrocity."

At the close of the case for the Defence, the President Invited Colonel Hastings to make his closing statement for the prosecution, who emphasised that it was no coincidence that both main prosecution witnesses had confirmed that Shiller was present at the barn at the time of the massacre and must have given the order for it to be carried out. Admitting that Tom had only recognised his voice, being unable to see him from inside the barn, but having heard him speak earlier that day his evidence was reliable. It was also unlikely that any other soldier in the SS Unit spoke such perfect English.

Acknowledging that Cpl. Kohl may have borne a grudge against an Officer responsible for his demotion, to respond in a way that would almost certainly result in the death of that individual was inconceivable.

Finally reminding the court that over eighty British soldiers were unnecessarily killed that day and the importance that the perpetrator be held to account for his actions.

Herr Muller then spoke passionately on behalf of his client, who he described as "a kind and caring husband and father of three children." He then began to challenge the main evidence against Shiller stating that he considered Cpl. Kohl to be "a bitter man who was intent on revenge against a conscientious and fair Officer who had been forced to discipline him." Asking the court to consider why no other members of the Unit had been willing to denounce Shiller all of whom having said that he had not been there, condemning Kohl as an unreliable witness whose evidence should be viewed with utmost suspicion.

Turning to Tom and looking straight at him Muller said, "Regarding Mr. Walton, both Herr Schiller and I consider him to be an honourable man who was subjected to unspeakable horrors on that day in 1940. We are both convinced that he has told the truth throughout this trial. However, we are also convinced that he was mistaken when he concluded that the voice that he heard shout from outside the barn was that of my client. It would in the opinion of the Defence be very dangerous to convict anyone charged with a capital offence on evidence of this type." He concluded that Herr Schiller was admired and respected as a teacher and by the community and considered incapable of the crimes with which he was charged. Looking directly at the members of the tribunal he said, "I believe it to be your duty to acquit Herr Schiller of all charges and allow him to return to his family and pupils from whom he has been separated for far too long."

The President Thanked Herr Muller and adjourned the court, stating that the Judge Advocate would sum up the following morning after which members would consider the verdict.

The Judge Advocate's summing up took just over an hour, during which time he reviewed both the prosecution and defence cases. The only real guidance he gave to the court, that given the diametrically opposing views, all they could do was convict or otherwise on whose evidence they considered most reliable. He did, however, state that Kohl's testimony should be treated with caution, given the bad feeling he had shown towards the accused.

Late in the morning of the fourth day of the trial, members of the tribunal retired to consider their verdict and Tom hoped that whatever was decided it would conclude that day. Waiting in a room outside the court, he was so stressed that he was unable to eat the sandwich lunch that he was offered, although he did manage to drink some water. He was relieved when his wish was granted at 3.30 in the afternoon, being informed that a verdict had been reached.

All parties re-entered the tense court room, to be joined by the members of the tribunal. Tom tried to assess their mood to guess what their deliberations had concluded, but they gave little away by their demeanour. The President ordered that Schiller be brought in and as always was flanked by the two Military Policemen. He looked towards his wife, who despite her obvious distress, smiled reassuringly. When everyone was settled, the President said, "The Judge Advocate will now read the verdict, will the prisoner please stand."

Almost immediately the Judge Advocate looking straight at Schiller stated, "This Military Tribunal finds the accused Guilty of all charges. The court understands that in the event of a Guilty verdict, Defence Council wishes to address the court prior to sentencing. Therefore, we will adjourn until 10 o'clock tomorrow morning to give Herr Muller the time to prepare his statement."

As the verdict was announced Frau Schiller began to sob uncontrollably, slumping forward with her head in her hands. This affected Tom deeply, knowing that the guilty verdict made it almost certain that Schiller would be sentenced to death and the consequences that would bring on his wife and children.

Hearing the guilty verdict, Tom felt that he had done his duty to his murdered comrades, but was surprised to find that he felt desperately sorry for Frau Schiller. Remaining in his seat for several minutes deep in thought, Hastings came across to him and shook his hand saying, "Well done Walton, you've been a great help in ensuring that Schiller didn't get away with it and he'll now get his just deserts."

Tom replied, "Thank you for your efforts, sir. It's just that I feel sorry for my mates and the guilty verdict has at least brought some kind of closure for their families, but I'll have to live with it for the rest of my life."

Sitting in the Courtroom deep in thought for several minutes afterwards, Tom realised that that only two other people remained, Herr Muller and his Assistant, who were deep in conversation. Approaching Muller, he said, "Excuse me sir, I know this may be inappropriate, but I have been thinking. Although I believe the guilty verdict to be correct, I do not bear Herr Schiller any malice and my sympathies are with his wife and children. I don't think that anything except revenge will be achieved by hanging him. That will leave his wife a widow and his children without their father and the war resulted in the deaths of more than enough husbands and fathers without adding to them. I also believe capital punishment to be morally wrong and I would be happy if you could make the court aware of my thoughts in your plea of mitigation."

After initially looking shocked, Herr Muller shook Tom's hand and thanked him.

Chapter 25

Thornton invited Tom to have dinner with him that evening, after which they went to the crowded Mess Bar. They were both quiet during the meal, but when they got to the bar, Thornton smiled at Tom, "Well done Walton, what a result, hopefully they'll finish the job and sentence him to hang." Tom made no mention of his conversation with Muller, thinking that Thornton would likely be upset and wanted to avoid a public altercation with him.

When the court reconvened the following morning, the first thing that Tom noticed was how Frau Schiller had seemed to have aged twenty years overnight, appearing to be drawn and pale, with the dark bags under her eyes suggesting that she had not slept.

Schiller was brought in accompanied by his usual escorts and like his wife looked like he had found sleeping difficult, but Tom could find little sympathy for him.

Herr Muller addressed the court on behalf of his client with his usual eloquence, stating that despite the guilty verdict his client still denied being at the scene at the time of the massacre and had indeed been appalled when he had heard about it. He had gone through the rest of the war, obeying orders as he had to but longing to return to his family and pupils in Hamburg. Since the war, he had become a pillar of the community and was much loved by those who he taught. He was a family man and he begged the courts mercy, not for him but his wife and three children. He then continued, "But the main strand of my plea is the opinion of Mr. Walton, who approached me after yesterday's verdict. He has been affected by this case more than anyone alive has and it says much for his character, that despite believing the guilty verdict to be correct, he bears my client no malice and thinks his life should be spared. He is against capital punishment and expressed the belief to me that little would be achieved by revenge when our two nations should be seeking reconciliation. I have to say that I believe Mr. Walton to be a very special human being and I ask the court to take notice of his humanity when considering the sentence."

The President Thanked Herr Muller and asked if Mr. Walton was still in court and if so could he stand. Tom stood looking straight at the President who asked, "Is what Herr Muller told the court correct?"

"Yes sir, it is."

"Thank you, you may sit, members of the court will now retire to consider the sentence to be imposed."

After what seemed an interminable amount of time, which in fact was just over an hour, everyone was called back into court. The President asked Schiller to stand and he seemed to do so with difficulty, visibly shaking.

Looking the defendant in the eye, the President began, "Paul Arno Schiller, you have been found guilty of the murder of over eighty British soldiers on 28th May 1940, in deciding the sentence to be imposed the court has considered the overwhelming evidence against you and your continued refusal to admit responsibility for the deaths of the unfortunate soldiers captured by your Unit. We have considered the plea on your behalf by your Counsel and Mr. Walton. Notwithstanding this, the court considers your crimes to be of such gravity, that the only appropriate sentence is Death by Hanging."

Schiller showed no emotion, but his wife was in a state of collapse screaming, "Nein" several times interspersed with body shuddering sobs, having to be helped from the court. Tom was shaken by this reaction and was disappointed that the court had not shown the mercy that he considered appropriate.

Thornton was waiting for him outside the court and with a face like thunder said, "What the fuck were you doing in there Walton, if ever anybody deserves to be hanged, it's that bastard and that's what we've been working towards for the past two years"

"I'm sorry Major, but I had to make my views known. I'm opposed to Capital Punishment and think it achieves nothing. I agree that Schiller is a monster and most people think he deserves to die, but I'm not most people and I want nobody's death on my conscience."

"Well thank God they did the right thing; I wouldn't want any of my money spent keeping him for the next thirty years."

There was no invitation to the Mess Bar that night and the following morning on the way to the airport little was said.

Just two hours after leaving Hamburg they were back at Northolt, where transport was waiting to take them into Central London. On arrival at Euston, Thornton shook Tom's hand, saying, "Look after yourself Walton, just try to put this behind you and have a wonderful life with your wife and family."

Knowing that would be easier said than done, but despite those misgivings, he was looking forward to seeing Barbara and the children, so it wasn't all bad. Finding a telephone box at the station, he rang Randell's shop to ask if Maud could tell his wife that he would be home in a few hours and then got on the next train north that stopped at Nuneaton. He had a short wait, for the local train that took him to his home village, a few stops down the line.

Walking the short distance down Station Road, he was soon through his front door. Hearing it open, Barbara rushed into the hall to greet him, throwing her arms around his neck and saying,

"I've missed you so much." Overcome with emotion, Tom sobbed in his wife's arms, I'm sorry love, but it was an ordeal that I could have done without. They found him guilty and sentenced him to death, but I got no satisfaction from it. I feel really sorry for his wife and children and spoke to his lawyer and told him that I didn't want a death sentence, he used it in his plea for mitigation, but they took no notice."

"Oh Tom, I'm sorry, but you've done your best me lad, going all that way to give evidence and I'm not surprised that you spoke up for him. You're back with us now and we'll look after you, won't we Petra?"

With the emotion of his homecoming, he hadn't noticed his six-year-old daughter clinging to his leg. He picked her up hugging her as she said,

"We've missed you Daddy, don't go away again"

"I've missed you too sweetheart and I won't be going anywhere without you, mummy and Jack."

Settling down to family life after Barbara gave him a homecoming that he wouldn't forget. Their lovemaking had always been enjoyable but Tom thought it to be conventional. But that night Barbara was passionate and demanding, so they got little sleep. After going to see his Mother and Maud over the weekend, he was back at the pit the following Monday throwing himself into his work, trying to put all thoughts of Hamburg behind him.

Chapter 26

The miner's annual holidays were as usual the last week in July and the first in August, the few that could afford it trooping off to Blackpool for a week, but Tom and Barbara decided to take up the invitation to visit Trevor and Grace. It was a real adventure for Petra and she seemed fascinated throughout the journey constantly staring out of the train window, giving a running commentary to her parents. As they got close to their destination, Barbara became unusually quiet and subdued, which Tom found understandable as this was her first visit to London since the war, with all the memories that it must have rekindled.

Trevor met them at the station in his car, making Tom very grateful that he was spared carrying the luggage to the house, which was over a mile away. Grace was beaming when she opened the door and immediately hugged Petra, who looked somewhat bemused by the lady who she clearly couldn't remember.

Grace greeted Tom warmly, immediately putting him at ease. They were shown to their rooms, a large double bedroom with a cot for Jack, with Petra having a brightly painted single room. Grace saying, "We hope that you like this room Petra, we've decorated it especially for you."

Petra smiled while saying thank you, seemingly enjoying all the attention she was getting.

Tom appreciated the warm welcome for his family, but was a little uneasy being surrounded by the numerous photographs of Peter, taken throughout his short life, ranging from the small boy in short trousers to the handsome blue-eyed young man standing in front of a bomber in his flying suit. Also, noticing that Barbara was unable to resist looking at them, although she swiftly looked away if she thought he had noticed.

When they went to bed that night, Barbara said to him, "Are you comfortable being here Tom, I know that I've been a bit distant since we arrived, but it's a strange feeling coming back. But never mind that let's enjoy our week and never think you're second best, because I love you more than you know."

Kissing her passionately, replying, "You're my whole life Barbara and don't imagine I'm jealous of Peter. If you hadn't have met him, we wouldn't have Petra."

That set the tone for what turned out to be an enjoyable week for them all; Grace couldn't get enough of the children, which allowed Tom and Barbara more freedom than they had ever experienced. Even being able to enjoy a day on their own in Central London, where Tom could pursue his interest in history, with a couple of hours in the British Museum and after lunch in a Lyons Corner House, went to the cinema in Leicester Square to see the new MGM musical "Easter Parade" starring Fred Astaire and Judy Garland, which they found enthralling. As they left the luxurious Empire Theatre, Tom reminded his wife," Fred was in the first picture we saw together, He's aged a bit but can still dance"

"Yes, it was brilliant, I'm glad we've seen it, it'll probably be next year before it gets to The Palace."

At the end of the week Trevor took them to the station saying to Tom, "It's been wonderful having you all here, you're all the family we have now and we really want to see our granddaughter grow up. Come again anytime you wish."

"Thank you we really enjoyed ourselves, if you and Grace want to see Petra more often you can always come and see us, we've got room."

CHAPTER 27

Refreshed by their holiday, Tom and Barbara were looking forward to getting home. Opening the front door, they found several envelopes lying on the doormat, but one immediately attracted his attention. Having never received a letter through the post with anything other than the King's head on the stamp, this one was totally different, red with a picture of a large church and the letters Deutche Post at the top and bottom. Calling his wife, prior to opening it Tom said, "I wonder what on earth this is?"

Taking it from him she replied, "Well, we'd best open it and find out."

The contents were neatly handwritten, realising who it was from he read it to Barbara.

Dear Mr. Walton,

Last week I saw my husband for the last time when I visited him in prison the day before he was hanged. Given the circumstances he was in good spirits and I am sure had made his peace with God.

He asked me to write to you and thank you for speaking up on his behalf after the verdict, even though it was your evidence that undoubtedly made a key contribution towards his conviction. I must tell you that Paul maintained his innocence to the last and swore to me that he had played no part in the massacre of your comrades, anyone who knew him would have believed him incapable of such a crime. I am convinced that he was innocent as throughout our years of marriage we have always been open and honest with each other.

He believed you to be a good man, but was adamant that you were mistaken in concluding that it was his voice that you heard on that terrible day.

My children and I are devastated at his loss as are the pupils in his school where he was much loved and respected. I must bring up my family without their father, but consider that I am in some ways blessed having had him for an extra two years after that terrible war, which resulted in so many women being widowed on both sides.

Like my husband, I bear you no malice and hope that you and your family have a happy life together. God Bless You.

Yours Sincerely,
Eva Schiller

Tom was shaking, asking, "What do you make of that? All I can think is what if I was mistaken, but I am so sure that it was his voice I heard."

"Well, you've nothing to reproach yourself for and as she says he was grateful that you spoke up for him even though you were convinced of his guilt. A lot of people did things that were totally out of character in the war and he was probably one of them"

Tom didn't sleep that night, being unable to get Frau Schiller's letter out of his mind. "What if he were Innocent?"

Having no intention to reply to the letter, of which only he and Barbara were aware, believing any correspondence would only prolong his anguish. It was not easy to get Schiller out of his thoughts, despite his contentment at work and home. To add to this, he had a nightmare in which he was locked in the barn with all his colleagues, clambering over their dead bodies trying to escape through the door that was always locked. When it was eventually opened, Schiller stood there with a pistol in his hand, but he stepped out of the way to let Tom escape saying,

"This is to prove I am not a murderer." Waking up shaking and sweating, with Barbara at his side trying to soothe him saying, "It's alright Tom, you're only having a bad dream. You're safe here."

Gradually over the next few months, he got back to something close too normal, despite Frau Schiller's letter being uppermost in his thoughts. The situation was helped when a short time later, Barbara told him that she was pregnant again. She joked, "Right me lad, three's enough for any woman, so you're going to have to find something else to keep you occupied."

He laughed and said, "Well I'll have to get myself a fancy woman then, mind I don't think that I could do it with anybody else but you."

"It looks like you'll have to take up stamp collecting then."

George was born the following summer and their family was complete. Barbara and Tom were blissfully happy and contented with their lot. When his wife asked him what he wanted for Christmas. Tom replied, "I don't want anything because I've got everything."

Almost a year after his fateful trip to Hamburg, another official looking envelope fell onto the doormat, Tom opened the envelope with trepidation.

Dear Mr. Walton,

On behalf of the M.O.D. and Commonwealth War Graves Commission, I am pleased to invite you and a guest to attend the unveiling of the memorial to those who lost their lives at St.jean du Becq, France on 28th May 1940.

The ceremony will be held at 11am on 28th May 1950, the tenth anniversary of the massacre. The memorial will be unveiled by HRH Prince Phillip, Duke of Edinburgh.

Wreaths of poppies will then be laid by those representing various organisations and as the sole survivor of those terrible events, we would ask that you lay a wreath on behalf of The Royal Warwicks, your own Regiment in which many of the deceased served with honour.

If you can join us, we will arrange for railway warrants and ferry tickets from Dover to Calais and return. Hotel accommodation, inclusive of meals will be arranged for the nights of 27th and 28th near Calais.

I am sure that you will wish to honour your fallen comrades and look forward to your acceptance. Please confirm your attendance by letter to the above address.

Yours Sincerely,
Emmanuel Shinwell

Secretary of State for Defence

"What do you think of that?" asked Barbara," It's a real honour for you."

"I know, I just don't want to go back there though, although I will because I owe it to my mates, but I want you to come with me."

"What about the kids?"

"Can't you ask your Mum to look after them, it's only for a couple of days?"

"I'll go around and ask tomorrow, perhaps Jean will help. Three might be a bit of a handful for Mum."

"OK, I'll wait to you've been before I reply."

When he got back from the pit the following day, Barbara confirmed that her mother would look after her grandchildren and Tom wrote the letter confirming that they would be honoured to attend. It was a couple of months until the event, giving Barbara the time to obtain a passport, something she never thought that she would need.

In the meantime, the local "Herald" found out and a reporter called wanting to do an article and take a photograph of Tom. Initially refusing, after speaking to Barbara he agreed, but refused to go into detail about what had happened to him. Seemingly happy with that, the young reporter came to the house to interview him and when the article appeared it was tastefully done, although he thought the headline, "LOCAL HERO TO HONOUR HIS FALLEN COMRADES", was a bit excessive. He was not surprised when one young "wag", called across the pit canteen. "I never thought I'd be working with anybody famous." Not reacting, his look must have made it clear how he felt about the remark.

It did provoke a positive response from his family, when his mother told him that she and Maud were proud, as was his Dad, who wanted to make it up with him, having admitted to her that he had been cruel to Barbara.

Telling his wife what his Mother had said, she reacted immediately by saying, "Well about time, but let's strike while the irons hot and ask them round to tea on Sunday and to make it easier for him, I'll ask my Mum and Dad as well."

Tom went to his parents' house the following day to issue the invitation, which was gratefully accepted although his Dad did say, "Are you sure she wants me in the house after everything that's gone on?"

Tom replied, "She wouldn't have asked you if she had any hard feelings, so let's put it behind us so that you can enjoy your grandchildren at long last."

Sunday came quickly enough and Tom could see that despite being the instigator of the invitation, Barbara was nervous. She had baked for much the previous day, making a sponge cake and scones, so by the time it got to 4.00pm the table was laden with sandwiches and the results of Barbara's labours. They were all dressed in their best, Tom in his Saville Row suit and Barbara in a straight skirt and floral blouse, both of which she had made herself. Seven-year-old Petra also wore one of her mother's creations, a pink summery dress, which complemented her blue eyes and blonde hair. While three-year-old Jack, looked the most resplendent of them all in a new "sailor suit", another product of Barbara's sewing machine. George was only six months old and sound asleep in his utility pram, when the guests arrived.

Tom answered the door, finding his father looking uncomfortable clutching a bunch of flowers. Trying to break the ice, Tom attempted to take them from him saying, "Oh thanks Dad, they're really nice."

"Get off, daft bugger, these are for my daughter in law, fresh from the garden."

"Well, you'd better come in and give them to her then."

Barbara and the children were waiting in the Living Room smiling, "Thank you for coming, Mr Walton, this is Petra and Jack. Say Hello to our guests, Petra."

Brimming with unexpected confidence Petra said, Hello Grandma Clara, is this man my Grandad?"

Before she could answer Henry laughed and said, "Yes, I am me duck and it's very nice to meet you. I've brought these flowers for your Mother and perhaps you'd like to give them to her for me."

Taking them, Petra turned to her Mother, who smiled nervously at her father in law before saying, "Thank you they're lovely."

Barbara's parents arrived soon afterwards and were invited to sit at the fully laden table, on which Henry commented, "By God Barbara, you've put on a good spread." Given what seemed to them all a considerable amount of food, it disappeared quickly, with the visitors seeming well satisfied. The three men went into the Front Room to smoke, leaving the women to clear the table and wash up. Barbara did say that she and Tom would do it later, but the two grandmas were insistent. When they were finished, they sat around the table with cups of tea, after Barbara had taken three cups into the Front Room for the men, who were engrossed in conversation about their common interest, the pit.

Towards the end of their exchanges, Henry asked, "When are you off to France then, Tom?"

"At the end of May, the ceremony is on the 28th, my thirty sixth birthday"

"Are you looking forward to it, lad?"

"Not really, what happened there still haunts me and I think always will"

"But they hung the bugger that was responsible didn't they"

"Yes, although he was insistent to the last that he wasn't there and that's another thing that worries me."

"Well, it shouldn't, you gave your evidence and the court believed you. They wouldn't have found him guilty if they hadn't been sure."

"The poor bugger left a wife and three kids, like all of my mates, they're victims too."

Trying to lighten the exchanges, Jack interjected, "Well our Barbara's looking forward to it, she's quite excited about going abroad."

Tom said, "I know and I'm really pleased that she's coming, it'll be easier with her there."

Henry closed the conversation with, "Yes, you've got a good one lad, pity it took me such a long time to see it. Anyroad it's about time we were going."

At that he was on his feet and through to the Dining Room, saying, "Come on Clara, we don't want to overstay our welcome. Thanks for a lovely tea Barbara, you'll have to come to us next time. And as for you, young lady, get your Dad to bring you round to see the pigs"

Thanking her parents in law for coming, she was rewarded with a kiss on the cheek from her mother in law and a hand shake from Henry."

Alone and the children in bed later that evening, Barbara said, "I think your Dad was really taken by Petra"

Tom laughed, "You're right, who wouldn't be? He realised what he's been missing."

Chapter 28

Writing to Trevor and Grace to tell them of their forthcoming trip, she had received a reply within days, in which he offered to make her a suit to wear at the ceremony, asking for list of measurements. Barbara asked Maud to help, thinking that it might embarrass Tom and sent back the information within a couple of days. Two weeks later, the parcel arrived containing a two-piece Navy blue suit, which fitted perfectly and was ideal for the occasion.

Travelling to London on the 26th May, after spending the night in the Bedford Hotel they caught the Boat Train from Victoria to Dover for the short crossing to Calais. It was an ideal day and they spent most of the time on the deck. As Barbara looked back on the White Cliffs, she had a lump in her throat thinking of what returning aircrew must have experienced during the war, believing that they had survived another mission. Then she thought of Peter and became increasingly upset, causing Tom to ask, "What's the matter, love?"

Thinking that if she answered truthfully, he may not understand, so she replied, "I'm alright, I just got emotional at the sight of the cliffs."

Tom put his arm around her and she settled, but thought that she would have to arrange to visit her lover's grave, even at the risk of upsetting her husband.

Arriving in France, there was transport to take them to the same Hotel that Tom had stayed in on previous visit, spending a comfortable night although the events of the following day were never far away from his thoughts. After an early Continental Breakfast, they were picked up and taken to the field near St. Jean du Becq, which held such terrible memories. The Barn had been rebuilt and outside the entrance was what was obviously the Memorial Stone, draped in a black cloth. A raised Dias faced the barn, either side of which chairs had been placed.

Tom and Barbara were shown to their front row seats, the remainder of which being soon mainly occupied by Military Officers. Several French Dignitaries were also present as where many civilians, which Tom was told were relatives of those who had lost their lives.

At approximately 10.45, soldiers from all the regiments concerned formed a Guard of Honour either side of the memorial on what was fortunately a warm and sunny day, very like ten years before. Ten minutes later two Official Cars arrived, from the first of which stepped Prince Phillip, looking resplendent in Naval uniform. The second vehicle had a plate with five stars on the front out of which stepped a General and his Aide de Campe.

Taking his place on the Dias, the Guard of Honour presented arms in royal salute. The Prince then addressed those present, "Ladies and Gentleman we are here today to honour those brave Officers and Men who lost their lives at this place in the service of their country. Many people were killed in the conflict, but these deaths that were the result of a criminal act should not have happened. There was only a single survivor of the massacre, Private Thomas Walton of the Royal Warwickshire Regiment, who enlisted voluntarily in 1938 and somehow managed to escape from the carnage, only to spend the remainder of the war a Prisoner. I am pleased to say that he is here today and will be laying a wreath in memory of his comrades. To the many relatives of the deceased with us, I hope that you do not think your loved ones gave their lives in vain, like all servicemen and women they made a vital contribution towards the final victory.

It is now my honourable duty to unveil this memorial to these brave men, may they rest in peace."

He then moved forward and pulled a cord, which allowed the monument to be uncovered. It was a tall marble stone and although Tom was too far away to read the inscription, it was obvious that the names of his comrades were listed. Following the unveiling the Prince stepped back and saluted and was then handed a wreath which he placed at the foot of the memorial, prior to giving a final salute and resuming his position on the Dias, the spectators breaking into spontaneous applause. Several wreaths were laid by Senior Officers from the Regiments concerned, by a single wreath by a French dignitary, with a Red, White and Blue Sash and chain of office. Finally, invited to step forward, Tom placed his tribute in the position in which he had been instructed, prior to stepping back and bowing his head. He was surprised that as he turned to return to his place there was applause.

After the Guard of Honour marched off Tom and Barbara were invited into the marquee, where they were presented to Prince Phillip, who Barbara was taken with. After she curtsied, which she had practiced several times, he said, "you must be proud of your husband Mrs Walton, I understand that you were in the services yourself."

Yes, sir, she replied I was in the WAAF's for a short time."

Prior to that he had shaken Tom by the hand saying, "I'm delighted to meet you Walton, I've heard a lot about you and that you travelled to Germany to assist in the war crimes trial."

"Yes sir, I was pleased to help, although it was quite difficult going over all that happened."

"I understand that you've gone back to coal mining since the war, you must enjoy it."

"Not much sir, but it's all I know and I do enjoy the comradeship and there's no better community to live in."

Barbara thought the Prince unlikely to agree with those sentiments.

Travelling back the following day, they arrived late in the evening, going straight to bed as Tom was due back at the pit at six o'clock the following morning.

CHAPTER 29

When he arrived home the following day, Barbara told him that when she took George to be weighed at the Welfare, she had been treated like a celebrity, having met Prince Phillip, with all the other "young mums" wanting to know what he was like.

"And what did you tell them?"

"Oh, I said how nice he was and that he was really good looking, but nowhere near as handsome as you."

Tom laughed, "There must be something seriously wrong with your eyes."

After tea, they sat at the table and it was clear to Tom that his wife was nervous about something so he asked, "What's the matter then, you'd better get it off your chest?"

"Well, I don't want you to get upset, but I would really like to visit Peter's grave. I've not been since his funeral and I think that I owe it to him to go and I also think that Petra should be taken as well."

"You can go if you want to, but I don't think that Petra should. It would serve no purpose."

"Well he is her father."

Feeling though he had a knife in his stomach he retorted, "No he's bloody well not, I'm her father and it would only confuse her. When she's older she can be told, and make her own mind up, but now I'm not having it. I'm off down the "Oak" for a pint."

Shocked at his reaction, crying after he had left, she was still determined to visit the grave, whether he liked it or not.

In the meantime, Tom trudged down to the pub, which was quiet so early on a midweek evening, bought his pint and sat at a corner table alone with his thoughts. Despite his love for Barbara and his happiness with her, he had always had pangs of jealousy of her wartime lover, knowing it irrational but always difficult to dispel. His wife seldom mentioned Peter, but this had brought Tom's envy to a new level and he realised that he had to calm down before he returned home, having a second pint to collect his thoughts.

When he arrived, she was sat knitting by the open fire, that was only lit in the evenings at this time of year. Neither of them said a word for the rest of the evening and when they went to bed for the first time in their marriage turned their backs on each other. He was up and off to work the following morning before Barbara woke feeling utterly miserable. Not knowing what to do, she went to tell her mother what had happened and was surprised when she came down firmly on Tom's side, saying, "That part of your life is long gone and you're damn lucky that Tom took you on after what happened. You should be ashamed of yourself reminding him that he's not Petra's father, because he is and she couldn't have a better one."

Back at home, waiting apprehensively for her husband to get back from the pit, when he arrived she threw her arms around his neck, bursting in to tears, saying," I'm sorry that I upset you, it was a bad idea and I think it best if we forget about it."

She was surprised by his answer, "I don't think it was a bad idea at all, you can go and I'll come with you but Petra isn't. So, we'll go in the pit holidays in August."

"Thank you, are you sure that you don't mind?"

"I do mind, but I love you and if you feel you should go so be it."

Nothing more was said, until in the middle of July, Tom telling her, I've booked us a room in The Bedford for the night of 3rd August, we'll go down to London that day and then get the train to Brookwood first thing the next morning and come straight back afterwards. "You'll have to get your mother to look after the kids."

August soon arrived, again travelling to Euston and after the night in the hotel went to Waterloo for the short journey to the Surrey countryside. Tom was amazed at the sheer magnitude of the cemetery, which was adjacent to the station. There were literally thousands of graves situated in park land, with a diverse variety of trees, many of which were unfamiliar to him. Even the section dedicated to the RAF was enormous with row upon row of white rectangular stones, marking graves that were all immaculately maintained. Having made enquiries prior to their visit, they easily located the place were Peter lay and Tom stepped back to allow Barbara to be alone at the graveside.

As she stood in front of the stone, she sank to her knees, sobbing uncontrollably, which Tom found disturbing, adding to his insecurity. Leaving her there for a few seconds, he lifted her to her feet putting his arm around her shoulders, she could barely say anything but did manage, "I'm sorry Tom, but it's just the pent-up emotion after all this time, just take me home will you."

Walking away arm in arm, she gradually stopped crying saying, "It was not just seeing Peter's grave that got to me, but all of the young boys lying here. I saw a lot from Binbrook fail to come back, who were so full of life with their whole future in front of them. What a waste."

After they got onto the train she smiled and said, "Thank you for bringing me, we won't come again." The journey back to the Midlands was uneventful, arriving in time to put their children to bed. Sitting together by the fire listening to the radio, Tom contemplated how lucky he was to have his wife, when it could have been so different.

Barbara didn't mention their visit to Brookwood, but despite this Tom could not forget the sight of her so distraught with grief over her lover who had been dead for almost ten years. Much to his discomfort, he began to feel that he had missed out by being so slavishly in love with one woman, thinking that she had looked elsewhere at the first opportunity. Despite knowing that it was irrational to be jealous of a dead man, as time went on it just got worse, because of which he became irritable with Barbara and could not make love to her without being plagued by thoughts of her and Peter together. Trying to put it out of his mind he began to seek extra shifts at the pit spending more time in the "Oak" and less with his wife and family.

Noticing the change in him, she was loath to mention anything, believing it to be just a passing phase. He had always returned from work in a happy frame of mind, kissing her as soon as he came through the door and asking about her day, before telling her about his. While the passion that had prevailed in the months following their marriage had waned, they had still made love regularly, but he seemed to have lost interest. Try to rekindle his passion, she bought a new nightdress out of the Universal

Catalogue, which he seemed not to notice the first time she wore it, causing her to ask, "Do you like my new nightie? "He gave her a cursory glance and said "It's OK." And switched off the bedroom light without saying another word and went straight to sleep, not noticing that his wife was lying next to him sobbing.

When he got home from work the following day she decided to confront the issue asking, "Why are you being so cruel Tom, you barely seem to notice me these days?"

He knew that she was right, but being in no mood to admit it and replied, "I've never been cruel to anybody in my life and you should be thankful that I spend all the hours that God sends at the pit keeping you and the kids fed. It's more than you deserve."

She ran out of the room and up the stairs and he immediately realised that he had gone too far, so followed her, finding her lying face down on the bed. Taking her by the shoulders, he put his arm around her before saying, "I'm so sorry, that was totally unfair, but my head's been all over the place since we went to Brookwood."

"Why?"

"I keep thinking about you and Peter together and to tell the truth, I'm bloody jealous."

"Well you shouldn't be, what happened, happened, but you're here and he's not, you and the kids are my life and I wouldn't have it any other way."

"I know that love, I've been irrational, but the visit to his grave brought it all back."

Kissing him she said, "I'm sorry, but I felt I owed it to him to go and apart from that Trevor and Grace were so kind to me in the war and since and consider us family, including you."

"I know that. They're brilliant to us and the kids and I should appreciate it more than I show. Just give me a bit of time and I'll get over it and by the way your new nightie is lovely, wear it again tonight."

And that's what she did, but it didn't stay on for long and by the morning they had well and truly made up.

Being ashamed of his behaviour, he did all he could to let his wife know how much she meant to him, with Barbara reciprocating by making sure that she cooked all things he enjoyed, baking his favourite "rock" cakes every weekend.

CHAPTER 30

Tom and Barbara's lives were relatively uneventful for the next two years, the most notable event being his promotion to Deputy, which resulted in him taking responsibility for a District underground. Barbara was busy bringing up her three children, with Petra, now quite a young lady of eleven, while Jack was five and his brother a lively three-year-old.

In the summer of 1953, they decided that they could have their first proper holiday and after a Boarding House in Blackpool had been recommended by a workmate, Tom booked for them to spend the first week of the Pit Holidays in the popular Miners holiday destination.

As the time of their departure grew closer, Petra became increasingly excited, having never seen the sea, while her parents looked forward to going away as a family for the first time. Mrs Ball who lived next door to Tom's Mother and Father always spent the first week of the Miner's holidays in Blackpool, as a side-line organised a coach each year, the seats on which were invariably all occupied. Reserving four places, deciding that they would take turns to sit George on their knees. It was a half mile walk to the pickup point, which was quite an effort, with Tom lugging two suitcases, Barbara carrying George and Petra holding Jack's hand. Only minutes after they arrived the red and cream charabanc drew up, with Mrs. Ball showing them to their seats for the three-hour journey to the North West. Showing Petra, a picture of Blackpool Tower, Tom told her to look out for it, as if she was the first on the bus to see it he would give her sixpence. Passing Preston, Tom told her to keep looking to the right and shout out if she saw it. With around five miles to travel, Petra shrieked, "Daddy, Daddy is that it over there?"

"It certainly is, I'll give you your "tanner", when we get there."

A few minutes later they drew into an enormous coach park, full of a variety of charabancs of divers colours, with fun seekers from all points of the compass emerging from the sliding doors. Prowling between the rows of parked vehicles were numerous boys pulling wooden trolleys, many of which were already piled with luggage. As Tom got off the bus, three of them gathered around shouting, "carry your cases to your digs Mister."

Having carried the two pieces of luggage only half a mile at the beginning of the day, the offers seemed appealing, so he asked, "How much.?"

"Where you staying?", asked the first one.

"Hornby Road."

"That's a right fair way, Mister, a bob."

The boy immediately behind smiled broadly and said, "I'll do it for nine pence."

The first boy looked as though he was going to punch his rival, before Tom stepped quickly in, put the two cases on the second boys trolley and said, "Right, nine pence it is then."

Spared the burden of luggage, Tom could carry George on the ten-minute walk to The Grove Boarding House, where they were to spend the next seven days. Their young porter, who had black unkempt hair, a spotty complexion and was dressed in short grey trousers, an opened neck check shirt, long grey socks that had fallen to his ankles and scuffed black shoes, led the way. On arrival at a tidy looking, freshly painted terraced house, with "Board Residence" sign in the window, under which hung another sign informing passers-by that there were "No Vacancies". Ringing the doorbell, they were greeted with a smile by their host, a short prematurely bald, rotund man of around forty, who shook Tom's hand saying, "You must be Mr and Mrs Walton, I'm Joe Hartley, me and my wife will do our best to look after you for the next week. How was your Journey?"

"Good", replied Tom, "but the boys were getting a bit restless towards the end, so we're pleased to be here."

"Well you can relax now", he said turning to Barbara, "What are the children's names?"

"Petra, Jack and the youngest one's George."

"Welcome to you all, I'll just call the wife, Bessie."

From the door at the end of the long hallway emerged a small thin lady, with short, well-kept grey hair, in a blue patterned pinafore dress.

Walking towards them offering her hand first to Barbara and then Tom. "We've been expecting you", she said smiling, "and hope you all have a nice holiday with us." Joe will show you to your room in a minute and leave you with the key and one for the front door, which you will need if you're out after ten in the evening. Breakfast is at 8.30, Dinner at one and Tea at five thirty, we sound the gong to remind you of the time. If the children want a glass of milk, before they go to bed, you should ask. I don't like to mention money, but you will need to pay the cost of your Board and Accommodation today."

"Not a problem" said Tom as he reached into his inside jacket pocket for and envelope, "I think you'll find that's the right amount."

Taking the envelope, which he handed it to his wife, Mr Hartley led them up the stairs carrying both cases, despite Tom's protestations. They arrived at a door, with a brass "Number One" screwed on the front, which they entered to find a large room containing a double bed, two singles and a large cot for George. Handing the key to Tom saying, "I hope that you have a nice holiday and the weather is kind to you. If you need anything just let me know. I almost forgot, we have an old pushchair downstairs, which you're welcome to borrow. It will help you get around with the little one."

Taking advantage of the offer, following a short rest, Petra constantly asking, when they were going to the sea, they were soon walking down Hornby Road towards the beach. The children were enthralled when after crossing the wide promenade, they got to the rails that looked down on the waves splashing gently against the sea wall.

Petra looking somewhat puzzled turned to her father and asked, "But where's the beach?"

Tom laughed, "Under the sea now, but there will be plenty of sand when the tide goes out."

"What's the tide?", interjected Jack.

Explaining the vagaries of sea that came in and went out twice every day, which placed some restrictions on sand castle building.

So, began their first of many holidays together, with Blackpool and The Grove to be their destination for the next ten years. The problem for Barbara was that at times it didn't seem like a holiday at all, as half the village was there during the Miners Summer Holidays. Despite this, she looked forward to going, relishing the idea of not having to prepare meals or clean the house for a whole week. The food that the Hartley's prepared was outstanding and Tom enjoyed having Bacon and Eggs for breakfast each morning. Most importantly, there was so much for the children to enjoy. As well as sand castle building and paddling on the beach, there was a profusion of Donkeys, trudging along the sands, conveying a variety of children of all sizes and shapes, providing their parents could afford the shilling fare.

One evening during the week the whole family embarked on one of the green and white tramcars that trundled along the promenade to the Pleasure Beach, which was an absolute delight for the children, the attractions surpassing anything that they had seen when the travelling fair visited the village on Wakes week each year.

The main bonus was that the sun always seemed to shine, so when they returned to the village at least they looked healthy having acquired tans on normally pale faces.

CHAPTER 31

Following that first holiday, Tom returned to work blissfully happy, thinking that life could not be better. He had a good well paid job, even though it was not what he would have chosen to do and he still dreamt of being able to get work away from the pit. Most importantly, he could provide for his family, with a wife he adored and three wonderful children, never thinking of Petra not being his own flesh and blood.

Then another official brown envelope arrived, opening the envelope thinking, not again:

> *Dear Mr Walton,*
>
> *It is requested that you attend an interview at the War Office in London on 2nd September 1953. This will be conducted by Officers from the Special Investigation Branch of the Royal Military Police and concerns the events that you witnessed in France on 28th May 1944.*
>
> *Please arrive at the War Office by 10am on the day of the interview. A reservation for the night of 1st September has been made for you at the Bedford Hotel in Southampton Row and a return Railway Warrant is enclosed. Any other out of pocket expenses, including loss of earnings will be reimbursed.*
>
> *It is unlikely that you will be required for more than three hours, enabling you to return home by the evening.*

Thank you for your anticipated assistance in this matter and I look forward to meeting you.

Yours Sincerely,
John Rea (Major)

Finding it unsettling as he had thought the matter closed, despite still being uncomfortable regarding the fate of Schiller and his insistence on innocence to the end. but nevertheless, confirmed that he would do all he could to assist by return of post.

Travelling to London on the afternoon of September 1st, as always, he tried to enjoy the interesting journey to Euston, the line running along the Grand Union Canal for several miles around the Tring area. The site of the barges reminding him of his teenage encounter with the giant horse on the towpath, although most of the animals had disappeared as the fleet had become progressively motorised.

After a restless night, he took the underground to the War Office arriving over thirty minutes prior to the designated time. Following a short wait, he was escorted to a first-floor office to be greeted by a short stocky, middle aged Officer, with a broad Scottish accent, who shook him firmly by the hand saying, "Thank you for coming Mr Walton, my name is John Rea, I work in the Special Investigations Branch of the Military Police. We will be joined by one of my colleagues Captain Charles Cockfroft and then we can get down to business."

Rae returned to one of two seats behind the desk, indicating that Tom should sit in the single upright chair immediately opposite. After sitting down Tom said, "Can I ask, what exactly is the purpose of me being brought back here. I thought that the case was closed four years ago?"

"Yes, it was, but new information recently emerged that has made it necessary to reopen it. I will elaborate in a few minutes, when Captain Cockcroft arrives. In the meantime, will you take a cup of tea?"

"Yes please", replied Tom, having had little appetite at breakfast time, "milk and one sugar."

Rae picked up his telephone asking for a tray of tea for three, not long after which there was a knock on the door, through which confidently strode a tall, thin, fair haired young Officer with three pips on each shoulder, who approached the desk and saluted his superior, before turning to Tom offering his hand saying, "You must be Tom Walton, excellent to meet you, I'm Charles Cockroft."

The Captain sat in the chair next to his superior, extricating a red file from his brief case, marked, SECRET. Placing the open file on the desk. "I'll get straight to the point Mr. Walton. Unlike ourselves and the Americans, our former Soviet allies did not release German prisoners of war soon after the cessation of hostilities. On the contrary they kept many of their former enemies in captivity until quite recently and many died in camps. Of those remaining several thousand were only released two years ago. Anyway, it transpires that one of them was a Sgt. Major Klaus Diedrich, who was thought to have been killed in Russia in 1943. You will remember that his name was mentioned at the trial of Paul Schiller in 1948. He was indeed present at the massacre near St.Jean du Becq and has admitted as such. However, the problem is that he is adamant that Schiller was not there and that it was another Officer gave the order to throw grenades and fire into the barn. If that's the case, an innocent man was hanged in 1948."

Tom's palms were sweating and his heart racing, finding it difficult to retain his composure he asked, "Did he identify the Officer who he alleges was there?"

"Indeed, he did, which again poses a problem, because the man he named is dead, we have verified that he was killed as the Russian advanced on Berlin in 1945."

"What was his name?"

"Walter Schubert, and apparently, he spoke perfect English."

Tom's was shaken asking, "What happens now?"

"Well, a final decision has yet to be made, but it's likely that the case will be reopened, which could result in Schiller's conviction being set aside. If that turns out to be the case, the shit will hit the fan. It may be that you will be required to attend any appeal hearing to give evidence and we thought it only right to make you aware of it, rather than springing it on you with not much notice. We have a transcript of your evidence and in the event of it being referred to appeal we'll be in contact and one of our lawyers will review it with you."

"I'm in shock", said Tom, "I gave my evidence in good faith and was and am still convinced that the voice I heard on that day was Schillers. Despite that, I've had nightmares about it since, particularly since he claimed to be innocent until the end, when he had nothing to lose. I don't know how I could live with the thought that I caused the death of an innocent man."

Rae got up from his chair and walked around the table, putting his hand on Tom's shoulder saying, "You've nothing to reproach yourself for Mr. Walton. As you said, you gave your evidence in good faith and it may be that this character Diedrich is just making bloody mischief."

Travelling back to the Midlands in a daze, Tom barely noticed the scenery. When he got home, Barbara immediately realised that something was amiss and hugging asking, "What's wrong duck?"

Slumping into an armchair, he told his wife about the disturbing meeting in the War Office, fearing that he might have been the cause of a miscarriage of justice.

"I'm convinced that the voice I heard outside the barn was that of the Officer who commanded the soldiers that we surrendered to earlier that day, but I have been worried since we got his wife's letter saying that he was still claiming to be innocent to the end."

Trying hard to comfort her husband, Barbara hugged him saying, "You told the truth Tom and you can't reproach yourself for that, you said that you owed it to your mates and it's unlikely that any man would admit something like that to his wife in any circumstances. He would have wanted her to remember the good things about him."

They were both quiet for the rest of the evening, finding it difficult to sleep throughout the night. It was with little enthusiasm that he walked along the pit lane the following afternoon, but the banter with his mates cheered him up. Despite this, Schiller was uppermost in his thoughts in the days that followed, while he was constantly on edge waiting for the War Office to contact him.

After what seemed an interminable wait, another letter arrived just before Christmas, informing him that in the light of Diedrich's testimony an appeal had been instigated by Schiller's lawyers. This was likely to be heard in the spring of 1954 and that once again Tom would be required to travel to Germany, it being likely that he would have to give evidence.

CHAPTER 32

Barbara was worried how much the ordeal was affecting Tom and did her best to maintain as much normality as possible.

When she had returned to the village with Petra in 1942, while being pleased to be reunited with her parents and Jean, she had received a far from friendly welcome from many of those she had known since she was a child. The first time she took her daughter to the Welfare, the staff were kind and considerate, but not even one of the other young mothers acknowledged her and arriving home close to tears, her mother to asked, "What on earth's the matter?"

When she told her what had happened, her mother dismissively replied, "Who the hell do they think they are, believe you me most of the girls in this village haven't lived like Nuns, including a lot of them who are pushing prams around. I wouldn't worry about it too much if I were you, they'll come round eventually and bugger them if they don't."

Many of them didn't, which made Barbara's life miserable, missing the friendships that she had valued so much when she was a WAAF. One person who did stop to speak when they met, was Tom's sister Maud and while she was delighted when she told her that he was on his way home in 1945, not for one minute did she think he would want to have anything to do with her. So, she was surprised when she and Jean came in one Sunday afternoon to find him and her Dad sitting in the living room smoking. In the meantime, Petra had grown into a beautiful toddler and Barbara was pleased with how well she took to Tom as she was normally shy with strangers.

They had sat down to tea and most of the time the conversation was restricted to the two men's analysis of what was going on at the pit and the prospects of nationalisation now that there was a Labour government.

Hardly saying a word to her throughout, he did smile briefly a couple of times, so as he was leaving she had decided to ask him out the following Sunday.

Happy when he agreed. When she told Jean, her sister laughed saying, "He still fancies you, I could see it in his eyes and he hasn't had a girlfriend since he came back from the war."

"I doubt it after all that's happened, I don't think he'd want to take me on with someone else's child."

"You might be surprised, Tom's a good bloke and I've never seen him with anyone else."

Unconvinced, but looking forward to the following Sunday when she put on the newest and brightest dress from her sparse wardrobe and was ready ten minutes early. Tom had arrived on the dot on a lovely early autumn afternoon and immediately put her at ease, making the most of the conversation, but never mentioning what had happened to either of them in the war. Finding herself enjoying male company for the first time since Peter had been killed, they chatted constantly, even laughing together a few times. Despite being pleasantly surprised how well they were getting on, it was like a bolt out of the blue, when he asked her to marry him and surprised herself by saying Yes straight away. Telling her to keep it quiet until he had spoken to her Dad, which had prompted her to say, "You don't need to do that, I'm not exactly a slip of the girl."

"I'd do the same if you were fifty, I may be old fashioned, but that's the way I do things."

"Well make sure, I'm not around when you come to ask him, I remember how embarrassed I was when you came round to ask him if you could take me out all those years ago."

"Don't worry, I'll catch him at the pit or in The Oak, with you well out of harm's way."

When she got home, Jean couldn't wait to ask how they had got on and Barbara just said that everything had been fine, without going into detail, which her sister found frustrating.

So, Jean was just as shocked as her mother, when a few days later her Dad came back from The Oak one evening and said, "Beth, you better dust off your best hat, because Tom Walton's just asked my permission to marry our Barbara."

Jean shrieked, "I knew that would happen, Tom has never looked at anybody except our Barbara, he'd still have wanted to marry her if she'd have come home with three kids."

Her mother said, "Well, she didn't, one's quite enough to be taking on if it's somebody else's."

They had got married in the local church, with just their immediate families looking on. The exception had been Tom's father, who had been totally opposed to his son getting involved with what he referred to as "damaged goods." Barbara was more disappointed for Tom than herself, who told her not to worry because he was just a "bigoted old bugger".

Despite her experience with Peter, who she knew would always be in her thoughts, she had been nervous on the wedding night. When they got to the bedroom in their new home, she wondered what making love to Tom would be like, but was shocked when he told her that he had never been with a woman.

Barbara took him in her arms and said, "Look Tom, despite what happened to me, I haven't had much experience, so it will be fun learning together. So, let's get undressed for the first lesson."

Taking off their clothes separated by the width of the new double bed, they had hardly looked at each other. Tom put the light out and got into bed where she was waiting for him. He had kissed her briefly, quickly putting his hand between her outstretched legs and soon clambering on top of her. She had said, "Just slow it down a bit love, there's plenty of time."

"If I wait much longer, it'll be over before I start", he had replied, his whole body shaking.

At that, she had guided him into her and while she was aware of him trying to slow down, within a minute he cried out, his body convulsed as he rolled away saying, "I'm sorry Barbara, I've made a fool of myself, but I was so excited."

"Don't worry, it was fine, but will be even better next time."

She had been right, because next time was less than an hour later and Tom was far more relaxed, careful and after what seemed like several minutes, Barbara had dug her finger nails into his back as they cried out together.

They had then drifted off into an exhausted sleep, but had recovered enough by the next morning for lesson number three.

Easily adapting to the routine of married life, Barbara found that she was treated far more amiably in the village, than had previously been the case. Tom adored Petra and was soon unprompted, calling him Daddy, which made her even happier.

When Trevor and Grace had asked to visit their granddaughter, Barbara thought that Tom may be upset, but was surprised by his reaction. Making them very welcome, they had obviously been impressed by him, Trevor saying to her, "You've got a good one there, Barbara, look after him", before they returned to London.

The birth of their two sons had made their family complete and she grew to love Tom more than she ever thought she could, even though she would never be able to totally get over the loss of Peter. She knew that what had happened to her in the war disturbed Tom, although he never brought it up. The only time that it did affect their happiness was when she decided that she owed it to Peter to visit his grave. While his initial reaction had been upsetting, he had been supportive of her when they did visit Brookwood, which she vowed never to do again.

Tom's war cast the main cloud over their happiness. When they got married, all she knew was that after joining the Army in 1938, he had been wounded and captured in France in 1940, spending the remainder of the European war in a Prison Camp in Germany. Only when he started receiving correspondence from the War Office he reluctantly made her aware of the shocking events following his capture, which he had been doing his best to forget. He had the trauma of revisiting the site of the massacre in France and then Germany for the trial of the German Officer who they thought responsible for it. Initially shocked by his antagonism to Paul Schiller, that had all changed after he had seen him sentenced to death and fully understood that despite everything, her gentle husband had tried to save his life. Afterwards, he had found the letter from Frau Schiller deeply disturbing, beginning to doubt that his testimony had been accurate. This was totally compounded when four years later another of those present at the atrocity had declared Schiller innocent and despite everything Barbara did to reassure him he was haunted by the thought that he had sent an innocent man to the gallows.

Chapter 33

Early in 1954 the inevitable happened, Tom being informed that he would be required to attend the appeal in Hamburg in March. He had hoped that it would be sooner as he found the wait almost unbearable, despite Barbara's support. The journey to the continent followed a familiar path, with the train journey to London and a bumpy flight in the noisy Dakota. This time he was accommodated in a Hotel in the centre of the city, where he was reacquainted with Colonel Hastings on the evening of his arrival, who explained that it was his job to defend the appeal to ensure that the conviction stood. The Officer also advised him that the appeal would be heard in a civilian court in front of three German and one British judge, with most of the proceedings conducted in German. Tom was guided through his original evidence by Hastings and told to answer questions from Schiller's lawyers with the same assurance that had been the case at the original trial. Hastings explained that the chances of successfully defending the appeal depended a lot on him being able to destroy the credibility of who he called, "that character Diedrich", who would "wonder what has hit him, when I get at him."

Driven to the court the following morning, he found that he would not be permitted to enter until he was called to give evidence, which would probably be on the following day. Fortunately, he had been pre-warned of this so was armed with a Zane Grey western novel to pass the time as painlessly as possible.

After spending all day waiting outside the court room, he was told that evening what Diedrich had said. Apparently, he was adamant that Schiller had not been present at the barn, never returning to his Unit after going to Field Headquarters to ascertain what was to be done with such a large group of prisoners. It had been when another SS Officer, who he had later found to be Walter Schubert arrived in the evening that they were ordered to start disposing of the prisoners, who had been responsible for the deaths of many SS troops in the battle on the previous days. Diedrich said that he had contested the order, but had been informed by Schubert that he had two choices, either kill the prisoners or face a court martial and be shot himself.

Diedrich had also stated that in his opinion Cpl Kohl bore a grudge against Schiller for disciplining him, which resulted in his demotion and had told others of his hatred for the officer and his determination to gain revenge. Hastings said that the former Sgt Major was very confident and had stood up well to his cross examination, so a lot depended on Tom's evidence.

The following morning, he was called into court, which had a similar configuration to that used for the original trial, but this time the bench was occupied by four middle aged men in black robes, one of whom wore a wig, who Tom took to be the British judge. He also noticed that Herr Muller, was again representing Schiller, whose widow was occupying a seat in the area reserved for the public.

After taking the oath, he looked across the courtroom towards Muller, who was studying papers, but after a short pause, stood up and smiled, saying, "Good Morning, Mr Walton, it's good to see you again."

Tom nodded in acknowledgement.

"Mr Walton, you are obviously aware of the grounds for this appeal and I will not expect you to comment, but I will again be asking you questions in respect of your original evidence. Firstly, given the fact that an eye witness to the massacre has given evidence that Hauptsturmfuhrer Shiller was not there, are you still totally convinced that it was his voice that you heard from outside the barn?"

"Yes sir, while I have found recent events unsettling, I was convinced at the time that the voice I heard that evening was that of the Officer who had addressed us after our surrender earlier in the day."

"But would you agree, that as you did not actually see Herr Schiller, that it is possible that you were mistaken?"

"Yes sir, I suppose I would have to accept that."

"Thank you, now you will recall that after the verdict in the original trial, you approached me and expressed an opinion that Herr Schiller should not be sentenced to death?"

"Yes sir"

"Was that because even at that time you were uncomfortable with a man being condemned on what has proved to be your flawed evidence?"

"No sir, I would argue that my evidence both then and now is not in any way flawed and the reason I expressed my concerns were twofold. Firstly, I had a lot of sympathy for Herr Schillers wife and children. I am also totally opposed to the death penalty."

"Are you also aware that Herr Schiller continued to maintain his innocence to the end?"

"Yes sir, I received a letter from Frau Schiller after he had been executed, in which she told me exactly that. While I did I believe her to be sincere, I am confident that the evidence I gave was correct."

"How will you feel if it is proven that an innocent man was hanged because of you being mistaken?"

Before Tom could answer, Hastings was on his feet and shouted, "Objection your honour, the question is unfair and bears no relevance to the outcome of this appeal."

"The judges conferred for around a minute, after which the President of the Court, speaking German, said, "The objection is sustained and the question should be struck from the record."

"Thank you your honour, said Muller, "I have no further questions for this witness."

Colonel Hastings, who was wearing civilian clothes and a gown, said to Tom, "Mr. Walton despite the new evidence that has been given on behalf of the appellant, you have never deviated from your belief that you clearly heard Herr Schiller's voice from outside the barn on that fateful night in 1940?"

"No sir, I have not, I will never forget that voice."

"You heard Herr Schiller give evidence at the original trial, did that reinforce your opinion that it was him that was present outside the barn immediately prior to the murder of your comrades."

"Yes sir, it did. I am convinced that it was him."

"Did you also identify him from photographs that you were shown during the investigation that resulted in him being charged."

"Yes sir."

"So, when you appealed for clemency on his behalf, it was in no way because of a lack of confidence in your evidence?"

"No sir, I stated my reasons both at the time and in my evidence to Herr Muller."

"I have no further questions, your honour."

The President said, thank you, Mr. Walton, you may stand down."

Having no desire to remain in Hamburg any longer than necessary, Tom was back on the Dakota to Northolt the following morning. Prior to his departure, Hastings shook his hand and said, "Thank you Walton, that must have been quite an ordeal for you, but you coped admirably. It's likely that these proceedings will be concluded in the next couple of days, but the Court will probably reserve judgement, which means they will give their decision later. The War Office will inform you of the result."

Although he had only been away for a short time, Barbara and the children could not hide their excitement when he walked through the door' Particularly Petra who was now twelve years old and always happy to help her Mother around the house. Tom loved her just as much as her mother and the boys, the only thing that blighted his happiness was the drawn-out saga that he hoped would be concluded by the dismissal of Schiller's appeal.

In the ensuing weeks, he became obsessed by what the postman pushed through the letter box, his heart skipping a beat every time he heard envelopes dropping on the doormat. It was around six weeks later that the by now familiar official brown envelope arrived, while he was on the Day Shift at the pit. Barbara had put it on the Mantelshelf above the fireplace. Seeing it as soon as he came in, his wife stood looking tense as he hesitated before opening it.

> *Dear Mr Walton,*
>
> *I refer to the recent appeal against the conviction of the former SS Officer, the late Paul Schiller for the mass murder of Allied troops at St. Jean du Becq, France on 28th May 1940.*

The Court in Hamburg delivered its judgement on Thursday last and I regret to inform you that it was ruled that given the new evidence presented to the court the original verdict of guilty was "unsafe" and therefore that the conviction be quashed and that Walter Schiller be granted a posthumous pardon.

I realise that the verdict will be a considerable disappointment to you personally, but I should say that the court did not in any way question your own integrity.

On behalf of the Secretary of State for Defence, I would like to thank you for your help throughout the long judicial process and can assure you bear no responsibility for its unsatisfactory conclusion.

I regret to say that the matter is now closed.

Yours Faithfully,
John Rae (Major)

Slumping into an armchair, Tom held his head in his hands and was immediately comforted by Barbara, who had prepared herself for this moment. Getting up, he took her in his arms, while saying, "How can I live with the thought of having sent an innocent man to his death?"

Looking at the letter, she replied, "You've nothing to blame yourself for. If it was a mistake on your part, it was genuine and the court obviously hold you blameless. Apart from that, they haven't said that it wasn't him, just that the conviction was unsafe. They probably thought that the new evidence had to be taken into consideration and that's why this has happened. Just put it behind you Tom, let's just look forward to the rest of our lives with the kids. We need you to be happy."

"What about Schiller's family, his wife and children must hate me, but no one will ever convince me that it wasn't his voice that I heard on that day."

"But you didn't see him that night, that's probably why they made the decision they did."

CHAPTER 34

The sight of the four judges entering the Court Room to deliver their verdict caused Eva Schiller's hands to shake uncontrollably. Having sat through two trials, she had endured evidence and arguments, regarding the vilest accusations against her beloved husband and childhood sweetheart. Whatever the verdict, it was too late to bring him back, but it was so important to her for his tarnished reputation to be restored.

Eva had known Paul since the day they started school, going out together from their early teens and marrying soon after they both qualified as teachers. Paul had been devoted to his job, so she had been shocked when he decided to join the military in 1938. He had been commissioned in the SS one year later and following the invasion of Poland had gained rapid promotion. After the successful campaign in France, he had remained on the Western Front until his capture by the Americans late in 1944. One year later, he was released and came back to their home near Hamburg, where he returned to his job as a teacher. Eva was soon pregnant with their third child and for the next two years, despite post war hardship, they had resumed their happy life together. Therefore, it came as a complete shock when Paul responded to a knock on the door early one Saturday morning in the autumn of 1947, to find two British Military policeman accompanied by a German official, stating that they required him to accompany them for questioning regarding an incident in which he had been allegedly involved in 1940. Despite being unsettled, Paul had assured her that he had nothing to hide and expected to clear the matter up and return home later that day.

Having spoken very little about his wartime experiences, Eva had not wanted him reminded of what he referred to as "a dark period of his life".

He later told her that he had been taken to a British Army base outside the city, where he was locked in a cell. When he had protested, he was told that it would only be for a short time as he would be interviewed later that day. True to their word, two hours later he had been taken a short distance to a small bare room, in which there was a rectangular wooden table with four chairs, those on the far side being occupied by two British Officers.

The first of them had introduced himself as Lieutenant Colonel Blackman, while he identified his colleague as Major Haldane. Blackman had told him that they were from the British Army Unit investigating war crimes and asked Paul to confirm his name. Having done so, he was then asked to outline his record of service in the SS from 1939 until 1945. Following his reply, Blackman making notes, asked if he could confirm his exact whereabouts in late May 1940. Telling his wife later that he had confirmed that he had been involved in the fighting in the Pas de Calais as British forces had retreated towards the coast. The extremely courteous interrogator had then asked if he had been involved in the capture of British soldiers. He had confirmed that after fierce fighting towards the end of May he had been in command of an SS Unit, to which a significant number had surrendered. Following that, he was asked what had happened to those prisoners. He had replied and assured his wife that his involvement with the prisoners had ended immediately following their capture, but had heard a rumour that they had been shot, which had appalled him. Returning to Field HQ to receive further instructions, he had been reassigned to replace a casualty, being told that the prisoners would be "taken care of".

At that Blackman, had allowed his colleague to ask the next question, "So you are telling us that you did not return to your Unit that was responsible for the care of the prisoners of war?" He had replied emphatically that that was indeed the case. "So, you did not re-join your Unit that had confined the prisoners in a barn near the village of St. Jean du Becq?" After repeating his denial, he was alarmed to be told, that it was alleged that he had returned and had been in command when the prisoners held captive were murdered, only one of them having survived. Realising the implications of the allegation, he denied returning to the Unit and knew nothing about what had happened apart from the subsequent rumours "Well, we have witnesses to the contrary and consider that we have enough evidence to charge you for being responsible for the "cold blooded" murder of 82 British prisoners of war."

Transferred to a nearby prison, he was visited by his wife, who he had told of his horror at the allegations that had been made, assuring her that they were without foundation and not to worry, but she recognised the seriousness of her husband's situation. The War Crimes trials of German wartime leaders and numerous military personnel had been well publicised; many having resulted in death sentences. Eva realised that the gravity of the charges if proven, would doubtless result in her husband's death, which horrified her.

As the date of the trial approached, she had become increasingly concerned and unable to sleep. This was only partially relieved, when Paul told her that Herr Muller, one of the leading criminal lawyers in Hamburg had agreed to take the case and had assured him that he had identified flaws in the prosecution case, which he thought he could exploit. Having said that, he had tempered his opinion by saying. "It is a pity that the trial will be before a British Military tribunal, which had tended to be extremely biased towards the prosecution in these cases."

The trial began it was conducted in English, with German translation, which Eva didn't need, because like her husband's, her English was near perfect. As the evidence was presented, she was horrified by the allegations being made and couldn't believe that German soldiers could have been responsible for such barbarity. It disturbed her that she thought the main prosecution witness, the only survivor of the massacre, to be convincing, giving his testimony clearly and concisely, looking lawyers in the eye with an air of confidence. The only aspect of the evidence that she felt weak, was that he had not actually seen the Officer in command of the SS troops at the barn, surely thinking they could not convict her husband because a witness thought it was his voice he heard eight years before, which she thought had been effectively exploited by Herr Muller.

Former Cpl Kohl, was a more serious problem, as he identified her husband as being in command at the time of the massacre. His motives were, however, repeatedly challenged by Herr Muller, making Kohl look increasingly uncomfortable as the cross examination progressed, which lifted Eva's spirits. It also seemed to have had a positive effect on Paul, who seemed optimistic when she visited him at the end of the day's proceedings.

Kohl was the final prosecution witness and Eva had convinced herself that the evidence was so flimsy that they could not possibly convict her husband. When Paul gave his evidence, he was confident and she thought he stood up to cross examination well. This had been backed up by several character witnesses, who testified to the respect he commanded in the community and his value as a teacher. Finally, Herr Muller appeared to cast doubt on the Prosecution case in a compelling closing argument, making her confident that her husband would soon be back with his family.

All her optimism had been shattered with the guilty verdict, thinking that she was going to faint, while her husband had been visibly shocked. Shaking his head in apparent disbelief, Herr Muller had quickly regained his composure and addressed the court, stating that he wished to make a plea on behalf of his client prior to sentencing. Agreeing to this, The President said that the court would reconvene at ten o'clock the following morning. After the verdict, she had been allowed to see him and while he tried to be cheerful, had told her to, "Prepare for the worst, because they are sure to want to kill me."

The following morning, having spoken briefly to Herr Muller prior to going into court, he had told her of the brief conversation that had taken place with Mr. Walton, which he would use on her husband's behalf, although he thought it would make little difference. He had been right, because despite Muller's eloquence, she had watched in horror as her husband had been sentenced to be hanged.

Following the sentencing, Eva had been appalled when she was informed that Paul would be taken to a prison controlled by the British Army in Hamelin, 200 kilometres south of Hamburg to await his fate. The authorities agreed to weekly visits and given travelling difficulties provided transportation for her. Despite his plight, Paul had maintained his optimism throughout and Eva was shocked that he seemed to hold no ill will to those who had condemned him and had asked her to endeavour to contact Mr. Walton to thank him for trying to save his life. Trying to comfort her when she had broken down, weeping uncontrollably during her final visit, he told her that she should marry again soon for the sake of the children.

Following her loss, Eva realised that she would have to work to support her family and the Principal of Paul's school had been pleased to give her a teaching job. Despite this, she had a difficult time, finding it hard to explain to her children what had happened to their father.

So many times, over the next four years she convinced herself that her husband had been telling the truth, but did have moments of doubt. Finding it difficult to balance her work with bringing up four children, she had enjoyed the support of the local community, who predominantly believed in Paul's innocence. There's and her own belief was bolstered, when one day in 1953 she was teaching when the Principal, Herr Steiger had rushed into her classroom waving a copy of Der Spiegel, which had a photograph of Paul on the front, with the headline, BRITISH GEHANGT, EINEN UNSSCHULDIGEN. "Frau Schiller, you need to read the article inside. A Sergeant who has been a prisoner of the Russians until recently had told Der Spiegel that Paul was not responsible for the deaths of all of those soldiers in 1940 and he knows who was." Grabbing the magazine, she asked Herr Steiger if he would look after her class for a few minutes. She was shaking as she went into the empty staff room and read the article. Afterwards she returned to her classroom and asked the Principal if it was possible to use the telephone in his Office." Of course, you can, the door is unlocked and I will wait here", he replied.

She knew the number for Herr Muller's chambers and was soon connected by the Operator. When it was answered, Eva asked if it was possible to speak to Herr Muller, but if not, one of his assistants."

"Herr Muller is in court, Frau Schiller, but I am sure that I can find someone who will be happy to help you."

After a short time, she heard a click and a youthful sounding male voice said, "Good Morning Frau Schiller, my name is Helmut Merk, I was Herr Muller's assistant at your husband's trial. Doubtless you are calling about the article in Der Spiegel."

"Yes, it was a bit of a shock after all this time and I was wondering what would happen next?"

"Well, Herr Muller spoke to me about it before he left for court this morning and we were going to contact you. We have always had serious doubts about your husband's case and we are keen to look at the new evidence with a view to lodging an appeal against the original verdict."

"Will it not be expensive?"

"Yes, but not to you, Herr Muller feels that we owe it to your husband to clear his name if we possibly can."

Eva's voice broke with emotion as she said, "Oh, thank you, you don't know what it would mean to me if he were declared to have been not guilty of that terrible crime."

Muller quickly lodged an Appeal, that was heard three months later, reviewing the original evidence, but with the significant addition of Sgt Major Diedrich's testimony. The Lawyer told Eva that he was more than hopeful of getting the guilty verdict overturned. Attending the hearing throughout, having been given leave of absence to do so, she tried to be optimistic. As expected, it was announced that judgement would be reserved and the court would reconvene two months later. Eva felt that these were the longest weeks of her life because she was desperate to have Paul's name finally cleared. Nothing could bring him back, but it meant a lot that the children would not grow up tainted by the fact that their father had been branded a war criminal.

The tension in the courtroom was palpable as the Chief Judge began to read out the result of their month-long deliberations, continuing as he summed up the two sides of the argument. Her hopes diminished, when it was stated that the only survivor of the massacre, Thomas Walton was reliable and truthful, but the fact that he didn't see the German Officer outside the barn did cast doubt on the validity of his evidence. The Court had, however, been less impressed by the evidence given by Cpl Kohl both at the original trial and appeal. Also, the fact that Sgt. Major Diedrich had cast considerable doubt on her husband having been at the crime scene rendered the guilty verdict unsafe and the appeal was upheld.

Eva was absolutely elated as Muller crossed the court room to congratulate her saying, "I'm so sorry that this evidence was not available at the time of the original trial. In fact, if it had been, I doubt that any charges would have been brought and your husband would be alive today. It's undoubtedly the worst miscarriages of justice I have encountered and someone should be held to account for it. It seems to me that Kohl's testimony was an absolute fabrication and he deserves to be charged with perjury."

Eva couldn't wait to get home to tell her children, the two eldest Klaus and Helga who were sixteen and twelve, being aware of her mother's torment over the past four years, while five-year-old Rudi had no memories of his father. Helga broke down in tears and hugged her mother, but Klaus reacted by thumping the table shouting, "Those English pigs, they killed our father for nothing. That man Walton, lied through his teeth."

Concerned by his aggression, Eva tried to calm him saying, "Look Klaus, this is a happy day for us, don't spoil it. There were a lot of victims of Hitler's war and your father was one of the last. He was not bitter towards Mr. Walton, who he thought truthful but mistaken and bore him no malice. You must realise what he went through on that terrible day in France, seeing his comrades shot in front of him and being wounded himself, your father bore him no ill will. If anybody should take responsibility for this, it's Cpl Kohl, who obviously lied deliberately."

Somewhat placated Klaus apologised, "I'm sorry for my outburst mother, but I can never forgive him for taking our father away from us."

Returning to school the following day, she was greeted by her colleagues, who applauded and hugged her. Herr Steiger spoke on behalf of them all when he said, "Welcome back, Frau Schiller, as you can see we are all delighted and have already been discussing ways that we can appropriately pay tribute to Paul's memory and the work that he did on behalf of the children in this school."

It was soon decided that a memorial plaque would be placed in the Entrance Hall to the Main Building and that the establishment would henceforth be known as "The Paul Shiller Elementary School." Eva was overwhelmed by the gesture and after giving it great deal of thought decided to write to Tom Walton for a second time.

Dear Mr. Walton,

You will doubtless have heard by now that my husband's appeal was upheld and I and all his former friends and colleagues consider him completely exonerated. Herr Muller told me that if all the evidence had been available at the time of the original trial, it is unlikely that charges would have been brought in the first place.

I have always retained my belief in Paul's innocence, but it has been very difficult for me and my children, living with the knowledge that he was branded as a war criminal. That is all in the past now and we are delighted that his school has been re-named in his honour and that a Memorial Plaque will commemorate his life and contribution to the education of children.

Despite all of this, neither me or my children bear you any ill will and believe that you acted honourably throughout and if you are ever in Hamburg again you would be welcome in our home. I personally remember with gratitude your efforts to save his life following the guilty verdict.

I hope that your own family are doing well and that all our children do not have to face the horrors of war that blighted our generation.

God Bless you.

Yours Sincerely,
Eva Schiller

Chapter 35

As soon as he saw the German stamp on the envelope, Tom knew who had written the letter and was not at all sure whether to read it, or alternatively throw it on the fire unopened. He placed it on the mantelshelf to give himself time to think.

Barbara had been out when the post arrived, but was aware that her husband was worried when she returned. asking what was the matter. Pointing to the envelope he said, "That's what's the matter, you know who that's from don't you. I don't know whether to open it or throw it away."

Barbara kissed him saying, "Well it's up to you, but if you don't, you'll always wonder what she has written."

"OK, let me open it with you here."

Tearing open the envelope, it revealed a single sheet of notepaper, Frau Schiller's neat handwriting being immediately recognisable. After reading it, he handed it to Barbara saying, "I can't believe it, she certainly is a remarkable woman. I don't think I would be so forgiving in her circumstances."

Quickly reading the letter Barbara said, "It obviously came as a relief when her husband's appeal was allowed and even if he's dead, his children will be able to remember him in a much more positive light."

"I'm going to reply to the letter this time, I think her attitude towards me deserves that."

"That's fine, but don't compromise your own belief that it was her husband's voice that you heard outside the barn."

"I won't, but the question is, did he deserve to die on the evidence given, the appeal judges obviously thought not."

Tom pondered for a week before putting pen to paper.

Dear Frau Schiller,

Thank you for your letter and good wishes to me and my family.

I did hear the result of the appeal and obviously must respect the verdict. I am still convinced that it was your husband's voice that I heard from outside the barn on that day, having heard him address us in English shortly after we were captured. However, I must accept that there is a chance that I was mistaken.

I am pleased that the verdict has brought comfort to you and your family and it is obvious that he was held in high esteem as a school master.

I absolutely agree with your sentiment regarding our children not having to experience those terrible times that we had to endure between 1939 and 1945.

I would like to wish you and your family every success in the future and hope that our two nations can maintain the excellent relations that have developed since the war.

Yours Sincerely,
Thomas Walton

Hoping that he had struck the right balance in his reply and that it had finally ended the trauma that had gone on for so long.

He was happy at the pit and the children were all doing well at school, while Barbara seemed contented being a housewife. She had mentioned getting a job, but Tom had not been particularly supportive of the idea, saying that a woman's place was in the home.

They kept in touch with Trevor and Grace and during the summer of her fourteenth birthday, they asked if Petra would like to spend a week with them during the school holidays. Petra didn't seem too enthusiastic about going such a long distance away from her parents, but after thinking about it decided that it would be an adventure, being the only one in her class that had ever visited London. Trevor said if they could put her on a train to Euston, he would meet her at the station. Tom was a little worried about her being on the train on her own, but Petra seemed totally unconcerned.

Taking her as far as Nuneaton on the local train, they only had a short wait before the Manchester to London express steamed into the station. She was quickly on board, finding a single seat in a compartment close to a door and was soon on her way, with Tom blowing kisses. It took two and a half hours to reach London, with stops along the way at Rugby, Bletchley and Watford. Looking out of the window for most of the journey, she almost forgot to eat the sandwiches that her mother had packed, becoming increasingly excited as she got close to her destination. Sure, enough, Trevor was waiting on the platform at Euston and they were soon in a black taxi with the driver asking, "Where to Guv"

"Charing Cross, please", came the reply. Her mother had explained that after she had been met they would as she said, "cross London" and catch another train to the suburbs. Trevor had greeted her with a handshake and remarked on how she had grown, also asking about her Mum, Dad and brothers. Not saying much while they were in the taxi, leaving Petra to look out of the window at the bustle of the city, she was absolutely astonished by the amount of traffic, wondering how on earth anyone managed to cross the road on foot. The journey only took a short time, but she was amused by the driver who tooted his horn and shouted at other road users several times.

Arriving at Charing Cross station, Trevor paid the" cabbie" as he called him and walked through the busy concourse towards the platforms. Asking how long it would take, causing her grandfather to smile and reply, "Don't worry, this a lot shorter journey than your last one, we'll be there in under half an hour." When they did get onto the platform, Petra was surprised that all the carriages where coloured green, rather than the red which she had become used to. Another concern was that there appeared to be no engines. When she asked where they were, he smiled and told her not to worry, because these were electric trains and didn't need engines.

They were soon on their way again and after leaving the station, were on a bridge crossing the widest river she had ever seen, prompting her to ask, "Is this the Thames?"

"It certainly is, it flows right through London down to the sea and some really big ships from all over the world come to the docks further downstream."

This was an alien world to Petra, whose experience of things that floated was the canal barges that chugged through the village.

Following several stops, they got off at a place called Catford Bridge and after a short taxi ride, pulled up outside a neat house, which Petra thought looked much larger than any in her village. Grace was waiting at the gate and hugged her as she got out of the car saying, "It's lovely to see you Petra, we're going to have a wonderful time together." Shown to her room, she was immediately taken by how big it was compared with her own at home, exclaiming, "Oh, yes", when Grace asked her if she liked it.

Looking around the house, there were numerous photographs, but the only person she recognised in them except for Trevor and Grace, was one of her mother with a baby in her arms and as she looked at it, Trevor said, "That's you with your mother when you were three weeks old." Many the photographs were of a young man, who was always smiling, including one of him in a group stood in front of an aeroplane. Fascinated, the following day she asked who the young man was. Trevor and Grace looked at each other and after he nodded Grace said, "That's our son Peter, who was killed in the war, He was your daddy."

"But my daddy is at home with Mum."

Grace replied, "Yes we know that and how much he loves you, but your Mummy met our son while she was in the Air Force and they had you, but unfortunately he was killed before you were born and you are our only grandchild."

Confused, she had never thought of Tom as anything other than her real father, but knew that her Mum would explain everything when she got home. In the meantime, Trevor and Grace couldn't have been kinder, taking her out every day sightseeing and buying her so many clothes that she wondered how they would fit into her small suitcase.

She had read a lot about London and when asked what she would like to see, listed the Zoo, Buckingham Palace and the Tower of London. Trevor said that could all be arranged but that they would have to make two trips "up to town".

Absolutely enthralled by the Zoo, she had seen pictures of many of the animals, but it was nothing compared with the actual sight and sound of them. It was astonishing to hear the roar of a Lion, Penguins being fed and to ride on an Elephant, thinking that her brothers would have loved to have been there.

On the way to Buckingham Palace, she asked if she would be seeing the new Queen and was disappointed when told it was unlikely.

But her favourite was left until last. Her favourite subject by a mile at school was history and the man in what looked like a skirt and stockings, with a funny hat, who she was told was a "Beefeater" made the visit to the Tower fascinating. Telling them what happened in the various parts of what Petra thought to be most interesting place she had seen in her life, they finished in a church were apparently many of people who had had their heads cut off on the green outside were buried. She had read about Henry V111 and his six wives, but to see the place where two of them lost their heads was spellbinding.

The week flew by and it was soon time to be taken back to Euston for the train that would take her home. She had kept a diary and was looking forward to telling her parents and friends about her adventures. In addition to this she went home with a larger case provided by her grandparents to accommodate a wardrobe that had almost doubled in size.

Throughout the return journey, she contemplated the fact that Tom was not her real father, but was happy when she saw that the train was pulling into Nuneaton and grateful when a kind man in Air Force uniform helped her with her case. Looking up and down the platform through billowing smoke, she soon spotted the man she had always thought was her father, waving and walking quickly towards her, lifting her feet off the ground in a hug and saying, "Oh, you don't know how much me and Mum have missed your happy smile."

They had to wait about half an hour for the local train to take them down the line to the familiar village station, followed by the five-minute walk to the house that had always been home. Her Mum was waiting at the gate and Petra got yet another hug and kissed her mother saying, "I've had a lovely time Mum, but it's good to be back with you and Dad"

"Where on earth did you get a case that size, what happened to the one that you went with?"

Explaining how much time she had spent in shops with Trevor and Grace, who seemed intent on buying her more than she wanted. When she opened it, her mother appeared a little annoyed by the contents that included three new dresses and two pairs of shoes. There was also a letter that Grace had handed to her, saying that it was for her mother.

After being given the letter, Barbara sat down and read it, looking concerned before handing it to Tom. Grace had written,

Dear Barbara,

We have had a wonderful time with Petra, who such a lovely, polite girl and a credit to you and Tom.

The only difficult aspect of her visit was that she asked a lot of questions about the photographs of Peter, so I decided to tell her who he was and that you and he had met in the war and that he was her father. She seemed confused at the time, but didn't mention it afterwards until she asked if she could have a photograph of Peter to take home with her. Trevor could see no harm in this and gave her a small photo of him in his RAF uniform, taken around the time that you met.

We are somewhat concerned as to how her relationship with Tom might be affected by the knowledge that he is not her real father and apologise if it is any way compromised.

Thank you for allowing our granddaughter to spend time with us, Trevor and I appreciated the opportunity to see what a fine young lady she has grown into.

With much love to you, Tom and the boys.

Grace

Tom gave the letter back to her saying, "She was bound to find out someday, but I would have preferred it if we could have been the ones to tell her. If she asks about it, we'll talk to her. Otherwise, it's not a problem."

Despite not being outwardly concerned; Tom was worried that his relationship with Petra would be affected although she continued to show him the same affection that had always been the case. This coming shortly after the setting aside of Paul Schiller's conviction and the subsequent letter from his widow, resulted in Tom not sleeping well for the first time in his life. Schiller was constantly in his thoughts and he was haunted by the thought that he might be responsible for the death of an innocent man. During fitful sleep, he had nightmares of being tried and hung himself for the murder of Schiller. On top of this the thought of Barbara with Peter was always on his mind, despite knowing that it was totally illogical to be jealous of a man who was long dead.

Barbara became aware of the change in her husband's demeanour as he became impatient with her and the children and one afternoon when he came home from day shift said to him that they needed to talk.

"What about", came the abrupt reply.

"You're not yourself and I'm worried about you."

"I'm o k, it's just the thought that Schiller might have been innocent that's playing on my mind."

Barbara hugged him saying, "Oh Tom, you've nothing to reproach yourself for, you told the truth."

"The truth as I remembered it. My God, his family must really hate me."

"You know that's not true from Frau Schiller's letters."

Unconvinced he replied, "Yes but her children will always know that I was responsible for their father's death."

"But they have never set eyes on you and are unlikely to do so, you need to move on Tom, for everybody's sake."

"That's easier said than done"

They left it at that, with Tom not wanting to bring up his other concerns, which he knew would only upset his wife.

It took time, but he gradually overcame his period of depression, giving quiet thanks every day for his happiness with Barbara and the children. Petra had been the only one from the village school to pass her 11 plus and caught the train each day to travel to the local Grammar School which was just one stop down the line.

She never mentioned what had happened in London although she did regularly receive letters from Trevor and Grace and despite always having a lot of school work always replied. Tom was surprised how studious she was and his and Barbara's visits to the school for parent's evenings were always a pleasant experience because of teacher's praise for their daughter.

It was when she was 15 that University was first mentioned by her Head of Year who confidently expected her to "sail" through O Levels and hoped that she would stay on for the extra two years. Tom and Barbara had difficulty taking it all in, because they could think of no one from the village ever going to University, but were determined to support her if that's what she wanted.

When they got back that evening, Tom said, "Your Mum and I are so proud of you, Miss Waterhouse said that you're good enough to go to University. What do you think about that?"

Chapter 36

Prior to her trip to London, Petra had often wondered who Trevor and Grace were. She had asked her parents about it and they had been evasive, so when she went on her holiday to London, it was a bit of a shock when she was told that the young man in the photographs was her father, always having known Tom as Dad. At least that explained, why she looked so different to her two brothers, with her almost blonde curly hair contrasting sharply with Jack and George's which was straight and dark.

Thinking about what she had found out, she didn't want it to affect her relationship with Tom, who would do anything for her, but did decide to confront her mother to find out exactly what had happened to her during the war. Waiting until Tom was on the afternoon shift, she returned from school one day and asked, "Can we talk about my real father, Mum."

Seemingly taken aback she replied, "What about him?"

"Well, I was surprised and upset when Trevor and Grace told me about their son, I love Dad so much."

"And he loves you, so please don't mention this to him because he will be upset."

"I don't intend to, but I do want to know something about my real father"

"Alright then, before the war your Dad, Tom and I went out together for about two years, but we had a fall out when he joined the army without telling me. So off he went and was sent to France in 1939. Then in 1940, when he didn't come back, everyone thought that he must have been killed in the fighting. I was terribly upset, but then quite relieved when we found out that he'd been taken prisoner. So, I decided that I needed to do my bit and joined the WAAF's. Well, after I'd done my training I was posted to

Lincolnshire and that's where I met Peter, he was a gunner on bombers. They flew over Germany and an awful lot of them were killed. Anyway, he came into the office one day and we chatted and a few weeks later met in a pub, when he asked me to go for a ride on his motorbike. I was reluctant to get involved with him because I knew that his future was so uncertain, but he was a real charmer and different to anyone I'd met before. So, we started going out and he soon asked me to marry him and I agreed. Then he asked me to go home with him and meet his mother and father and that's when you happened. We'd arranged to get married and to come here so that he could meet my Mum and Dad, but he was killed the day before we were due to come. I soon found out that I was going to have a baby, but when I wrote and told Mum and Dad, they didn't want anything to do with me. I was desperate and went to Trevor and Grace and they were kind to me, looking after me until after you were born and then persuaded my parents to take us back. There was real shame in having a baby when you're not married and I had a hard time here, but I don't regret it. I loved Peter and you're his legacy. He would have been so proud of you."

There were tears streaming down Petra's face as she hugged her mother asking, "How did he get killed"

"It was really bad luck, they were on their way back from a raid over Cologne, when the plane crashed only a few miles short of the airfield, three of them survived and three were killed."

"Where's he buried?"

"In a military cemetery in Surrey."

"I want to go."

Her mother sighed, "I can understand that, but we'll have to speak to your Dad about it. It might upset him."

"Look Mum, this in no way affects how I feel about Dad, but I think that I should visit the grave. How did you and he get back together anyway?"

"I think it was fate really, he came back from Germany in 1945 and a short time later unbeknown to me your Grandad invited him round. You and he hit it off straight away and we went out for a walk the next weekend and he asked me to marry him. I was shocked, but said yes and he's made me very happy. Your Dad is a wonderful man."

Petra was determined to visit her real father's grave, but decided to let her mother speak to her dad, when she thought the time was right. Knowing that her academic ability was outstanding compared with the others in her class, her Head of Year, Miss Waterhouse had spoken to her about staying on after she had passed GCE exams and then going to University. In her village, she knew very few people who stayed at school after they were fifteen, let alone go to University. Nearly all the other girls she knew couldn't wait to leave school and get a job, despite knowing that they would have to hand over their unopened pay packets to their parents and depending on their generosity be handed back "pocket" money.

Petra wondered what the attitude of her own parents would be, having already said that she would probably be able to get a job in an office or bank, because she was a grammar school girl. As soon as Miss Waterhouse had mentioned the prospect of University, she was desperate to achieve her ambitions, but didn't mention it to her parents. So, when her Dad asked her what she thought about University, following the parents evening, she couldn't control her enthusiasm saying, "Oh did she say that, I want to get the qualifications, but haven't mentioned it because I thought that you and Mum would want me to finish school when I'm sixteen."

Tom smiled. "Not likely we don't, having someone go to a University from our family will be brilliant. Me and your Mum will back you all the way."

"But, I won't be bringing any money in."

"It doesn't matter, we've talked about it and even if she has to get a job for us to help you, she'll do it. You can pay us back when you're a lawyer or a Doctor."

Petra was elated and flung her arms around her father, thinking that she could not have better parents.

She couldn't wait to tell Miss Waterhouse the following morning, who didn't appear surprised having discussed it with her parents the previous evening.

"We really need to sit down next year and talk about what you want to do with yourself after University, because that will determine what GCE A Levels you need to take. But first things first, you really need to work hard when you come back in September to make sure that you get top marks in all of your Ordinary Level exams next summer."

Not needing any motivation, Petra couldn't wait until September so that she could get back to her studies, but during the summer holidays, after the family had spent their usual week in Blackpool, her mother surprised her one day by saying, "I've spoken to your Dad and told him that you want to visit your real father's grave, so you and I are going to London on the Train next Tuesday morning and will stay in a hotel overnight. We'll go on the train to Brookwood the next morning and come straight back here in the afternoon."

"What did Dad say."

"Nothing much, just, if that's what she wants, who am I to stop her."

Tom said nothing to Petra, but walked with them to the station the following week and waved them off on the 8.34 to Nuneaton, where they had a short wait for the express to Euston.

Travelling to the capital for the second time in two years, Petra wondered what her mother had thought when she came for the first time during the war, also thinking if the war hadn't happened she wouldn't have either.

They had some time to look around the shops in the afternoon, that displayed a quantity and range of goods, that they could only dream about at home. Petra was enthralled by the fashionable clothes displayed in the shop windows, but knew that she could only look. The only thing that they did buy was a bunch of flowers, that they took back to their hotel and put them in water in the sink in their twin-bedded room.

Travelling on the underground the following morning, they emerged into the cavernous terminus that was Waterloo and soon found the platform for the train that stopped at Brookwood. It took about forty minutes to reach their destination and then a short walk to the cemetery. Given its size, Petra was surprised that her mother could take her straight to the grave which was towards the end of a long row of uniform flat white headstones.

"How did you find it so easily?" asked Petra.

Her Mum replied with tears in her eyes, "I've been here twice before and didn't think that I'd come again, but I'm glad that we have."

Stooping beside the grave, Barbara said, "Hello my Darling Boy, I've brought our daughter to see you, I named her Petra after you."

Petra looked at the stone and saw that her father had been killed on 17th August 1941, just eight months before she had been born, and reading the inscription at the foot of the stone,

"In ever loving Memory of Peter a young man with a great heart"

She repeated it to her mother and asked, "What was he like, Mum."

"Always happy with a glint in his eye and he was the handsomest man I ever met. I really loved him and still think about him every day, He would have been so proud of you"

She hugged her mother and began to cry, thinking of how different her life would have been If the "young man with a great heart" had survived.

They placed the bunch of flowers on the grave and walked away arm in arm, not speaking to each other until they reached the station.

Petra was still deep in thought as the train chugged into the village Station that evening, but was happy to see her Dad waiting for them on the platform. He had a beaming smile on his face and hugging them both simultaneously, said, "You don't know how much I missed my girls."

Barbara said, "It's only been two days Tom."

He grinned again, "It seems like two bloody months."

The rest of the holidays seemed to drag, because as far as Petra was concerned she couldn't get back to school quickly enough. She hadn't mentioned her trip to Surrey to anyone, but felt she would like to share it with someone who was trustworthy. So, on the second day back asked Miss Waterhouse if they could have a chat after school.

The Head of Year was a little older than her parents, tall with sharp attractive features and shoulder length jet black hair, which was flecked with grey. Strict with her pupils, but Petra found her easy to talk to, as she seemed to have a lot more time for those who were termed. "clever."

They sat down in one of the classrooms after school with the teacher asking, "Well, Petra, what did you do with your six weeks off?"

I was bored most of the time Miss and couldn't wait to get back, but we did go to Blackpool for a week, which was a lot more enjoyable for my brothers than me. We've been going to the same boarding house for years; my Mum and Dad love it there. It's another thing that I want to tell you about, one of the best but saddest days of my life. My Mum, took me to Brookwood in Surrey to visit my real father's grave."

Well, I always thought that Mr. Walton was your father

"So did I until recently and I feel a bit guilty about going, because he's brilliant to with us all. I just hope that I haven't upset him, but now I feel that I should honour my real father by taking his surname."

"I doubt that's a good idea, knowing your Dad, he's such a happy family man."

"My real father was called Peter Stanford and was killed when his plane crashed in 1941, my Mum met him when she was in the WAAF's, they weren't married."

"I didn't know, but that happened a lot in the war. My Father was killed in the First War and I never a knew him, but my Mother married again and I had a happy childhood with her and my stepdad. I know what your father thinks of you and he was beaming with pride when I talked about you possibly going to University."

"Yes, I know that they're both really pleased about it and I'm determined not to let them down."

The school year flew by, with Petra totally immersed in her studies, homework being her priority every day after school. She was rewarded the following year with excellent grades in every O Level that she took and decided that she would try to do the four A Levels, including French and German, that Miss Waterhouse thought her capable of, rather than the usual three. That proved to be sound judgement as she excelled in all of them and easily got the grades that would enable her to study Modern Languages at Kings College, London. The capital was her preferred choice after Trevor and Grace offered her a room for as long as she wanted. The cost of the short commute from Catford, being a lot less than what she would have had to have paid for food and accommodation, wherever she chose to study.

Prior to her departure, she decided to tell her mother of her decision to change her surname to Stanford and was surprised when Barbara told her, that was the name on her Birth Certificate, on which Peter Stanford was named as her father. However, Barbara was concerned that it would make Tom unhappy, and was nervous when she mentioned it to him that evening.

Surprisingly Tom seemed completely unconcerned saying, "If that's what she wants, I don't have a problem with it. I'll always think of her as my daughter, whatever she calls herself."

Chapter 37

Barbara tried not to show her daughter how upset she was on the day Petra left to begin her three-year degree course, but with little success. Tom said that he would make the short but familiar walk along Station Road with her and was surprised when for the first time in her life turned and kissed him on the lips, saying, "I'll miss you Dad."

Tom hugged her and she was quickly on the train, leaning out of the open window waving and blowing kisses as it pulled away from the platform. Reflecting on the love he had for this girl, who was a product of his wife's wartime romance, but thought no less of either of them for that. She had an obvious talent for languages and had stated her desire was to have a career teaching them.

When he got home, Barbara was busy cleaning a house, that was already immaculate, saying nothing about Petra's departure. They had agreed to write to each other every week and when a letter dropped through the door a few days later, it was addressed to them both and Barbara handed it to her husband saying, "You read it first love"

Tom opened the envelope,

> *Dear Mum and Dad,*
>
> *Well, here I am my grandparent's house and as you would expect, they have made me feel very welcome. My journey to London was fine and I'm pleased to say that, now that I'm almost an adult, Trevor didn't meet me at Euston and I made my own way across London and onwards to Catford.*

I went to the University yesterday where I met my tutor, Professor Coleman and the other students on my course, who except for me and a girl from Brighton called Sarah Medwin, are all men. That says a lot about the inequalities of the British education system. I also signed up for two extracurricular activities, the rowing club and a group that is in favour of the U.K. joining the European Economic Community, which is generally known as the Common Market.

I hope that Jack and George are both alright and trying hard at school. It would be good if two more of our family get to University. I'm settling in well here, so you mustn't worry about me, but I'm already looking forward to coming home for Christmas.

I've already thought about want I want to do after University and I hope that you won't be disappointed that I want to teach. I've gained so much from my own teachers and it would be gratifying for me to help young people achieve what I did at school. Hopefully I will be able to get into a school near home.

Give my love to my brothers.

Lots of Love,
Petra

Smiling Tom handed the letter to Barbara, who after reading it, shared her husband's happiness.

The remainder of the family slipped back into their routine, but with the boys getting older, Barbara decided that she had enough time to go back to work for the first time since she had been discharged from the WAAF's. Maud managed Randall's shop, with the proprietor having given her that responsibility, on his retirement five years earlier. It had been a surprise causing her to ask," I'm really delighted, Mr. Randall, But why me?"

The old man had smiled, "Because you've been here since you left school and know the shop inside out and what's more, you're much better at spelling than your brother."

When she had told Tom, her brother had laughed, "Well, my spelling's fine now, are you going to give me a job?"

When Maud told them that one of the girls was leaving have a baby, Barbara saw her chance and asked, "Can I have her job then?"

Maud had to make sure that Randall was agreeable, but was happy to employ her sister in law, to whom she had become increasingly close over the years. She also doted on her nephews as she and Les seemed unable to have children, despite years of trying.

When Barbara told Tom of her plans, he seemed far from happy, saying, "I don't know why you need a job. I get a good wage and am perfectly capable of supporting my family."

"I know that, but now the children are getting older, there's not enough to keep me occupied at home and I don't fancy joining the Women's Institute. As well as that, with Petra at University, we could do with the extra money to help her. So, that's why I'm getting a job."

Tom knew that it would be futile to argue with his strong-willed wife, so despite his misgivings, Barbara had her own way.

In his late forties, Tom was one of the most experienced Deputies in the pit with many of his colleagues coming to him for advice. As well as this he was also active in his union NACODS and had joined the Labour party, having become increasingly frustrated with Tory attitudes to the mining industry. He was nevertheless surprised, when he was approached by the local party Secretary asking, if he would be prepared to stand for Labour in a County Council election. He immediately agreed and told Barbara that night and it was her turn to express concerns.

"Do you think you'll have the time, it's probably quite a commitment?"

"Probably not, but I want to give something back to this community and I don't want life to pass me by. I'll soon be fifty"

"My God", said Barbara, "I'll have to trade you in for a newer model, but before I do that, I'll vote for you."

Enjoying campaigning for the election, he particularly liked knocking on doors and speaking to people, many who he had known all his life. It was no surprise that he got a positive reaction in what was a predominantly Labour Ward, but he was still nervous on Polling Day that not enough of his supporters would turn out and that his Liberal or Tory opponent might sneak in by default. Needing not to have worried, he got over fifty percent of the votes in a low turnout. Barbara was pleased for him and when he wrote to tell Petra, she responded, "That's brilliant Dad, you'll soon be a M.P."

Chapter 38

Petra's first year at University flew by, confirming that she had a real gift for languages and was soon fluent in both French and German. Also, making her mark in the Women's Rowing Club, she was soon participating in regattas. Much to her delight she was selected for an eight at Henley, with Tom and Barbara travelling from the Midlands to support her. Barbara wore a new summer dress and Tom bought a blazer and flannels from Burton's, but gave a brusque response to his wife's suggestion that he should wear a "Straw Boater".

"Can you imagine what they'd say at the pit, if they saw me in one of those. When I said that we were going to the Henley Regatta it was bad enough."

Petra's team performed well to finish fifth in their class and her Mum and Dad were proud, meeting her and her team mates with some other parents afterwards. They included a Conservative M.P and his wife, with whom they got on with well, much to Tom's surprise. Meeting in a marquee, for which Petra had managed to get them tickets, they were offered and tasted champagne for the first time in their lives, with Barbara commenting, "My goodness, I could get used to this, you'll have to buy me a bottle on our anniversary, Tom."

Petra came home for the whole of the long summer holiday, but declined her parents offer to accompany the family on the annual pilgrimage to Blackpool. She agreed to look after Jack, who like his sister had decided that he was, as he put it, past joining the "bucket and spade brigade". Having left school that summer, he was due to join the R.A.F as a Boy Entrant in September to train to be an Airframe Mechanic. This had delighted Tom, who had always expressed determination that his sons would not follow him into the pit, humorously telling them that he saw them on the pit top looking for a job he would, "throw them down the shaft without the cage."

Barbara was not so enamoured with the departure for South Wales of another of her children, but Jack had reassured her, "Don't worry Mum, I'll get plenty of Leave."

Prior to going back to London, Petra told her parents that she was hoping to spend some time developing her Language skills in Germany in the following spring, as part of an exchange scheme with the University in Heidelberg. She told them that she had saved almost all the money she had earned from her part time summer job at Randall's, but would need them to help her subsidise the cost.

Tom was somewhat sceptical, but Barbara was surprisingly enthusiastic exclaiming, "What an opportunity, I wished I'd had similar when I was your age."

Continuing to excel in her studies and looking forward to what was to be a full term in Germany, beginning after the Christmas holidays. She had never been abroad before, finding applying for a passport exciting and more so when the hard-covered navy blue document arrived. She found that she would travel by train to Dover and boat to Ostende, after which she faced what she considered a daunting ten-hour rail journey to her destination, involving changes at Brussels and Frankfurt.

Trevor saw her onto the early boat train from Victoria for the relatively short nonstop journey to Dover Marine, where she found that she had to go through passport control, before walking up the gangway of the black and white single funnelled cross channel ferry. The boat was quite crowded on a bitter January morning, but Petra decided to brave the cold as it set sail to have a good view of the White Cliffs. Fortunately, due to the weather the deck was quite empty, but she was relieved to get inside the salon where she managed to buy a cup of hot chocolate to have with the sandwiches, which Grace had made for her. Just over two hours later they sailed into the Belgian port and she stepped onto foreign soil for the first time.

After passing through customs and immigration, where the Officer who stamped her passport had been impressed by her fluent French, she was soon on the Belgian train that took her to Brussels. When she arrived in the Belgian capital, she wished that she had more time to enable her to explore the City, but there was only forty minutes before the international express, taking her as far as Frankfurt departed on what turned out to be a five-hour journey. Petra was fascinated by the fact that she had her passport checked a further twice during the journey, initially by the Belgians and then a German Immigration Officer, who asked,

"Where are you travelling to, Miss?"

"Nach Heidelberg"

The Officer was obviously impressed that she had replied in German so continued he conversation in his own language, "Fur welchen Zweck?"

"Ich bin ein Sprachschuler und Nach Heidelberg werde studieren"

"Wunderbar", exclaimed the smiling officer as he stamped her passport, "your German is already excellent, good luck in Heidelberg."

Petra was quite tired as it was already seven in the evening when the train pulled into a very busy station in Frankfurt, but relieved to find that the final leg of her journey took only an hour and a half. She had been told to get off the train at the Old Town Station and was relieved to see a tall middle aged man, with gaunt looking features and grey hair at the exit gate holding a card with her name on it.

Approaching him, she smiled, which he did not return or offer his hand but greeted her brusquely in English, "Welcome to Heidelberg, Miss Stanford, I am Doctor Lowe and I will be your tutor while you are here. It is only a short walk to the University. You must be very tired. I will carry your suitcase."

Petra was grateful for that as there was snow on the ground, but, unlike in England, all of it had been cleared from the foot paths."

Doctor Lowe said little throughout the ten-minute walk, only the she would be accommodated in France Hall, which was for women only and would share with a German language student, Eva Heller, who would look after her throughout her stay.

When they arrived, Lowe showed her to her room, where a short Jolly looking girl, with dark curly hair was waiting for her, "Guten Abend, ich bin Eva, ich hoffe, dass wir gute freunde sein"

Petra replied, saying that she was sure that they would be good friends and asked if there was any way that she could get some tea or coffee, having survived on Grace's sandwiches for over fifteen hours.

Unfortunately, she was told that she would have to wait until breakfast time as the canteen had closed hours ago, but there was plenty of water in the tap. Taking Eva's advice, she drank two glasses and was so exhausted that all she wanted to do was get into bed, having no difficulty getting to sleep.

In what seemed no time, she woke in the Spartan room with two beds, with Eva still fast asleep. The room was sparsely furnished but there was a wash basin in one corner. Getting up straight away, she went out into the corridor to search for the bathroom and was back and dressed by the time her roommate woke up. Eva was out of bed quickly, swilled her face and dressed in less than ten minutes saying, "Let's get going, I need some breakfast before we start work.

In the large canteen, which was full of students, they were fed croissants and coffee, which Petra devoured as if she hadn't eaten for a week. During breakfast, she found that she would be attending lectures and tutorials with Eva.

As they walked through the Old Town, Petra's enjoyment was not spoilt by snow flurries as the traditional buildings on either side of the narrow streets tended to provide some protection from the bitterly cold wind. There were shops but these were easily outnumbered by the numerous restaurants and bars. Petra commented on this to Eva, who explained, "This is a student town and the bars are full, particularly at weekends. There are also a lot of Americans based close by, but you need to be wary of them, they're only after one thing."

"What about the students?"

"They're very much the same, but it's better to stick to the devils you know"

Petra laughed, contemplating what the next three months would bring.

Chapter 39

Initially finding the lectures and Tutorials challenging, Petra soon began to feel more at home and found Doctor Lowe an excellent teacher, who despite hardly ever smiling, had a dry sense of humour and was popular with his students.

Heidelberg was a place, the like of which she had not seen before, with the Old Town on one side of the River Neckar, which was crossed by two bridges, to more modern developments on the opposite side. The Old Bridge that was close to the University dated back to the 18th century and could only be crossed on foot or bicycle. It had been blown up during the war by retreating German troops, but had since been fully restored. Fortunately, that was the only damage suffered by the Town as the Allied bombers completely avoided it and the overlooking castle.

Quickly hitting it off with Eva, her new friend liked to go into town at least three nights a week and had a taste for "Grosser Biers". After one attempt to keep up with her companions drinking, Petra decided the pain she suffered the following morning was not worth it, only having a small beer every time Eva ordered a large one. Usually going out in a large group, most of which were boys, it being Eva's opinion being that there was "safety in numbers". They usually found a large table to sit around, the beer being regularly complemented by boisterous singing.

Petra enjoyed these nights out and became friendly with several male students, but thought it best not to get seriously involved with anyone as it would prove totally impractical when she returned to London in a few weeks' time. As Eva had warned, she was propositioned by a number of Americans, being invited to their Starlight Club on the banks of the Neckar on several occasions.

Her plan went well until four weeks prior to returning to the UK, she was out with their usual crowd at a bar called Cave 54, which was in a vault below a Jazz Club and very popular with students. Towards the end of the evening, Petra spotted a tall dark haired man, somewhat older than her usual companions, who she thought was the most attractive she had ever seen. The feature that she found most appealing were his piercing brown eyes and when he caught hers, he smiled and when she returned it, walked towards her. Offering his hand, he said, "You're the English girl, aren't you? I asked about you when I first saw you on campus."

"Oh, did you, and why would you do that?"

"Because I thought you were the most beautiful girl I've seen since I arrived in Heidelberg."

Petra laughed, "I've met flatterers like you before and Mum told me to be wary of them."

"Well, your mother would have no need to worry about me, my intentions are entirely honourable. But I would like to take you out, not in a group, just the two of us."

"And why would I want to do that, I've only just met you."

"I'm safe, you can ask anyone about me, I've been here doing a Medical PhD since September, my name is Klaus Schiller."

"Well, Klaus Schiller, my name is Petra Stanford and I'm going back to London in a month's time, so there's no real future for us."

He smiled again, "That's not a problem, I only want to take you out not marry you."

Flattered by this attention, she agreed to go out to a restaurant with him the following week, but was warned by Eva to be wary of him as he had a reputation on campus. Apparently, being such a charmer most girls would "crawl over coals" to go out with him and was usually seen with a different one every week.

It was with Eva's advice on her mind that Petra met him outside of France Hall the following Thursday evening, for the short walk into the Old Town. Having quite a restricted wardrobe available, she had only packed the practical items that she would need at the University, but had one dress just in case she did receive an invitation like this. The temperature had been gradually rising over the past two weeks, making it pleasant during the evenings and their walk much more enjoyable.

They arrived at The Hackfaulle Restaurant, in a narrow noisy street, not far away from the river embankment. It was quite busy, but Klaus had booked a table in the wood panelled dining room and received a friendly greeting from the waiter, suggesting that he was a regular visitor.

"This is my favourite place in Heidelberg.", said Klaus, "the steaks are wonderful."

Petra chatted about her family telling him about her two brothers, Mother and Stepfather and their ambitions for her to qualify as a language teacher. He was interested to know that her mother had met her real father in the war, who had been killed before she was born, she didn't mention that they hadn't been married. Asking how her mother had met her stepfather, she explained how they had split up before the war, for most of which he was a prisoner in Germany and how they got together when he came back. "We're really lucky, he's the most kind, loving man that I know and I think no less of him for not being my biological father."

After she had done most of the talking she smiled across at him saying "You're turn now, go on tell me that your Dad's a millionaire."

At that he frowned for the first time since they had met, I'm afraid that my father died in 1948, he was a teacher."

An embarrassed Petra reached over and took his hand saying, "Oh I'm so sorry, how stupid of me to have made such a flippant remark."

"It's alright, you weren't to know, it's a long time ago anyway. My Mother has not married again; she is also a teacher and a good one at that."

"What about brothers and sisters?"

"I have a younger sister and a brother, my sister is around your age and is at University near our family home in Hamburg. I hope to go back there myself, when I qualify as Doctor, I really want to make a difference to my own community."

As well as his good looks, Klaus was coming over as an understated serious man, who she found herself attracted to. They talked about a lot of things during the rest of the evening, including Eva's warning about him. At that he had roared with laughter saying, "She's so right, I should have a danger sign pinned on my chest."

Continuing their banter on the way back, when they arrived at The Hall, Klaus asked, "I've enjoyed tonight, can we do it again next week?"

"I've enjoyed it too, but Eva told me you have a different girl every week."

"She's right, but I like you so much that you can have two weeks."

Laughing, she agreed to meet him again the following Thursday. He lent forward kissed her briefly on the lips and was gone, finding herself regretting that it hadn't lasted longer.

When she got into bed she lay awake for a couple of hours not being able to get Klaus off her mind. Arguing with herself that nothing could come of it as she would be back in London in a few short weeks. She still thought about him throughout the weekend, despite being invited to Eva's home in Frankfurt, whose parents made a fuss of her.

Arriving back in Heidelberg on Sunday evening, she realised that she was counting the hours until Thursday, wondering if he was thinking about her. When Eva told her that she had seen him out with another girl on Monday Night, she thought probably not. Thinking about trying to call their date off, unfortunately she didn't know how to contact him and decided it would be unfair to just not turn up.

So, on Thursday evening, she put the same dress on, making her way to the doors of the Hall, where she was pleased that he was waiting for her. They repeated their walk to the Hackfaulle on another spring like evening, to be greeted by the same waiter, who said, "Good to see you again Herr Schiller, and you Fraulein."

Showing them to the same table by the window, Petra found a Red Rose laid between the cutlery on her side. She was lost for words, but Klaus smiled saying, "A Red Rose for a rose of England"

Petra immediately regretted replying, "Oh yes, did the girl that you were out with on Monday get one as well."

He laughed, "News travel fast, Elsa is a girl I know from Hamburg, we went to the same school and we do meet from time to time. I love her so much that I gave a whole bunch, which really upset her boyfriend, who is my flat mate."

Feeling embarrassed, she apologised, hoping that she had not already spoilt their evening.

She need not have worried, as Klaus seemed to brush it off and was soon chatting away, about his family, Hamburg and his ambitions for the future. While she told him, how she lived with her real father's parents in London and how profoundly affected she had been when visiting his grave. She went on to tell him about the circumstances of his death and that he and her mother had not been married and how her own parents had disowned her for a time.

Klaus was sympathetic, "Damned wars, so many young people had their lives ruined by them. How could two countries so alike as ours fight each other twice in the same century. Mind there were good things that happened a s result of the last one."

"What for instance"

"You Petra, if the war hadn't happened, neither would you."

She laughed, thinking, smooth talking so and so. To move the conversation on, she asked, "Did your father fight in the war?"

Like the previous time she had mentioned him, he frowned and explained that he had been in the German army throughout the war, had come home afterwards and resumed his career as a teacher, only to die in 1948.

Petra thought it best to leave it there as he was visibly uncomfortable and very vague when his father was mentioned.

Following that brief upset the evening passed quickly, with them laughing most of the time and when they left the Restaurant, he put his arm around her shoulder and she immediately put hers around his waist. When they arrived at her halls he took her in his arms and kissed her gently but deeply, she felt his tongue move slightly inside her mouth causing her to shiver. Pulling back, she said, "Thank you for my rose."

"You're welcome, same time next week? You can be my Thursday girl."

"Not for much longer, I'm going back to London in three weeks' time."

"We'll have to make the most of the time we've got left then and anyway it's not that far to London."

Her head was spinning now, could anything come of this, she had experienced long distance romances amongst her friends in London, most of whom had arrived at University leaving boy friends at home, almost inevitably splitting up as they developed new relationships. Apart from that, he was so flippant and she wondered just how many different girls he went out with each week.

The next three weeks seemed to pass a lot more quickly than she had hoped, with their meetings increasingly frequent. Their embraces were becoming more passionate by the day and Petra found herself dreading leaving Heidelberg and the probability of never seeing Klaus again. A few days before, they sat having a coffee one lunch time and taking her hand he said, "Look Petra, I've never met a girl like you before, I have always liked to go out with as many as possible while the going's good, but that's all changed since you came along. What about if I come and see you in London during the summer holidays.?"

Petra's heart skipped more than a couple of beats, considering afterwards that she had replied too enthusiastically, "That would be wonderful, but I won't be in London during the summer as I'll be going home to my family in the Midlands, but I'm sure that my Mum and Dad would be really happy to let you stay with us."

"That's settled then, providing they're OK with having a foreigner in the house, I'll write to you about the arrangements after you get back to London. Before that, I've got something else that I want to say to you and I'll understand it if you say no. My flatmate is away this week and I'd really like us to be together the night before you go."

Petra hadn't expected that and said hesitantly, "How together do you mean?"

He looked straight into her eyes, "That's up to you, I think too much of you to pressurise you into anything."

"I'll come to your flat, but I don't really want to stay all night."

"That's fine, we'll make it like one of our normal dates, I'll collect you and take you back as normal, it's not much of a walk."

Telling Eva that she was going out with Klaus as usual, but was apprehensive as to what might happen. What if he had said that he was going to visit her in the summer, just to make sure of yet another "notch" on his bed post. Apart from that, she was nervous, having been out with a good number of boys, the furthest she had ventured was let them explore the inside of her blouse if she liked them.

When they arrived, and climbed the stairs to the first floor flat, the door opened straight into quite a small room that looked as though it would benefit from a coat of paint, but was surprisingly tidy with both beds neatly made. A narrow corridor led to a small kitchen containing an oven, a plain wooden table and two chairs, while further along was a tiny bathroom and lavatory.

He grinned, "Welcome to my castle, where many a maiden has been ravished, but on this occasion my intentions are honourable."

Petra quickly replied, "Well that's alright then, because it's the wrong week for ravishing this maiden."

She looked for signs of disappointment, but didn't see any. "Don't worry, they'll be plenty of time for that after we're married."

Petra laughed, "Is that a proposal then.?"

"It certainly is, I've written to my mother and told her that I've met the girl that I'm going to marry."

"And what did she say?"

"She would obviously like to meet you, but I have told her that you are going back to England, so that it won't be possible for a while, but she said that you will be welcome in our home any time."

Sharing a bottle of Riesling, Klaus spoke about his own future and ambitions, but said that the most important thing was that they were together. After that they lay on one of the beds kissing and clinging onto one another, making Petra wish that she hadn't lied about her period. But at around 11pm, knowing that she faced a long journey in the morning, she told him that she would have to go. He wanted to go to the station with her in the morning, but she told him "No", as she preferred to say their goodbyes in private. He did walk back to the Halls with her, but when they got there she was surprised, when he just kissed her lightly on the cheek and was gone.

Telling Eva, how the evening had developed and of her deception, which made her roommate laugh, "You mean to say that you've never been with a boy, how have you managed that?"

"Because I've never met anyone that I liked enough until now"

"Well, why didn't you?"

Petra sighed, "I don't know, I'll probably regret it all the way back to London."

Lying awake for a long time, Petra's thoughts were full of the future, wondering if Klaus would keep his promise and visit her in the summer and was never far from her thoughts as her train sped towards Ostende. It was late in the evening when she arrived at her grandparents' house, who were obviously delighted to see her, with Grace saying, "Thank goodness your back, the house has been so quiet without you."

Petra was pleased to see her grandparents, but didn't mention Klaus, thinking that they might be upset that she was involved with a German. Neither had she mentioned him in her letters to her parents, but now with him planning to visit, she felt that she had to, so wrote the following evening,

Dear Mum and Dad,

Well, I'm back with Trevor and Grace after my interesting and enjoyable three months in Heidelberg. It's such a wonderful place and a miracle that it escaped being bombed in the war.

As you know, I intend to come home for the summer and am looking forward to it, but I need to ask if it will be alright for my boyfriend who I met in Germany can come to stay for a couple of weeks. Klaus is a little older than me and is close to qualifying as a Doctor, I like him and I'm sure that you will too. I am not sure the exact dates that he intends to come, but I have told him to avoid the week that you will be in Blackpool.

I have not met his mother, who is a widow, but she has apparently told him that I will be welcome to go home with him anytime. He has a younger sister and brother.

On that note, I hope that my own brothers are doing well, I'm looking forward to seeing them. Also, I wonder if you could ask Auntie Maud, if there may be a summer job at Randall's for me, I could certainly do with the money.

I'm longing to see you both.

Lots of Love,
Petra xx

Chapter 40

Barbara was pleased to see an envelope with her daughter's neat handwriting and a British stamp on the front, confirming that she was safely back in London. Opening it enthusiastically, she immediately wondered how Tom would react to Petra's news and the fact that she wanted to bring her German boyfriend home. Not needing to have worried, because he laughed and said, "Good for her, write back and tell her that we are looking forward to meeting him."

"So, you don't mind that he's German?"

"Not at all, it's getting on for twenty years since the war finished, we need to move on."

She wrote back the next day and soon afterwards Petra told them that their visitor would be staying with them for the second and third weeks of July. In less than three months' time. Barbara thought the timing ideal, as it was before their annual trip to Lancashire and Jack's summer leave from the R.A.F, so they would have a spare room for him.

Tom joked, "Yes, and we'll lock the bugger in, we don't want him doing any moonlight flits along the landing to Petra's room, I'm far too young to be a grandad."

Responding to his humour, Barbara replied, "Well I wouldn't mind at all, it would be nice to have a grandchild to look after, because you're hardly ever here these days."

Realising that his wife was referring to his increasing council commitments, Tom himself felt that he would like to spend more time at home.

Petra came home in the middle of June, having successfully completed her second year. Maud had been happy to give her a part time job as her niece had proved to be hard working and popular with customers the previous summer. She found her Aunt really easy to talk to, expressing excitement at Klaus' impending visit and hoping that her parents would like him.

As the date approached, Barbara became more and more apprehensive and wondered how they would get on, having thoughts that were not quite as conciliatory as Tom's. But she made sure that his room was in pristine condition as was the rest of the house and garden prior to his arrival.

Petra said that Klaus intended to stay in London on the night of his arrival, travelling to the Midlands the following day, his train arriving at 3.40 in the afternoon and she would meet him at the station. Working in Randall's until 1.00pm, she had difficulty concentrating and was relieved when the time came to go home. Skipping lunch, she had a bath put on a blue and white floral summer dress that she had bought in Nuneaton the week before, especially for this day. Fortunately, it was warm and sunny for the short walk to the station. Arriving on the platform ten minutes early, three expresses roared through, before the bell sounded to indicate that a local train was due. Her excitement increased as the two-car diesel drew into the station and she found herself trembling with anticipation. Then she saw him leaning out of the window, waving his arms and as the train stopped he jumped onto the platform, running towards her, lifting her off her feet to hug her, saying, "Three months have seemed like three years, I've missed you so much."

Petra, tears running down her cheeks replied, "Back in Heidelberg, when you said that you would come over, I didn't really believe it, Thank you."

Setting off down Station Road, Klaus carried his suitcase with his right hand and held Petra's right hand with his left. Barbara was smiling at the gate waiting for them and offered her hand to Klaus, who shook it a little more vigorously than she had expected saying, "I'm so pleased to meet you Mrs Stanford, thank you for letting me stay in your home."

Giving her daughter a puzzled look, for some reason deciding not to correct him straight away, as she would do so when Tom returned from work. Going through the front door into the airy hall way, Petra leading the way up the stairs to Jack's bedroom, where he put down his case and turned and kissed her asking, "Where is your stepfather?"

"At work, but he's due home shortly, let's go down, because Mum's bound to have the kettle on."

Her mother shouted from the kitchen, "Take Klaus into the front room, the tea's nearly ready." As they went through the door, it occurred to Klaus, how immaculate the house was. The room they went into being furnished with a red settee and two armchairs on a floral deep piled carpet, with the sun shining through the large bay window. Just as he was thinking how lovely the room was, he saw on the wall, what was obviously a photograph of a slightly younger Petra, two boys who were as dark as she was fair, her mother and a man he was alarmed to recognise. Almost shouting, "Is that your stepfather?"

"Yes, of course it is, the photograph was taken just before I went to University."

"I'm sorry Petra, I can't stay here, that man was responsible for the death of my father."

Petra froze as her mother came into the room carrying a tray laden with a teapot, milk jug and three cups.

"What do you mean my Dad, wouldn't harm a fly?"

Not knowing what was going on, Barbara interjected, "What's the matter?"

Looking at her, Klaus said, "It's your husband, his lies led to my father being hanged for crimes he didn't commit and I must leave, I'm sorry."

At that he left the room and Petra slumped into a chair, "Stop him Mum, he must be mistaken."

Barbara didn't know quite what to do, "Is his name Schiller?"

"Yes."

"It's a long story about what happened to your Dad in the war, we've never thought that there was a need to tell you about it."

They heard Klaus coming down the stairs and out of the door without a word. Petra jumped up and followed him, almost running up the road towards the station, she caught him, "You can't do this to me Klaus, not without an explanation."

Seeing anger in his eyes he said, "You said that your surname was Stanford, so there was no way I could connect you with your stepfather, who I saw in the courtroom in Hamburg, when my father's appeal against his conviction for war crimes was allowed. That would have been fine, but he had been hanged four years earlier and the main witness was your stepfather, Thomas Walton. There can be no future for us Petra, thank goodness he wasn't in. If he had been there I would probably have punched him."

"Where are you going now.?"

"To London on the next train and then back to Germany tomorrow. I'm sorry."

At that, she left him on the platform, waiting for the south bound train, walking slowly back home, thinking that her life was in ruins. When she arrived, Barbara was waiting for her and doing her best to comfort her daughter said, "You're Dad will be home soon and he will be able to explain to you the connection between our two families. But you must believe me when I say that your Dad did nothing wrong."

Barbara was still trying to console her daughter, who was no longer crying, but the redness of her eyes immediately alerted Tom that something bad had happened. Making him aware of the afternoon's events, Barbara suggested that he needed to tell Petra the whole story from the start, thinking the consequences were never likely to end.

Tom beckoned Petra to sit by him on the settee and holding her hand began by outlining the events of May 1940 and the aftermath. All she had known before was that her father was taken prisoner in 1940. Learning of the circumstances that led to his capture shocked her, also being surprised that he showed no apparent bitterness towards the perpetrators. He went on to tell of his return to France and the subsequent trial of Klaus' father in Hamburg. Having always known of his avid opposition to the Death Penalty, she was nonetheless again surprised that he appealed for mercy for the man he fervently believed to be responsible for the deaths of his mates. The last and he thought final episode in the story had been the Appeal hearing ten years ago, when, because of new evidence, the court had declared Paul Schiller's conviction unsafe and he had been granted a posthumous pardon. Tom remembered that Frau Schiller had been accompanied by her teenage son at the Appeal, and that is why he had recognised him in the photograph. Petra also learnt of the exchanges of conciliatory correspondence between Frau Schiller and her father, who said that he was not surprised by Klaus' reaction as he would probably have felt the same in similar circumstances. He concluded, "This has blighted my whole life and now it's affecting yours. I'm so sorry."

Petra hugged him saying, "You've nothing to apologise for Dad", thinking of the horror he must have suffered seeing so many killed around him. Together with the additional trauma of his escape, wound and capture and spending the next four and a half years as a prisoner, not knowing when or if he would ever get home. She also knew that he would have told the truth at the trial, but was still haunted that he may have been mistaken, after hearing the additional evidence at the appeal. Despite her anguish, she now knew that there was no future for her and Klaus, who she would probably never see again, regretting her deceit on that final night in Heidelberg.

Following a sleepless night that compounded her misery, she went back to work the following day, where her Aunt did her best to cheer her up, "You want to get off to Blackpool with your Mum and Dad, there are loads of lads there. They'll be queuing up outside the Boarding House for a girl like you."

Taking her Aunt's advice, it did take her mind of things, despite the queue failing to materialise. The remainder of the summer holiday seemed to pass slowly and she was pleased when the time came to go back to London for her final year. Intending to apply for a post graduate teaching course, after which she hoped to realise her dream of becoming a language teacher.

CHAPTER 41

As always, Barbara and Tom were sorry when their daughter went back to London. They worried that following her traumatic summer, she had seemed changed, being much quieter than the bubbly girl they knew.

Tom still felt responsible, despite being told by his wife not to be too concerned, Petra had plenty of time to get over it. A few weeks later they received a reassuring letter, telling them how much she was enjoying the start of the final year and had been out a few times with a Law Student, who she had met at the Student's Union. David Austin was from South Wales, where his father worked as a miner, so she felt that they had plenty in common and apparently made her laugh.

Just a few days later, arriving home from work before his wife, Tom found a single envelope on the doormat, picking it up he froze when he saw the German stamp and Frau Schiller's familiar hand writing. Not wanting to open it himself, he decided to wait until Barbara came in so they could read it together. As was his usual routine after getting up at five in the morning for a day shift, he sat in his armchair to take a nap, which he found refreshed him for the rest of the day. Unusually, he could not get to sleep and after half an hour decided to cut the front lawn and prune roses in the surrounding beds, the aromas from which tended to relax him.

He was still in the garden, when Barbara breezed through the front gate, walking straight onto the grass to kiss him. "Had a good day then?", she asked."

"Not bad, but there's a letter from Germany on the mantelshelf, I didn't want to open until you came home."

"We better have a look at it then" she said going into the house with Tom following, kicking off his gardening shoes at the door. Sitting together on the settee, Tom opened the envelope.

Dear Mr. Walton,

I felt that I had to write to you, following my son Klaus' recent visit to your home in England. Prior to going he had told me about meeting an English girl at University, saying that he was determined to marry her in the future. He did of course tell me that her name was Petra Stanford, so there was no way I could identify her connection with your family.

When he returned unexpectedly, just a few days after leaving, he of course told me what had happened and he seemed and remains extremely sad that he could no longer look forward to a future with Petra. I have told him of the representations that you made to the court to try and save his father's life, despite believing him to be guilty. As I told you in a previous letter, I truly believe that we need to put the divisions caused by that terrible war behind us.

I have discussed with him the circumstances that brought you and his father together in 1940 and the terrible experiences that you went through. As you know, I never believed that my husband was responsible for the crimes of which he was accused and my beliefs were reinforced by the evidence and findings of the Appeal Court. Klaus has always been angry about his father's death despite my efforts to placate him, so it is no surprise to me that he behaved as he did when he found that you were Petra's step-father. Although he did accept my rebuke, regarding the upset he must have caused her.

I believe that we owe it to our children to join forces to bring them back together, as an act of reconciliation between our two families. I have not spoken to my son about it, but I wonder how you would feel if I invited Petra to visit us in Hamburg, when hopefully I can help them both put the differences between our two families behind them and enjoy the future they deserve.

If your daughter is agreeable, I will speak to Klaus and then hopefully we can plan for a visit soon. I hope that like me, you believe we should make every effort to bring them together as their happiness should not be blighted by the events in the war, for which we all paid a high price.

Yours Sincerely,
Eva Schiller

Barbara was the first to react, "My goodness she really is a remarkable woman, given all that's happened to her. Do you think that we should tell Petra?"

Tom sighed, "I'm not sure, she was really down in the dumps before she went back to London, but seems to be getting over it and has been going out with this new lad. If they were to get back together, there's always going to be tension between him and me, despite his mother's attitude."

"I know that, but I do think that we should let her make her own decisions."

"Yes, as always, you're probably right, she must see the letter, before we respond."

"She's coming home the weekend after next, so let's wait until then."

They always looked forward to their daughter's visits, but both worried that the news from Germany might upset her and almost changed their mind, when on the following Friday she seemed to be back to her normal self after the upset of the summer holidays. Having discussed it again, they sat down together the following morning and gave Petra the letter to read.

"Oh Mum, I was just getting over this, I don't know if I want to put myself through it all over again and If Klaus wants me he must accept the whole package, including you Dad."

Barbara hugged her daughter, "Well you need to think about if you love Klaus enough to try and repair the relationship and if you want to. What about this Welsh boy, David who you wrote to us about?"

"Well, I've only known him for a few weeks, but he's funny and I really like him. I look forward to seeing him and it's mainly because of him that I've got over what happened."

"But" asked her mother, "Do you love him?"

"It's too soon to say, but I think I could and he seems a lot less hassle than Klaus"

Tom interjected, "And his Dad's a miner, so he's got an advantage to start with."

"Yes, we've got loads in common, like me he's the first in his family to go to University."

"So, do you want me to reply to Frau Schiller?"

"Yes, you should reply, she seems to be kind and forgiving lady, but I wonder if she spoke to Klaus before writing. I saw hate in his face that day in July and I'm finding it hard to imagine him ever getting on with our family. In fact, if you wish, I'll write the letter."

Her parents looked at each other, nodding in agreement, with Tom thinking that they were so lucky to have a daughter who was confident to take responsibility for her own decisions.

Having thought about it, Petra sat down the following day to write,

Dear Frau Schiller,

Thank you so much for your recent letter to my Father.

While I was in Heidelberg, Klaus and I went out together for several weeks and became very close. In fact, I thought that I had found the man that I wanted to spend the rest of my life with. Hence, when he said that he intended to come to England to visit me, it made me happy and I was delighted when my parents agreed that he could stay with us.

As you now know, when he found out who my stepfather was, he stormed out of the house and while I can understand his reasons for doing so, I was shocked at the hatred that he has for my father, who is the kindest and most considerate of men.

I was upset at the time, feeling that I had lost the man I loved. However, I have gradually recovered from the shock and am now back at University enjoying the final year of my language course. Reading your letter was a bit of a shock for me and while I very much appreciate your invitation and efforts to get Klaus and I back together, I do not feel that he would ever have the same attitude to my lovely Dad as you do. I have therefore concluded that there is no future for us and hope that he can find happiness in the future.

I enjoyed my time in Germany earlier this year and got on well with people, thinking that our two nations have a great deal in common, despite what has happened in the past. If Klaus and I had got married, I would have been happy to come and live over there, despite the thought of being so far away from my family.

I wish you, Klaus and the rest of your family every happiness in the future and very much regret that it is most unlikely that I will have the opportunity to meet you.

Yours Sincerely,
Petra Stanford

Petra caught the train to London the following day and was back in Catford by the middle of the afternoon, telling Trevor and Grace what had happened. She was looking forward to getting back to College the next day and hopefully meeting David at lunchtime, thinking that the letter to Frau Schiller had brought the curtain down on her unhappiness.

CHAPTER 42

The next day she caught the train to Charing Cross, having to stand as was normal, with many passengers attempting to read newspapers or books, while hanging on for dear life. She was glad to get back into the fresh air for the short walk to college, where she had a morning tutorial. Having a free afternoon, she had arranged to go with David to St. James' Park at lunchtime, providing the weather was reasonable. Petra enjoyed the wide-open spaces, away from the bustle and was pleased that the October day was unseasonably warm and sunny, with leaves on the trees turning from the green of summer to the various shades of autumn.

Petra looked across at her companion, who was so different from Klaus, being around her own height, with short Jet black hair, dark complexion and muscular build. She was surprised that he still retained a Welsh lilt to his voice that reminded her of Richard Burton, which she thought would go down well in courtrooms, should he realise his ambition to be a Barrister. The main appeal that he had was his almost perpetual smile or laugh and a tendency to take nothing too seriously.

"How was your weekend at home, a bit relaxing after this place I'll bet?"

"It was fine, I love being with my parents, but I missed you."

"Laughing he said, "Well, I didn't miss you at all, I went out with three different women over the weekend and slept with all of them. I'm bloody exhausted, I'm glad that your back so I can have a bit of a rest."

"Good for you, because there's no chance you'll get to sleep with me."

"Believe you me girl, if I am ever lucky enough to get you into bed, we won't get much sleep."

Their banter continued, David telling her that as usual, he had played Rugby on Saturday, followed by the usual ritual of downing several pints and sleeping it off on Sunday. "Bloody marvellous weekend." Was his conclusion.

After her disappointment with Klaus, Petra hoped that her relationship with David would develop into more than a friendship, but she didn't want to rush things, despite his obvious enthusiasm. A lot of girls she knew, were in serious relationships and at times she wondered, at the age of 21, if she was the only Virgin in the entire college. The fact that she had been illegitimate concentrated her mind, being determined that the same thing would not happen to her. Living with Trevor and Grace helped, as those who were in Halls or rented flats had far more opportunity to entertain partners.

As much as she liked David, she suspected that the sexual innuendo in his humour suggested that he would very much like to get her into bed and was determined not to be coerced.

During the week, they saw each other most lunchtimes and went out together at weekends and while their embraces became more passionate as time went on towards the Christmas break, that's as far as it went.

About a week prior to the end of term, they had to see the latest Hitchcock film "The Birds", which she enjoyed, despite having a phobia of them flying too close. Afterwards he took her back to Charing Cross and just before she walked through the barrier he surprised her,

"I've spoken to my Mum and Dad about us and they can't wait to meet you, they've asked if you'd like to spend Christmas with us. It's fine if you want to have a think about it."

Taken aback she replied abruptly, "Oh, I couldn't do that, I want to be with my own family at Christmas."

At that, looking disappointed he brushed her cheek with his lips, "OK, I'll see you next week then."

During the journey, back to Catford, gazing out of the window oblivious to anything going on inside the crowded carriage, she regretted being so instantly dismissive of David's invitation, thinking that she should at least have given the impression that she would consider it. The fact was, that she knew that her family were looking forward to seeing her, as were both sets of grandparents, who were all now in their early eighties. As a compromise, she decided to suggest that after spending Christmas at home, she could travel down to Wales for a few days over the New Year, to spend time with him and his parents.

Meeting him on Monday lunchtime, she asked him to thank his Mum and Dad for their invitation and offered her alternative suggestion, explaining that she felt that she wanted to be at home with her parents at Christmas, grinning he said, "They'll be fine with that and you'll enjoy it, we always have a great night in the Miner's Welfare Club on New Year's Eve, dancing, singing with a lot of them doing their best to drink the place dry."

"Not too much drinking for me I hope, three Babychams and I'm anybody's".

"That sounds good."

"Don't get your hopes up."

Going their separate ways at the end of term, she arranged to travel on 28th December and would stay until 2nd January. She was looking forward to visiting South Wales, having never been there before, but was sure that she would feel at home in a mining community. Christmas at home was very much as it always was, the highlight being a family party hosted by her Mum and Dad on Boxing Day, carrying on a tradition started by his parents, who a few years ago had decided that they were no longer able to cope with catering for so many.

On the morning of the 28th, Petra took the local train to Birmingham New Street, which was without doubt the busiest railway station she'd ever encountered, much more so than Euston. There were countless platforms, with trains constantly arriving and departing for all parts of the country and she was relieved that there was a 25-minute wait for the express to Cardiff, which gave her plenty of time to locate the right platform. It was quite crowded when it finally pulled in, but she managed to find a single seat in an otherwise crowded compartment, in which most passengers were smoking. It was some relief, that the small sliding window was open, at least giving some respite from the smoke lingering in the compartment. There was space on the luggage rack for her small suitcase and she was happy to accept the offer of a soldier in uniform to lift it for her.

Entering a conversation with him, she found that he was from Derby and on his way, back to his camp in Chepstow, after being at home for Christmas. He seemed interested that her brother was in the R.A.F and that she was a language student, speaking both French and German. Suggesting that she could get a good job in the military, having those skills. Petra laughed saying, "Oh, I don't see myself in uniform, I wasn't even in the Brownies."

She was sorry when the train arrived in Chepstow, as the journey had passed quickly in his company, also having enjoyed travelling along the banks of the Severn as the train approached Wales. After bidding her companion farewell, there was only one further stop at Newport, before arriving in Cardiff, where David was to meet her, prior to taking what he had called a Rhondda express to Trehafod, where his family lived close to the Lewis Merthyr Pit.

True to his word, he was there enthusiastically waving as she stepped off the train, breaking into a trot and hugging her, saying how much he had missed her over Christmas, pledging to make the most of their next few days together. Grabbing her case, he said, "Come on, we've only got five minutes until the Trehebert train and we need to change platforms."

As soon as they had climbed the steps to Platform Six the local train clunked noisily into the station and they were quickly on their way. Travelling north from Cardiff she had little time to look out of the window, being in constant conversation with David, but did notice how different it was to the area where she had lived all her life, with several pits surrounded by row upon row of terraced houses, there being hardly a garden in site. Arriving at Trehafod, she noticed that despite being in a valley, the village was dominated by the pit, the focal points being a tall chimney and the twin winding gantries, David telling her that it provided work for nearly all the men in the community. The surrounding hills provided a stark contrast to the industrial scars that they overlooked.

It was only a short walk to David's parents' terraced house, which looked very much the same as all of those surrounding it, but when they got inside Petra was quite surprised at the amount of living space there was. They were greeted by David's mother, a quite large with short grey curled hair and wore a pinafore dress, who Petra thought looked a picture of domesticity. "Welcome to our home, lovely, David has told me and his father so much about you. First time in Wales, is it?"

"First time in South Wales, Mrs Austin, I went on a Sunday School outing to Rhyl once."

"She laughed, "Oh, there a funny lot in North Wales, you'll like it a lot better here. My husband will be home from the pit soon, so I'll put the kettle on."

At that she disappeared into the kitchen, leaving her and David in what was quite a large room, with floral wallpaper, furnished with a comfortable but worn looking three-piece suite, a newer looking polished table, four chairs and a sideboard. The front window looked straight out onto the pavement, enabling conversations of those passing to be clearly audible. David saying, "It's hard to keep secrets in this village."

As promised, David's father arrived a few minutes later, having obviously just finished work, stocky and well-muscled like his son, he wore an old dark suit, with a striped shirt, no collar, boots and a flat cap, which he removed as soon as he came in. "Hello Petra, I'm Alun, I suppose Cath told you how much we have been looking forward to meeting you. I hope he's looking after you." He said nodding towards his son. "Strikes me, he's a lucky bugger."

Talking together while they had tea, Cath said, "You'll be sleeping in David's room lovely and he's on the sofa "and looking at him said, "and you make sure you stay there."

"Don't worry Mam, I know that the secret police upstairs will keep an eye on us."

The following day they were back on the train to Cardiff, which Petra liked. It seemed quite clean compared with Birmingham, having an excellent shopping centre. David also showed her the castle and they rounded an enjoyable day off by going to the Cinema. Being made to feel welcome, she was enjoying herself, feeling at home. On the next evening, they went for a drink with David's parents in the Miners Welfare Club, where everyone seemed to know him as Dai. Apparently, they were out for a quiet drink, prior to the serious business of New Year's Eve, but Petra couldn't help noticing that David and his father, "put away" six pints each in less than two hours.

New Year Eve was heralded by a cold but sunny day, David saying that they would climb the mountain, which she enjoyed, with the air fresh compared with the valley below. Petra had packed her newest blue and white dress for the festivities, which had a belt to emphasise her waist and a knee length full skirt. She had bought it in London, specially to wear at Christmas and was flattered when both David and his Dad said how nice she looked. There was quite a large room at the rear of the club, with a stage, where they apparently had to arrive early to make sure that they got seats. Early meant 6.30, causing Petra to speculate on the amount that David and his father would drink between then and Midnight.

The hall was soon crowded, with no seat being unoccupied by seven o'clock. The music was provided by three guitarists and a drummer, who were from Cardiff and apparently known as "The Matadors." Petra was intrigued, wondering if any of them had ever been anywhere near Spain, looking at their somewhat pale complexions, she thought, probably not. Everyone seemed to be enjoying the entertainment, with the dance floor packed, with gyrating couples of all shapes and sizes. There were groans of disappointment, when at 9.15 it was announced that there would be a forty-five-minute break for Bingo.

At least it also allowed time for some conversation, while the four people who each won five pounds were also more than happy. Just after the break, Petra went to what was pretentiously called the Ladies Room and washing her hands at the next sink was a quite an attractive dark haired girl, who being judgemental, Petra thought could have gone easier on the makeup.

"You with Dai Austin are you love?"

"Yes, I'm staying with his parents, we met at University."

The girl grinned before saying, "I'd be careful of him if I was you love. I went out with him at school and just before he went off to London, he said he wanted to marry me. Then the night before he left, he had his way with me and I haven't heard a word from the bastard since."

Taken aback by the girl's intervention, Petra wondered if she was just trying to spoil things for her old boyfriend. Nevertheless, she thought of little else for the remainder of the evening, during which David and his father seemed to be competing to see who could drink the most. By the time it got to midnight, it was obvious that the older man had prevailed, because he walked purposefully onto the Dance floor for Old Lang Syne, while David's progress was less controlled, resembling someone crossing the deck on a cross channel ferry in rough seas. She joined in linking hands with the two men, while they sang in another year, after which David grabbed her, kissing her unlike he had ever done before, pushing his tongue between her teeth, so far into her mouth that she almost regurgitated her three Babychams.

The party carried on for another half an hour, when it became obvious that the club was closing with the bar extension having expired. David had spent the whole time slumped in his chair grinning at her and she was pleased when it was time to leave. His parents had gone home immediately after midnight, leaving them to make the ten-minute walk by themselves. It was quite cold and David put his arm tightly around her shoulder, Petra thinking he had done so because he needed support.

Eventually getting back to the house, which was already in darkness. David fumbled with the key, but didn't seem to be able to locate the hole, so with a suppressed giggle she took it off him and unlocked the door. They were soon indoors, but he didn't put the light on, with the moonlight through the window giving sufficient light to locate the settee, where he pulled her down beside him, kissing her and slurring, "I told you it was good in the club on New Year, have you had a good night?"

"It was really nice", she lied, "everyone was very friendly, but I'm tired now and I want to go to bed."

"Not so fast girl, we haven't said goodnight properly yet." Pulling her back towards him and putting his left hand inside the top of her dress and squeezing her breast.

"Stop it David, you've had too much to drink and you'd do better to sleep it off."

"I'm fine and I've got something for you." he said taking her hand and pulling it onto the front of his trousers so she felt his erection.

Alarmed she said, "Look David, I don't want it like this, you'll regret it in the morning."

Laughing softly, he pushed her down on to the settee slurring, "There's no way I'll ever regret what we're going to do now."

CHAPTER 43

Klaus was distressed, looking back on his short trip to England, knowing that his reaction to Petra's stepfather meant that they would never be together. He had been bereft when she left Heidelberg, wishing that he had spent more time with her and hoping that they had a future together. Telling his mother about the English girl that he was convinced that he would marry one day, had provoked a typical response, "Well if she's the one, make sure that you don't lose her."

As soon as Petra had gone home, Klaus arranged to visit, after being told that her parents would be pleased to have him as a guest. It had worked out really well, completing his Post 'Graduate Course in Heidelberg in June and having qualified, was due to take up a junior post in the Accident and Emergency Department of University Medical Centre, Hamburg in early September.

Increasingly excited, anticipating his first visit to England, he had dismissed the opportunity to spend a few days in London, prior to travelling to the Midlands, wanting to maximise his time with Petra and get to know her family. Leaving Hamburg, he had decided to ask her to marry him when she graduated from University, thinking that she could probably make a good living teaching English if she moved to Germany.

Getting off the train and seeing her waiting on the platform, his heart had leapt, thinking that she was even more beautiful than he remembered. He had never been so happy walking hand in hand with her towards her parent's house, which quickly turned to despair.

Storming out, he knew that he was hurting her, but that he could never forgive the man who he blamed for his father's death. It had made him feel even worse when he had dismissed her pleas, but was not surprised by her loyalty to the man that she had always known as her father.

On the train, back to London, it took a great deal of self-control to supress tears. Spending as little time in the capital as possible, he booked train and ferry tickets for the next day and after an early start arrived in Hamburg late in the evening, to the astonishment of his mother.

Looking shocked she asked, "What's happened?"

Finally giving way to the emotions of the previous day, he said, "I couldn't stay with Petra's family, her stepfather is Thomas Walton. Fortunately, he was not at home or I'd probably be in prison by now."

"And what about Petra?"

"She was heartbroken and chased me up the road and when I told her what Walton had done, she stuck up for him."

"What do you expect Klaus, she's his daughter."

"But to me he's a murderer, so there's no future for Petra and me."

At that, he went to his room, not wanting to share his misery with anyone.

Brooding for the rest of the summer, he was relieved to start his first job, which was so demanding that his mood began to improve, but when his shift was over, when he returned home, so did despair. He had no enthusiasm for a social life, declining invitations to go for drinks with colleagues and resisting the flirtations of nurses, who he thought must consider him to be a loner.

After a family dinner, a few weeks later his mother came to his room and sitting on the bed said, "I've done something that may upset you, but I can't bear to see you in such a morose mood all the time. So, I've written to Mr. Walton to try and get you and Petra back together. I've corresponded with him before and while we are not friends, our exchanges have always been courteous and conciliatory. I don't blame him for your father's death, he found himself in a horrendous situation and I am sure did think that your father had been responsible. But never forget, despite that, he did make a plea on his behalf, trying to save his life. I don't want what happened in the war to ruin your life as it almost did mine and I'm sure there's not a day passes when Mr. Walton is not haunted by what happened to him in 1940."

"You're wasting your time; he will know that I could never forgive him for what he did and if I marry Petra, he will be my father in law."

"You're being stupid Klaus, I could understand your anger when you were younger, but I would expect you to have a more mature attitude now, don't let what you perceive as the sins of fathers, destroy your happiness."

Klaus sighed, "I'll be astonished if you get a reply."

Arriving home from work a few weeks later, she gave him an opened envelope, with a British stamp on the front and he immediately recognised Petra's handwriting. Reading the letter, he was disappointed, though not surprised by the content and handing it back to his mother said, "Well that's it then, it was kind of you to try, but I've hurt her too much, there's no future for us. She's probably got a new boyfriend by now."

"Looking resigned his mother kissed his cheek saying, "Well, I've done my bit, if she's the only one for you, swallow your pride and put things right, before it's too late."

CHAPTER 44

Petra knew that she would never forget the first day of January 1963, her life having changed forever. Afterwards she wondered why she hadn't screamed while he was forcing himself on her and knew she couldn't forgive him. All he had done afterwards, was roll off the settee and was asleep by the time she sat up and went to her bedroom, where she sobbed silently for most of the night.

The house was quiet when she got up and washing and dressing as quickly and quietly as she could, packed her things and was out before anyone stirred, noticing David still asleep on the floor next to the settee. Walking briskly towards the station in the winter chill, wishing that she would never see him again, but knew that she would be unable to avoid him in London.

Fortunately, she only had to wait for around twenty minutes for the train to Cardiff and was on her way to Birmingham within the hour. Sitting in the corner of the compartment, she asked herself if she had led him on in any way. Having often wondered what it would be like to be with a man for the first time, she had never imagined it would be so violent and painful. Knowing that she couldn't tell her parents what had happened, she did her best to compose herself and just say that she was home early because she felt unwell.

Arriving in mid-afternoon, she was relieved that the house was empty and after making herself a cup of tea, went upstairs and ran a bath. She had only had time to wash her hands and face that morning and wanted to cleanse anything of David that remained on her body. After a while, she heard footsteps on the stairs, followed by a knock on the door and was glad to hear her Mother's voice, "Is that you, Petra?"

Petra shouted, "Yes Mum, I came home early because I wasn't feeling well. I'm going to lie down for a while when I've finished in here."

"Alright love, I'll bring you a cup of tea later."

Feeling a little better after a bath and relieved to be in the safety of her own home, she got into bed and was soon asleep, it being dark by the time she woke up. Turning on the bedside lamp and looking at her watch, she found it was almost seven o'clock. Having had no food since the previous evening, she thought that she would have to try and eat something. Going down stairs in her Dressing Gown, the whole family were sat watching, Opportunity Knocks on television. Her brothers didn't seem notice that she had come into the room, but both her Mum and Dad were on their feet, hugging her. "Are you feeling better now love", asked her Mum. While her Dad also interjected, "Did you have a good time with all those Welsh miners?"

Despite being on the verge of tears, she was doing her best control herself for the sake of her parents, so replied, "I am feeling a bit better. It was OK down there, but I'm glad to be home."

Barbara knew that something was amiss, but didn't press her daughter, thinking if she wants to talk to me she will.

But Petra didn't want to talk to anyone about what had happened, just wanting to get on with her life. It had been like a bad dream, but there was nothing that she could do about it.

Going back to London in mid-January, she was pleased to see Trevor and Grace, having been relieved when her period started a couple of days earlier. At least that was one worry out of the way.

This was the final full term before graduation and she was determined not let what had happened spoil her efforts of the past three years. When on her second day back, he was waiting at lunchtime in his usual place. Trying to avoid a conversation, she walked in the opposite direction, but chasing after her grabbed her arm saying, "Not so fast young lady, you owe me an explanation."

Incredulous Petra looked him in the eye, "I owe you nothing, what you did that night was unforgivable and I just don't want you in my life."

"I only did what you wanted and by running off like that you upset my parents."

"Well, I'm sorry about that, but they would have been even more upset if I'd have stayed and told them what you did to me."

"You were gagging for it, Petra, you have been since we met."

"You are unbelievable, just keep away from me, go and spoil someone else's life."

"Fuck you", he said and turned and walked away.

She was shaking, wondering if all men had similar streaks in them and was in no hurry to find out, thinking that she would never trust another.

Keeping herself away from the social scene for the remainder of the term, she was confident going into her finals, which was not misplaced as when the results were published she was ecstatic that she'd got a First. The graduation ceremony was planned for early July and she was pleased that she would receive her certificate in Southwark Cathedral, arranging tickets for Trevor, Grace and her parents. She had returned home after her finals, but was back in Catford a few days prior to the Ceremony, while her Mum and Dad arrived the night before.

The day before, she had sat in the garden with Trevor, who said, "It's a big day for you tomorrow Petra, you've done so well and I can't help thinking how proud your father would have been, had he lived. But you should also be grateful to your Mother, she had a difficult time in the war and you couldn't have wished for better parents than her and Tom. I know how proud they are of you and tomorrow will be a wonderful day for us all."

Seated with other graduates in the front pews of the Knave in the ancient building by 10.30 am, with the remainder occupied by proud parents and guests. The proceedings passed quite quickly and after about two hours she was reunited with her Mum, Dad, Trevor and Grace in the summer sun outside, all hugging her in turn. She felt so happy with those she loved all around and Tom being the last to embrace her said, "Darling girl, we're all so pleased that you've done so well and we couldn't have wished for a better daughter, but if you look round there's someone else here who wants to congratulate you."

Confused for a moment, Petra turned and her heart seemed to burst out of her chest, when she saw Klaus smiling broadly, standing a few feet away. Rooted to the spot, as he walked towards her, she thought for a moment that she must be dreaming. But when she felt his arms around her he said, "I had to come back, I couldn't not be with you on this special day.", she knew that she was safe and could be happy again.

Tears streaming down her cheeks as she said, “Oh my god, how did this happen?”

“Divine intervention”, he replied, “in the shape of your father and my mother.”

CHAPTER 45

Barbara and Tom has been concerned when their daughter had returned from South Wales obviously distressed, despite her efforts to suppress emotions. It became clear that it was something to do with David, as when Barbara asked after him, Petra snapped, "That's over, I don't even want to hear his name." Despite this, she seemed in a lot better mood on the morning that she went back to London and Tom being on the afternoon shift carried her case to the station, seeing her off on the local train to Nuneaton.

Still worried, soon afterwards Tom was surprised to receive yet another letter from Germany, this time not recognising the neat handwriting.

Dear Mr Walton,

Let me introduce myself, my name is Klaus Schiller and you have corresponded with my mother on several occasions in the past. As you know, I met your wonderful daughter, Petra in Heidelberg last year and we became very close. When she returned to London, I arranged to visit her in the summer, you and your wife kindly agreeing to allow me to stay in your home. You will be aware what happened, when I arrived and found that you were her stepfather. I have been deeply ashamed of my behaviour ever since. The last thing that I wanted to do was upset Petra, who I adore.

When I returned to Hamburg and told her what had happened, my mother, who holds you in high regard, appraised me of the full circumstances surrounding you and my late father, urging me to try and repair the hurt that

I had caused Petra. As she felt that I would not have the confidence to do this myself, she wrote a letter to you in the autumn, to which Petra replied. I was not surprised that she declined to accept my mother's invitation, feeling that my attitude to you was inexcusable. On reflection, I must say that I understand her sentiments and would therefore like to personally apologise to you for my attitude and behaviour. My mother, who is a wonderful lady, has always believed in reconciliation between our two families and countries, which were so badly damaged by two world wars and despite my earlier anger, I have come to agree with her.

It is my heartfelt wish to be reconciled with Petra, because I think that we could have a future together. When we met in Heidelberg, I knew that she was the one for me, telling my mother that I had met an English girl who I wanted to marry. Since the summer, I have been truly miserable, thinking that I had lost her for ever and with your permission and perhaps help, I would like to come to England again to apologise to her and to yourself face to face. I want to be with her, believing that it will also bring our two families together.

My mother sends her Best Wishes.

Yours Sincerely,
Klaus Schiller

When Tom showed the letter to his wife, she said, "Well, that's a turn up for the book, what do you think."

"After what happened in the summer, I thought that was that, despite her being so unhappy. But then she thought that he would never be able to accept that I was her Dad, which no longer seems to be the case."

"I don't think that she really got over him and it certainly didn't work out with that Welsh boy. I'd never seen her so happy when she was waiting for him to come last summer or so sad afterwards. So, I think that we should try to help them."

Ending the conversation Tom said, "Let's do it then, I'll reply to him tonight."

Dear Klaus,

Thank you for your letter regarding our daughter.

Like you, Petra has not been happy since last summer and I know that she was deeply upset by what happened. As you rightly say, we have corresponded with your mother several times over the years and My wife Barbara and I have a great deal of respect for her.

Petra's future happiness is important to us and we are therefore willing to help you. She is currently preparing for her final exams in London and we do not want to distract her at what is an important period in her life, but we have a suggestion to make.

Providing, as we expect, she graduates, she will receive her degree in London this summer. We think that the day would be an ideal opportunity for you to see her and if you are able we would like to invite you to come to London on that day and surprise her after the ceremony. Of course, there is a risk that she will not react well, but we are confident that it will not be the case. I realise that you are now working as a Doctor, but hope that you can arrange the time off to come over, probably in mid-July.

If you agree, we can correspond further to make the arrangements.

We look forward to meeting you.

Please pass on my best wishes to your mother.

Yours Sincerely,
Tom and Barbara Walton

They received Klaus' reply about ten days later and were not surprised by his enthusiasm for their scheme. Asking for confirmation of the date as soon as possible, he was confident that he would be able to arrange the time away from work. Providing the reconciliation was successful, Tom invited him to back to the Midlands with Petra, so that he could spend the remainder of his holiday with her.

As soon as they could inform him of the arrangements, Klaus confirmed that he would arrive in London on the day before the Graduation and meet with them before they went into the Cathedral, obviously doing his best to avoid Petra. After the ceremony, he would wait close by until they were reunited with Petra and would approach her then. He added that his mother was delighted and was hopeful that everything would go to plan.

As the day got closer, Tom and Barbara became increasingly nervous and hoped that Petra didn't turn up with another boyfriend, although they were sure that she would have told them if there had been one. Petra was excited, but nervous on the day as they all travelled in from Catford, taking a taxi to the Cathedral from Charing Cross. After she had gone inside, they only had to wait a couple of minutes before, a tall dark young man, dressed in a smart blue suit approached them, offering his hand to Tom saying, "How do you do, Mr. Walton, I'm Klaus and I am pleased to meet you.

Impressed by the formal nature of the greeting, Tom replied, "I'm fine Klaus, how are you? I believe that you briefly met my wife before."

"Yes sir", he replied turning to Barbara, "briefly and I must again apologise for my behaviour."

Shaking his hand, Barbara thought that he was undoubtedly one of the best-looking men that she had met and was not surprised that her daughter had fallen for him. Introductions were made to Trevor and Grace after which parents and grandparents went into the Cathedral, with Klaus left waiting outside on what was fortunately a fine warm day.

The proceedings lasted around two hours and Tom was on edge when they left the Cathedral. Soon the new graduates were reunited with their loved ones and a beaming Petra hugged the four of them, beginning with Barbara.

Petra looked momentarily confused when Tom said that someone else was there to congratulate her, but he immediately knew that they had done the right thing, by the look on her face when she saw Klaus. They seemed to hug each other for a full minute, before she turned to Tom, saying, "How did you manage to pull this off, Dad?"

Laughing, Tom replied, "Oh don't thank me, Klaus made the running urged on by his mother and we thought that it would make you happy."

"Well, it has, I couldn't be happier", she said, arm in arm with Klaus, seemingly never wanting to let go.

Tom and Barbara were delighted to see their daughter so happy and were grateful to Klaus for his determination to get back with her. Returning home, he was to stay with them for the following ten days, during which time they hoped to get to know him better. It proved difficult to wrestle him from Petra's grip, but Tom did manage to get him to "The Oak" on a couple of occasions. One of these was two nights before he was due to leave and he was not surprised when their guest asked if he and Barbara would have any objection if he asked Petra to marry him.

Tom laughed saying, "Having seen you two together, I'm not surprised and I'm sure that Barbara and I would be delighted."

Smiling Klaus said, "It will probably mean living in Hamburg, but with her language skills she will make a good living."

"I'm sure she will and while me and her Mum will miss her, we'll be able to travel across and visit."

"Fine, the only problem then is getting her to say yes."

CHAPTER 46

The following day, Klaus and Petra walked hand in hand into the wood, where at the height of summer the trees blocked out much of the light, but the numerous clearings allowed them to feel the warmth of the sun. Sitting down together, with their backs against an Oak tree, Klaus leaned over, kissed her gently and pulled a small black box from his pocket.

Realising what was about to happen, she gasped as he opened it and offered her a diamond ring saying, "Do you think that you've forgiven me enough to marry me?"

Momentarily she panicked, thinking that Klaus would expect to marry a virgin and knowing that before replying she had to tell him what had happened with David.

"Something happened a few months ago, that you need to know before we go any further."

Klaus was confused, wondering what on earth it was that was clearly upsetting her at what should have been a happy moment.

Telling him everything about that night in Wales, he held her hand listening intently and she noticed him grimacing several times, finishing by saying, "Knowing that, I'll quite understand if you don't want to marry me."

"The fact that you're not a virgin Petra, is no big deal. But what happened to you is, the bastard should be in prison, why didn't you go to the police?"

"Because, it would have been my word against his, all I wanted to do was get as far away from him as possible. I saw him once when we got back to college, but as far as I was concerned he was dead. I just wanted to get on with my life and have told no one until now. The only regret that I have is not staying with you that night in Heidelberg."

He kissed her again, putting the ring on her finger and saying, "It makes no difference, I have wanted us to be together since the first night we met and nothing or no one is going to get in the way."

They sat in silence for another twenty minutes before he stood up and helped her to her feet saying, "Come on, let's go and tell your parents. They'll probably throw me out."

Barbara was delighted when they told her, but Petra was alarmed when she started to talk about a "big church wedding" the following summer, which was the last thing that she wanted. Telling Klaus, she said, "We spoke about me coming to Germany to meet your family in the autumn, do you thing that we could get married quietly in Hamburg while I'm there?"

Klaus couldn't wait to marry her, but was concerned that this would damage his recently repaired relationship with her parents, but Petra was adamant, "I just don't want any fuss and the sooner we are married the better. If we had a church wedding, it would be covered in the local papers and I just don't want to risk them making the link between our two families."

Seeing the sense in it, he asked, "What are you going to tell them.?"

"Nothing until afterwards, if I do they'll try and stop me. Don't worry I'll tell them that the whole thing was my idea and that you tried to talk me out of it. It will be a shock, but they'll be happy for us."

So, when he left for home the following day, Petra's birth certificate was in his luggage. He was looking forward to telling his mother the news, but thought that if her parents were not aware of the marriage neither should she, so he went ahead with planning, telling no one.

The following day, he went to the Magistrates Office in the centre of Hamburg and began the process required, arranging the ceremony on 24th October, a week after her arrival.

His mother loved Petra from the moment she saw her, having travelled with Klaus to the Airport to meet her. After he kissed her, Petra turned to his mother and offered her hand, but was happy when the older woman kissed her on each cheek saying, "I've heard so much about you Petra, I know that we are going to be good friends."

They got on well from the start, even going on a weekend shopping trip together. She found it difficult not to mention the wedding and hoped that it would not affect their relationship.

It was Klaus' day off from the hospital and telling his mother that they were going for a day out in Hamburg, no suspicion was aroused. Telling Petra that he had arranged for two friends who were nurses, Johan and Irma, to meet them at the Standesamt Office to act as witnesses. The appointment was for mid-day and Petra felt nervous when they arrived, finding Johan and Irma waiting for them. After a short wait in an Anti-Room, they were ushered into a larger wood panelled room with a desk at the far end, with around twenty chairs arranged in rows in front. They were greeted by a tall, bespectacled, middle aged man, wearing a dark three-piece suit, who Petra thought wouldn't look out of place in an Undertakers Office. Despite this he had a pleasant demeanour, smiling a lot throughout the short ceremony, concluding with the words, "I spricht man Mann und Frau", After signing the register they, bade farewell to their witnesses and after a celebratory lunch, were on their way back to break the news to Eva.

A week later Petra was on the short flight back to London, wondering just how her parents would react when they saw a wedding ring on her finger. She and her new husband had been concerned as to how his mother would react, but after her initial shock had been happy, agreeing with the logic of keeping their union low key.

Whatever the reaction of her parents, nothing could spoil the blissful week that she had just experienced. After the wedding, she had moved into Klaus' room, where on the first night she had to overcome her apprehension to how she would react to intimacy after her experience in Wales. Seeming aware of this and after they had undressed, Klaus led her to the bed, where he held her in his arms, gazed into her eyes before kissing her gently for several minutes. Caressing her body, gradually moving down until he was stroking the inside of her thigh. He felt her tense as he gradually moved his hand between her legs, while kissing her and whispering, "If you don't want to go any further tonight I'll understand, we've got a lifetime so there's no hurry"

Petra was tempted, but said, "I love you Klaus, just be gentle".

She wondered how two experiences could be so different. Klaus' had been so considerate and soon after he had entered her with no pain, she gradually became more relaxed and excited before experiencing an explosion of emotion, trying to suppress cries of delight. After it was over, she had gone to sleep in his arms, knowing that she would always feel safe with this wonderful man.

When she got home, both her mum and dad sat beside the fire, but were quickly on their feet as she walked through the door, "Hello princess." Said Tom, did you have a good time?" While Barbara was soon hugging her saying how much they had missed her.

"I did have a wonderful time, but I've got something to tell you both and please don't be angry Dad, but Klaus and I got married last week."

Her parents looked at one another shocked but to her relief, he said, "How could I be angry girl, if that's what you both wanted, you'll have our support, although we're sorry that we weren't there."

Petra was relieved, explaining their logic, doing it quietly without any fuss, not wanting anyone to drag up the previous history between the families, also explaining that they hadn't told Klaus' mother until afterwards. After which she handed them a letter.

> *Dear Mr and Mrs Walton,*
>
> *I suppose that you will be as shocked as I was, when Petra tells you what she and Klaus have done. But I am sure that like me, when it sinks in you will be delighted for them both. I am confident that they can look forward to a wonderful life together.*
>
> *I must say that I loved Petra from the moment that we met and was impressed by her thoughtfulness regarding the possible consequences of there being publicity around their marriage. I'm sure that you both agree that is the last thing they needed was what had happened to their parents all those years ago to overshadow their own wonderful relationship. I do feel now that our two families are truly reconciled and while we can never forget the past, the future happiness of our children is more important.*

I understand that for the time being, Klaus will continue in his current position in Hamburg and that they intend to rent an apartment together. I realise that it will be difficult for you with Petra living so far away, but I am sure that she will be able to make a good living teaching English and London is only one and a half hours away by air. I understand that it is Klaus' intention to come over at Christmas, to enable Petra to spend it with you, before she travels back with him in January.

When they do get settled, I hope that you will come over to visit. It would make me very happy to meet Mrs Walton for the first time and you in happier circumstances than has previously been the case.

In closing, I must say that I am very happy and proud for my son and consider him fortunate to have married your wonderful daughter.

Yours Sincerely,
Eva

CHAPTER 47

Lying in bed in his lonely room fifty years later, Tom reflected how fortunate he had been in his long life. Apart from Barbara, he had loved Petra most of all, despite not being her natural father. Bringing so much joy into his life and through her marriage some sort of closure to those terrible events in 1940.

After her marriage, she had as expected gone to live with her husband in Hamburg, where they had raised two children, Paul and Matilda. Tom thought it ironic, that after his wartime experiences, he had two German grandchildren that he and Barbara had done their best to visit every year, until advancing age had made it impossible.

They had become good friends with Eva and although the celebration wedding party never materialised, enjoyed some special times together, before she died in 2004 well into her nineties, a month after his beloved wife.

He had been inconsolable when Barbara died, wondering how he would go on without the woman who had been his constant companion for almost 60 years. Petra and her brothers had been supportive, but Tom didn't have a clue how to look after himself, so didn't argue when they had suggested that he would be better off in a Care Home. As he had been ninety-two at the time, he expected not to have to put up with it for too long.

But here he was eight years on, lying in his cell like room alone with his memories. He was thankful that most his life had been joyous and fulfilling, counting himself blessed to have been with Barbara, his only lover, for so long. She had given him three wonderful children, whose achievements had filled him with pride. If only he had not been in that place in 1940.

Often lying awake thinking about what had happened, tonight was no exception and he wondered if his torment would ever end. "Don't worry you won't be in there for long and there's plenty of room where you're going." Those seventeen words had been enough to send a man to the gallows, deprive his son in law of his father and his daughters two children of a grandfather. Every night he tried to convince himself that it was Paul Schiller's voice that he heard, but the appeal hearing had concluded that it wasn't, by which time it was too late.

Having got to know Eva, although she never mentioned it, he knew that she was convinced of her husband's innocence and he had been astonished that they became friends. Petra had adored her mother in law, who had been delighted when she and Klaus called their son Paul. He had got on well with Klaus, but at times thought that his son in law suppressed his resentment, for Petra's sake. There were times when he had wished that his daughter had married a local lad, but never had any reason to doubt her happiness.

Craving the peaceful sleep that he was often denied, finally drifting off, only to find himself back in France. He relived the events of that day as he had done countless times before. As always, it was Schiller who addressed them, prior to the horrendous march to the barn and he was certain that it was the same voice that he heard just prior to the doors being flung open as the shooting began. Then he was again running away from the barn, experiencing the intense pain when he was hit in the shoulder. Feeling the cold water as he jumped into the pond, he could distinctly hear the voices of his pursuers, who all bypassed his refuge. The exception was a tall soldier in a peaked cap who came to the edge of the pond, Tom thinking that he was sure to be discovered. Totally submerged, except for his head, he could only see the outline of the Officer. But suddenly his face was illuminated for the instant that he took to light a cigarette. Tom couldn't mistake the familiar features of Paul Schiller as his own life finally ebbed away.

Lightning Source UK Ltd.
Milton Keynes UK
UKOW02f2332200317
297117UK00001B/104/P

9 781524 678616